THE BUTTON COLLECTOR

M.M. COCHRAN

THE BUTTON COLLECTOR

A Thriller

IngramElliott

Published by IngramElliott, Inc.
www.ingramelliott.com
9815-J Sam Furr Road, Suite 271, Huntersville NC 28078

This is a work of fiction. The names, characters, places, or events used in this book are the product of the author's imagination or used fictitiously. Any resemblance to actual people (alive or deceased) events, or locales is completely coincidental.

Book design by Maureen Cutajar, gopublished.com
Cover design by Jeanine Henning, jeaninehenning.com
Editing by Abbie Payne

ISBN Hardcover: 978-1-952961-23-6
ISBN Paperback: 978-1-952961-24-3
ISBN E-Book: 978-1-952961-25-0

Library of Congress Control Number: 2024934213

Subjects: Fiction—Thrillers_Suspense.
Fiction—Mystery and Detective_General.

Published in the United States of America.
Printed in the United States of America.
First Edition: 2024, First International Edition: 2024

To my faithful readers

Acknowledgments

The Button Collector was alive in my mind long before it hit the ground running in 2020, when I got it on paper.

I was working as an intern at a newspaper during my last semester of college, and I'd spent most of my hours on the clock writing this book in the office's conference room. By summer of 2021, I had a complete manuscript and only one idea of what to do with it—get it published.

This book sat on the back burner until my publisher discovered it, asked me for it, then put *The Button Collector* under contract. Since then, I've wanted to tell this novel something very important: You've challenged me. You've pushed me. You got me out of my YA comfort zone, and you set me on a new path. Thank you.

I have many people to acknowledge who encouraged this book and were simply a source of joy for me as I got this tale on bookshelves.

Mom and Dad: you two have been the root of my success in writing since I was a kid. If you both hadn't pushed me to keep writing when I wanted to quit, I wouldn't be the daughter you know today. Thank you for reading my roughest drafts, answering my questions, and listening to my story ideas. You two planted a seed in me at a young age to chase my dreams, and I did. And I'm never going to stop thanking you for that.

To several other family members—Grandma, Katie, Wren, Matthew, and Wyatt—I acknowledge you here on this page because each of you have, in some regard, endorsed my journey to becoming an author. Thank you, and thank you in advance, for still being on this journey with me.

Austin Joyce: you tend to make my words go away, but I'll try to find them here. I've never met a better listener, gentler speaker, or patient dreamer. You inspire me daily, so I must offer my most wholehearted gratitude to the person I love most in the world. I mean it when I say I couldn't do it without you. Leaning on you holds me up, and walking this life with you keeps me steady. Thanks for being my most passionate reader.

Bethany Nelson, Citlaly Arevalo, Cassidy Lappin, Claire Grider, Lauren White, Josue Lopez, Cameron Clark, and Fernando Liriano: I thank each and every one of you for being my best friends. I hope to always return the endless encouragement and support you've given me since I've known and loved you.

To my publishers at IngramElliott Publishing, thank you for believing in my book again and so quickly becoming a fan of this story. Working with you is, as it always has been, a pleasure.

Once again, I lift my glass to *The Button Collector*, to the people who stand behind it and before it, to my dearest readers, and to all my stories to come.

Cheers, to the next chapter!

Yours,

The first thing I feel when I step outside my apartment building is his eyes on me.

They burn. They haunt. They're always there, somehow finding me almost every day since the first murder.

Long shadows stretch over the brown patch of grass before my building. They're soft on my boots and heavy on the winter flowers that need sun. Rain pelts down the petals, but I'm too cold to get my fingers wet and shake the water off the weak flowers.

The thick weather clouds the feeling of his surveillance, but I still close my eyes to escape it.

Count backwards from ten.

Nine.

Eight.

Seven.

Okay, it's gone.

Now open your eyes, I instruct myself.

It's time to catch a cab. "Time to catch a cab," I say.

Leave me alone. "Leave me alone," I say.

~

The office buzzes with fluorescent lights over rickety desks made for half-hearted journalists. I slide between their narrow spaces and make my way to the associate editor's desk. The editor in chief smokes in his office, and Della can tell me everything he knows, so I avoid him and his stench. It's not something I can handle this morning, though on a good morning, I'd crave the smell of his cigarettes.

"Della, John wanted to see me? Why?" The tip of my umbrella taps the ground, sprinkling cold drops of leftover rain onto my pant leg.

She doesn't even look at me, doesn't even jump at the opportunity to comment on my red lipstick that's too dark or my unshapely long coat. "He's in his office."

"But—"

"Jessica."

The smoke in John's office rolls onto me in waves of foggy white. My automatic response is to cough, clear my throat, but it would be nothing more than for show. He knows I'm used to it.

"Knight. Come here, I've got somethin' for you." He fingers me in and motions for me to take a seat. The dark leather on the chair does everything but absorb the moisture from my wet thighs.

He nudges a stack of papers in my direction. "Here're some stories for the week that I came across over the weekend. Fire and Crime section looks like it'll be good and full next issue, but I'd like you to start on this Button story. A profile about him to follow-up his murder we reported on last week. It'll take some research, so I want your time and attention on this one. All week." He taps the folder with his index and middle finger, keeping his cigarette in place between them. "Make it good. If you need me to get some intern on the other stuff, you just let me know, Knight. Let's focus on this Button profile, and make sure to really center it around the freakshow killer more than the victims."

John takes a long, focused drag off the cigarette. Blows it in a thin streak over his shoulder. Eyes me with a glare that's crimped with sixty-year-old crow's feet.

"You alright, Knight?"

"Fine. But why do you want me for this? I'm not investigative, just—"

"A hard crime reporter. I know. But you really proved yourself with investigative journalism skills after you covered that murder trial last month. I want to spread your wings a little more. Cover this Button story, Knight. It's going to sell a lot of papers. Keep it up, and we'll change your title to Investigative instead of just Crime Journalist."

"Thanks, John, but I'm comfortable with my position."

"I'll give you a little raise, dear." He wraps his lips around his cigarette and blows the smoke over his shoulder again. "And I'll hire one of those interns to take over hard crime. Okay?"

"Alright. Thank you."

"Well, we'll see how this Button story goes."

I nod.

"You sure you're okay, Knight?"

"Yeah, fine."

"Then shake that look off your face and get to work. I'd like to have that story by Thursday; I want the designers to arrange A1 layout around it. This'll generate a lot of attention, you know. People are all over this Button Collector thing."

"The word count?" I ask. I usually don't have to talk word counts with him, but with big stories like this—like that trial—he always has some requirements to meet.

"Give me nine-hundred, no less."

A knock on the door diverts his attention to behind me. "John," the receptionist says, "a young lady would like to speak with you about advertisement."

John pushes back his chair and stands, surrendering his cigarette to the dusty ash tray. "Stay here, Knight. I'll be right back."

My next breath is stifled by the smoke that folds into my face when he walks by. He leaves the door cracked behind him.

Just then, it splits all the way open again, squeaking, spilling out the smoke onto the main office floor.

"Hi, Jessica." The voice makes me jump; I know exactly who it is.

Ben, with skin too white for his black hair and a poise too hunched and unsure for a man only five years older than I am.

"Morning." I turn back around to face John's desk so Ben can't see me head on.

"How was your weekend?"

"It was okay," I say.

His faint voice moves closer, settling on the nape of my neck. It strangles me. "I didn't do anything over the weekend. I saw a movie but went by myself, so that doesn't really count." A quick schoolboy laugh slithers from his narrow lips. "What did you do this weekend? Actually, uh, what are you doing this coming weekend?"

I pretend I don't hear his question. Instead, I pat some heat into my frozen legs and stand, taking my umbrella in hand. "It was nice speaking with you, Ben."

"Where are you going? Perhaps I could help."

"Research. Only conducting some research for a story. Nice speaking with you, Ben," I say again. I try flashing him a small smile hoping he gets the hint. He doesn't, but then again, he never does. I push past him to leave. John will never miss me, and he'll forget all about the file of useless information for me. I've been doing my job long enough to find my own stories, but he's never been good at disguising his favoritism.

When I reach the cool street, I snap my black umbrella into an open canopy overhead, creating my solitary safe space that envelops and offers me protection.

"I'm going to the library," I tell the Collector if he's out there watching. But I turn and go home instead.

❧

4

There, a moment alone. On my gray couch in my storm-tinted apartment, dull noises seep through my ceiling from the family above. A stool moving from here to there, or a pot clattering on the stove, or a toddler's drowned-out temper tantrum. It's okay, because it all fades by the time it soaks through their floors and into my living room.

I heard somewhere that when you live alone and don't often see friends or family, your voice grows weak due to the lack of frequent use. Sometime over the past three years, I suppose it happened to me. I didn't talk much to my foster family after my parents died, and when I turned eighteen and lived with a friend for the summer, I kept to myself. My college roommate and I weren't friendly, and finally, I got my own place after graduation.

A bachelor's in communications didn't treat me well, either, so perhaps a cup of hot tea would warm up my throat.

"You're back," I say.

Because the truth is, he never really goes away. No matter the lies about where I tell him I'm going, he always finds me.

The steaming tea splashes over my thumb and down my wrist at the sound of my doorbell resonating through the apartment. I dry the burn on my way to the door and put my eye to the peephole.

It's Melanie, from across the hall. It's annoying, how straight she stands, already smiling on the other side. Her cardigan is slipping off her shoulder, but she doesn't bother to fix it. Single mother of one living in a moldy apartment building—why correct a petty blunder?

"Hey, Jessica. I made some cherry pies, and, well, I had a whole leftover one, so here you go." Offering it to me, I try to hum something out as I take it with both hands.

"Thank you. I appreciate this." I hope she doesn't notice how my words are void of emotion.

"It's fresh out of the oven." The pie isn't very hot in my palms, though.

"Thanks." I pull together a smile.

She remains idle, flipping around her messy brown hair. I'm being rude.

"How's your daughter?" I say, but I don't care and never have, no matter how many times the silence obligates me to ask.

"Oh, Marge is good. She goes back to school in a few days. Christmas really flew by. She's finishing fourth grade this year; can you believe it?"

"It has flown by." It hasn't, really. My mind shifts to my five family members who have died in the last seven months. It's the kind of thing that slows life down.

John doesn't know the details, of course. He doesn't know how personal the Button case is to me or he never would have assigned me—one of our three crime journalists—to the serial killer's story. But a raise? A promotion if I make the story remarkable?

I glance at the old water stains around my doorjamb. I could use the money. I sigh, annoyed that Melanie's still here.

"So, tell me, since you work at the paper—any word on that Button Collector thing? My gosh, it's really dangerous out there, isn't it? I read online that he might still be in the city. Is he that kind of killer that revisits the crime scene?"

"I've got nothing on him, no." The key to getting rid of Melanie is refusing engagement.

Finally, she gets the message when I put my hand on the doorknob, and she leaves. I set the pie underneath my dim kitchen light bulb and force myself in front of my computer to type *Chicago, The Button Collector* into the search bar. Our newspaper article is one of the first links to appear.

It's dated back to one week ago. Clark, our investigative guy, reported it. I called in sick the week that murder happened because I knew John would want someone to write about it, and I could sense he had been trying to reel me into investigative stories. I didn't lie to him when I said I was throwing up all morning. What I had called the stomach flu was actually six drinks the night before to numb the panic of being the Collector's next victim.

I read the article.

On December 28 at 11:28 p.m., Chicago Police Department officers and Cook County Sheriff's Office deputies were dispatched to an incident on W. 87 Street.

Martha Pax, 89, of the Gresham area of Chicago, was found murdered in her home, making her the fifth victim discovered since June with a similar pattern of injuries. In each case, the killer follows a unique ritual, and authorities have established a profile, naming him the Button Collector based on the signature he leaves behind.

Pax, in a similar fashion to other victims, was cut by a knife on her neck. She was found with a button from an accessory sewn to her lips. Investigators said a second button was stolen from the accessory and allegedly collected by the killer. The Cook County Coroner's Office determined loss of blood and trauma as the cause of Pax's death.

Though police do not have any leads on the killer's identity, the Button Collector's ritual is very specific, they said. According to authorities, this killer is notorious for stealing a single button from his victim's clothing or accessory and sewing it onto their lips, as well as collecting an additional button for himself. Other known Button killings have taken place in Hermann, MO; Spooner, MI; Denver, CO; Cedar Rapids, IO; and most recently, Chicago, IL.

Authorities have established a victim pattern, concluding that each murder victim is of distant relation in the same family. While the general public is considered safe at this time, police urge citizens to remain vigilant.

I close my laptop. I've read enough.

It started with my cousin, Robert. We met only once. He was a senior in college when I was a senior in high school, so we had a little in common. After the family reunion was over, I never went to another one; I was eighteen, freshly moved out of my foster home, thinking it would be healthy to get involved with my "loved ones" again. But with dead parents and not even a foster family anymore, I didn't see the point in attending another one. Then I went to college, and the only person who kept up with me was Rosa's mom: my aunt Deborah.

Rosa was next. She was Aunt Deborah's daughter, only fourteen years old. When Deborah called me in hysterics to tell me the news, I wondered who could take the life of a shy fourteen-year-old in such a brutal way. The button on her lips had come from her cardigan sweater.

Third was my great aunt Julianne, whose button had been an artificial diamond from her blouse.

Then came Uncle Josh. They said he was too drunk to fight off the Button Collector. There wasn't even a struggle. The killer took a copper button from his jeans to silence him forever.

Last week, it had been Martha Pax, the only member of my family who wasn't actually blood related to any of us. She was my grandfather's third wife, but I had never known him. He died long before my parents did. I haven't spoken to Martha since she gave me a quick kiss on the cheek at my parents' funeral over a decade ago. She moved to Chicago after that, but I never called her when I moved to the city for college. In all fairness, she never really contacted me about anything either.

The relationships between me and the victims are too distant for John or anyone else at the *Post* to track back to me, especially since I never bring up the topic of family.

But this trajectory hasn't gone unnoticed by me. I know the truth: I'm the only person tying my parents' sides of the family together. The collector is moving closer to me, one aunt, uncle, and cousin at a time, until I'm the last one standing. He's watching me. I can feel it. So close, in fact, that his stare burns into my skin.

My lungs constrict, yearning for air.

I launch off my mattress, but the skin over my eyes only stretches when I try to open them. They remain locked, closed by—what... crust? Dried mascara?

I try to suck in a breath, but only a thin stream of air slips through the small creases between my lips, between thin layers of thread that refuses to rip apart when I scream, unable to tear when I claw at it, leaving my nails caked with dried blood. A button dangles from a string attached to my upper lip, and two more rip off my eyelids, thick, red tears gushing down my cheeks. All at once, my body hits the floor, shaking me, and the carpet shudders with tremors from the weight of my body.

Then I wake up on my bed, cold from the sweat of my nightmare, and shaking from my frantic heart rate.

It's just a phone call, nothing more than a series of brief little vibrations on my pillow.

Aunt Deborah.

I pick up the phone from underneath my pillow and answer, "Hello?" I try to keep my voice steady in case it's him. "Hello?"

"Jess? Jessica?"

"Deborah, hi."

"I'm calling late, I know."

"It's fine." The clock says it's fifteen after ten. Late for Auntie.

Her voice shakes, and I imagine she's rolled into a blanket and tucked into her closet, somewhere where she can't be found by an invader. "I want to check in on you. See how things are."

I tell her I'm doing well, but she doesn't buy it.

"You're afraid too. I'm scared, Jessica, and you know something. For Christ's sake, dear, you work at *The Chicago Post*; you've got to know something. Tell me, please."

"Aunt Deborah, I was assigned the story today, so I don't know anything. Are you okay?"

A woman like Deb should smoke. Not someone like John, just a stressed-out news editor who sleeps with all the journalists.

"I'm—I want to invite you to come stay at my place, at least until all this is over."

"I have a job, Deb. I can't just leave."

"Forget Chicago. You don't need to be alone right now in that city where the killer is."

"We don't know that he's still here," I say, even though the truth is that he always returns to me.

"I'll keep you up," Deborah pleads.

The line falls silent, and I rub my eyes to reassure myself that they haven't been mutilated by the Button Collector.

God. I'm humiliated by my own paranoia.

"Tell someone, Jessica." She becomes quiet, pressing the phone to her cheek, I imagine. "Tell the police you're related to the victims. They can take precautions that way and protect you. Think of Martha Pax, dear. Your grandmother."

"Step-grand—"

"They'll put it together at some point. Just spill it."

The thought had crossed my mind after Rosa died, but the police weren't protecting the rest of the family. Why would they protect me? They can't shelter an entire family, especially knowing this case's foundation is laid on the fact that the Button Collector must have some sort of personal issue with us. The protection would be never ending.

"Jessica?"

"I can't, Auntie. I'll call you soon." I hang up and struggle to get back to sleep.

~

First thing in the morning, I phone the Fuller Park Police Department, the one I know is closest to Martha's house.

"Hi, my name is Jessica Knight, and I'm with *The Chicago Post* doing research about Martha Pax's murder—um—specifically, about the Button Collector. I'm writing a profile story on the killer, following up on the Pax murder that occurred over a week ago. May I ask someone a few questions regarding the killer's signature?"

"Let me put you on with the chief. One moment," the lady says. Sixty seconds later a voice booms across the line: "Chief Reed." Again, I explain who I am and what I'm doing. Trying to do.

"I can tell you a few things, yeah. I'd like for you to come down to the station if you need the information."

"Oh, um, sure." I have no excuse to not go. Last night, it started to snow, but traffic is still moving, and the snow isn't sticking to the ground yet. "I can be there within the hour."

He agrees, and we hang up.

In my bathroom mirror, my icy reflection stares back at me. I'm too cold in the winter to be any other color but snow white, except for the lilac rings that act as permanent fixtures around my eyes. My brown irises provide a heavy contrast, and the dark tones of brown in my hair only accent how pale I am. The summer my parents died, I chopped it all off with kid scissors standing over a sink, and I kept it short like that through high school. When I moved to Chicago, I needed the warmth it provided, so I grew it back out. I've worn it long ever since.

I throw on a knitted hat, my long coat, and a dash of red lipstick. Best keep all the color I can.

∾

Instead of a mirrored interrogation room like I expected, Chief Reed—a thick-armed man with a broad chest—leads me into his office. The shade over his single window is pulled shut, but light spills through in thin lines.

Another man stands in the corner, his hair greased back in one blond swoop, and his bullet proof vest puffing out his chest. He appraises me upon arrival, so I tuck into my coat when I take a seat. A man who looks thirty-something should be married, but his wedding ring finger is bare.

The chief sits behind his desk and folds his hands together. The little bulb light on the desk casts both men's shadows largely on the wall. They loom like monsters over me.

"Ms. Knight, this is Detective Michael Bradley. He's familiar with this case and can best answer your questions," says Chief Reed.

Right. I forgot I'm here to ask, not to answer. I didn't even bring my notepad. Strike one in earning my promotion.

Detective Bradley smirks, and heat spreads into my cheeks because he can see how uncomfortable I am. Ripping off my hat to allow some airflow, I fold it and refold it five separate times in my lap.

"Actually, I'd rather you just tell me everything you know," I say. "I can work better from there."

"What exactly are you writing about?" Chief Reed asks.

"It's a profile story on the killer as a follow-up to the Pax murder."

Chief Reed rolls back in his chair, motioning to Detective Bradley. "Care to spill?"

Their shadows—they move and spill and contort through the room. My paranoid imagination turns them into demons trying to attack me from above, so I hunker deeper into my coat and turn my ear toward Bradley.

Bradley pushes himself off the wall with the heel of his foot and crosses his arms next to Reed. "What do you already know?" he asks.

The light from Reed's lamp colors Bradley's face with a yellow glow. A shadow covers half of it, though I can still make out the stubble of a beard and mustache. Why is it so dark in here?

My nerves sense an interrogation, but despite my discomfort, I pull together a quick little pitch. "The chief editor of the *Post* wants a profile on this guy, the way he kills, the way he works. I know the victims are all killed the same way—asleep or in bed, caught off guard—and they're all related to each other somehow or another."

"Exactly. Therefore" —he steps closer, his knee knocking the desk— "we've concluded that these murders aren't random. He has a motive, but we don't know what it is."

"Is age a factor?" I ask, even though I know it's not. Coming here feels useless.

"No," says Bradley. "Not that we've concluded."

Reed nods along. He reminds me of John, with his height and graying hair, but John is skin and bone. Not tough or thick like Reed. "And since the victims are both male and female, it isn't about gender either," Reed says. "Or sex, for that matter—he hasn't raped any females so far. There's been absolutely no trace of his DNA found on any of his victims. Not a single hair."

"You're right, though—they're all killed the same way," Bradley says, "and at the end, he sews their mouths shut with a button from their clothes, then takes another one for himself. The most unique murder that's happened is the Pax murder. She's not blood related to that family, and her button came from her purse, not an article of her clothing. We're doing some heavy investigating."

"That's all we can do, at this point," Reed says.

When will they find out I'm her husband's granddaughter?

"Is that all?" They haven't told me anything I don't already know, except that they've pieced the murders all together well and given me a few solid quotes about the killer, which is what John wants from me, really. Anything to settle the readers and sell papers. I try to memorize what they've said, since I forgot my notepad.

Detective Bradley's arms open, and he puffs out his cheeks as if to ask, *Are you serious? We gave you a lot.*

"I don't mean—"

Chief Reed takes over. "I know what you meant, and yes, that's all we've got. You'd think we'd have more in seven months, huh?" He slaps Bradley on his belt, trying to joke but failing to smile with it. His chair squeaks as he rests his forearms on the desk.

Bradley doesn't acknowledge him. Instead, he leans in, a faint shadow crossing him once more, and says, "Chicago is filled with crime, so we know a lot given how busy we are."

"In all fairness," Reed says, "we don't plan on solving these murders or finding this guy. He passed through here on his way to a bigger job, probably. We just need to make the city feel safe. Once we've investigated, done what we can do here, we'll pass the information on to the next municipality where the killer strikes."

"But we're doing all we can," Bradley adds.

"We are," confirms Reed. "I didn't want to tell you over the phone all of this information, light as it seems. Sorry to call you out in this whether; I never talk to media over the phone."

"Of course." I shuffle in my seat, eager to put my hat back on and leave. "Great. Well, thank you for your time. You've given me a lot to write about." Standing, I almost offer Chief Reed my hand but pull it back because it's too cold and shaky. I give him a pathetic wave instead, and he rubs his vest.

"Stay safe," he says, as if he had rehearsed it.

Detective Bradley doesn't speak to me, but I dart out of there before he can change his mind about it.

On the street, I adjust my hat and blink snowflakes out of my lashes. They flutter over my cheeks and down my shirt, my body heat melting them, which causes my cleavage to dampen. I wipe it away, but the coolness only smears, and I shiver as I zip my coat up to my chin.

Step, step, step. Heel, toe.

He knows. He watches. *I don't have anything you want.* "I don't have anything you want." *I was only in there for my job.* "I was only in there for my job."

So I hail a cab and dive through the yellow door, and the driver takes me to my apartment. Before I get out, though, I hesitate on the handle, trying to see out the foggy, iced window.

No one. Nothing. Just like every time I look for him, he's not visible.

FULLER PARK POLICE DEPARTMENT of Chicago Police Department (CPD) claimed on Tuesday morning that they have no leads on the unidentified serial killer's motive for the brutal murders of five people in various states since last June. The murders are still under investigation by law enforcement agencies across the country, as they examine the signature of whom authorities and media have deemed the Button Collector.

Detective Michael Bradley of CPD says, "These murders aren't random. We just don't know what his motive is."

Because each victim is part of the same family line, authorities have concluded that there are connections with the victims, which pose a threat among the rest of the family. These similarities include lacerations of their throats and a button from an article of their clothing or accessory sewn to their lips.

"It isn't about gender or sex," Chief Reed of CPD says, a conclusion he drew due to the unequal number of males and females murdered thus far, as well as the fact that there has been no evidence that points to rape or sexual abuse.

In addition, "age is not a factor," according to Detective Bradley. The victims of whom authorities are calling the Button Collector range from 14 to 89 years old, leading country-wide police departments to believe the unidentified murderer's motive lies beneath the surface.

Last week, Martha Pax, 89, was murdered in her home late at night; however, Chief Reed says that due to evidence collected at the scene, the murder is unlike any other.

"This is a unique murder...[Pax] is not blood related to the family, and her button came from her purse, not an article of clothing," he says.

The Pax murder is currently under investigation with CPD and Cook County Sheriff's Office.

"We want Chicago residents to feel safe," he says.

Police, however, are concerned with the lack of DNA or evidence left behind at each crime scene, noting there has been no trace of skin, bodily fluids, fingerprints, or hair found thus far.

I keep going for a hundred words about the past murders, just to recap, then I add some fluff to what I'd previously written about Martha's murder. Grandma Martha. Part of me was relieved when Grandpa died so we'd stop having to visit the woman who tried so hard to pretend she loved me like one of her own.

I don't mention the fact that this morning, Chief Reed said they weren't planning on solving the case, and I choose to ignore it myself. It kind of pisses me off that they're letting the killer slide by with the expectation that he's moved on to another city, but with every murder, he only moves closer to me. My feelings don't lie. My intuition isn't false.

At nine-hundred words, I email the article to John. He responds in an instant. I can almost smell the cigarette from here, held between his loose lips, the tip of the white stick lost in the darkness behind his teeth. He reminds me in his email that he's got some interns on my usual stories so I can focus on the Collector one, but I distract myself anyway with a handful of stories on shootings, the recent statement the mayor made about the spike in crime. John's email says, *Stay remote today, remember,* as if it's a demand. He didn't mean it like that, though I do appreciate my hybrid position. I'll appreciate my promotion too.

I pour into my work for a few hours then lie on the sofa to watch the evening news with a cup of black coffee. The headline on a local channel restates almost everything I've just written, excluding only some of the direct quotes. Chief Reed's and Detective Bradley's responses were rehearsed, as I'd suspected.

I shake my head, snap off the power to the TV, and watch as the screen shutters black. A stool stomps overhead, its sound dulled through my ceiling. Six steps follow the noise, then fades into silence.

Peering through my window, I notice the ground four levels down is pale, covered with a thin layer of fresh snow. Still, the Collector isn't somewhere I can see. That's the point, isn't it? His theme? To go unseen, unheard, without leaving a hair behind? Besides, it's evening, and he doesn't come until dark. Perhaps I'm safe until then. But I think that every night. It's become a routine. Go to sleep, wake every few hours, see that he isn't here, and then close my eyes again. Nightmares come and go. Unpredictable. Breathing becomes difficult at sunset, once the light of day slips behind the city. After the first murder—Robert's—it was assumed by everyone that it was a fluke. Of course, the situation was new—nothing in his home stolen, no evidence of any abuse other than the Collector's signature move to slash his throat and sew his lips together with a button from his polo. It was Rosa's death, the same brutal nature of his work, that tattooed my brain with the fear that this was by his design. Whoever he is, whatever his motivation is, these killings were no coincidence. This is intentional. He is climbing down my family tree one branch at a time. I wondered if the rest of the family had made the same connection. For the first time since my parents' lives were taken in the crash, I was grateful to be alone. I'm actually thankful I don't have anyone to worry about except myself.

My cell phone ringing on the glass coffee table pulls my attention away from the cool window.

I answer without looking at the caller ID. "Hey, Aunt Deb—"

"Hi, Jessica. It's Ben." My blood turns cold.

"I—I know who it is."

"Oh, my number must be in your con—"

"From the last time you called me. Last week."

The sound of his shuffling feet snakes through the line, his version of a stutter. "Well, you never got the chance to answer my question about this weekend. You know, about what you're doing?"

"I've got quite the workload." The lies roll off my tongue without any effort. "John's given me a ton to do outside of my regular stories."

"Maybe Sunday evening—"

"I've asked you not to call my personal number, Ben."

The line fuzzes with stillness, both waiting for the other to explain.

"I just thought—"

"Stop calling me at home, Ben. We're just coworkers."

He exhales a breath of frustration and ends our call by slamming it down. It rattles against a hard surface before it disconnects, and I imagine it made a mark given the force of his actions. I imagine there are probably dozens of other marks there too, each left behind where he's smashed his phone in a rage after my rejections.

I set down my cell gently with shaking fingers.

Ben didn't used to obsess. It began when I moved up to his floor at the office three years ago, and I was assigned a desk nearby his. He'd asked me out more than once, but I had turned him down. The first few times I'd made excuses, but he continued to persist until ultimately,

I gave in. Sure, he was attractive to me back then, but his overbearing nature was already turning me off from him. Ben was something of a curiosity to me. While I hadn't necessarily wanted to go out with him, I determined he was the type to shut up if I just gave him the chance to see that after one date he would realize I'm not very likable. His disposition was sweet toward me—all the flattery was nice—but something growled underneath his pushy mannerisms. It lurked like a predator waiting for his prey.

The next time I showed up at work after our date, I tried to avoid him, but one morning I walked in on him in the break room. He shot me an angry glance and threw his mug in the sink so hard that it shattered. That following day, he'd smiled as though nothing had ever happened, as if he'd never said that he would kill me if I told anyone what happened that night. It was an empty threat. Ben was only thirsty and desperate. Obsessive. He's no Button Collector.

John's office is warm, but it might just be the cloud of his smoke blanketing me in heat. It comforts me in a strange way, how it coils in fine kinks before settling over my shoulders. On Thursday, the snow succumbed to a light rain drizzle that is still falling on this dreary Monday morning.

"Good job on the Button story, Knight. You killed it." He lights a new cigarette, the tip glowing to life. "No pun intended."

I take a seat in front of his desk. This room is always dark, barely lit by a golden lamp that sits on top of his filing cabinet. It reminds me of a pub without the alcohol.

John leans back and takes a long drag off his cigarette. "The cops say anything good about Buttons?" He crosses his legs.

"They said they weren't planning on solving the case. I suppose because the murders have been so spread out."

"Well, as soon as they do, I want you on that story." He even points to me with his ring finger to prove it. His thin, gold band is fogged over with years of a dirty marriage, barely noticeable anymore. "You add something to this case, Knight, and I think our readers like it. We sold two-thousand extra copies on Sunday."

"Thank you." I say it more like a question. "It's an interesting case."

"I'll have you write an update on it next week, another follow-up piece."

"What if there is no update?"

"So get a few more quotes from the police. Contact people outside of Chicago. Get to the bottom of why there's no update, should that be the case. You're the journalist, Knight. Not me." He turns his chair back to face his computer, silently dismissing me.

Back at my desk, I open my list of new stories: CPD press releases I've been sent, all stand-offs, domestic violence arrests, a rapist suspect. Same old. I pause for a cup of coffee three hours later and stretch my feet until they are kicked out under my desk. It's a rare treat to get an undisturbed moment in the bustling office, so just as I am relishing the calm, my desk phone rings. I expect to hear Ben's voice on the other end but remember he's only a few desks down from mine.

"Hello, is this Jessica Knight?" Still, I'm surprised that the voice on the other end belongs to a female.

"This is she."

"I'm Detective Morgan with the Eau Claire Police Department in Wisconsin; however, I'm in Spooner today. This concerns your aunt Deborah." Her voice is stern, softened by a refined touch of sympathy.

My legs lose feeling, the numbness crawling up to my waist. The immediate image that forms in my mind is painted dark with blood, her body lying face-up on her braided yellow rug with her hair tangled in gray knots from the Collector's grip. She's dead. I know it. Why didn't I get a call from anyone about my other family members? Martha Pax? They should've definitely called me about her; I share the same city with her. *Shared*, rather. They must be calling me because I was the last person in Deborah's call log. Her cell was probably tight in her hand when the police found her. She was probably trying to call me, to warn me. But I'm not sure whether I would have picked up the phone if she had called.

Sour bile sizzles on the back of my tongue, and I want to stand up, run to the bathroom to vomit, but I force it back down; the cord on the phone won't let me leave this desk.

"Ms. Knight, Deborah has asked us to inform you of an incident." She *asked*, which means she's alive. I begin to breathe again.

"Is. . . is she okay?" I stammer.

"Ma'am, at one o'clock this morning, 911 operators received a call from her residence claiming that the Button Collector had tried to murder her. She has had quite the traumatic experience—her throat has been slit, and her lips were sewn together. She injured herself by tearing the button off with her own hands. The slit on her neck was not severe, which saved her life. Had it been any deeper or closer to her artery, she would have bled out like the rest of the Button Collectors' victims."

"So you're sure it was the serial killer?" Hot tears sting my eyes, but I blink them away. Fear wraps my airways in a tight hold, ropes me into the belief that I'm next, that I'm running out of family members, and it's coming down the line to me.

"After authorities' initial investigation early this morning, they confirmed in a press conference around noon today that it was the Button Collector who broke into the home and attempted to murder the victim."

The woman stops, takes a breath.

"As of now, your aunt is stable in the Eau Claire trauma center, but you were her emergency contact. She asked for you as soon as she could speak. She's really unable to communicate now due to the bandages."

"So she's going to be okay?"

"Remarkably."

"Do you know how—I mean, what happened? Did they catch him?"

"No, ma'am, but authorities will be at the hospital soon to try and ask her a few questions. We are optimistic about finding him now that someone has seen him."

"But" —my face falls into the cup of my palm, rubbing away the disbelief— "she survived? How did she survive?"

"I'm not at liberty to share these sorts of details with anyone until we know more about this case. The case is still under investigation with Spooner PD and Eau Claire County Sheriff's Office."

"Um." I lower my voice, hunching over a sticky notepad and pen. "Can you tell me what hospital that is again? Can I visit her?"

"In many situations, a niece wouldn't be allowed at this time, but since she considered you to be her immediate, closest family, you're the exception."

My skin prickles at her words. *Immediate, closest family.* Another reminder that I must be next.

I rub my finger over the button on my sweater sleeve, a soft wooden circle with a knot of thread holding it in place.

It's an hour flight to Eau Claire, Wisconsin. The four-and-a-half-hour drive would've been cheaper, more practical, but without a license, I can't go far. Perhaps if my parents hadn't died in that pile-up before I turned sixteen, I'd be a little more useful.

John reassigned some of my stories to the interns, and I made the tough call to Ben to ask if he could take over that domestic violence and rape story I had started researching. I hated even asking, considering the subject matter. But I'm certain he's thought about it—sleeping with me without my consent. Ben was gracious and agreed to take my stories on such short notice. I told John I'd be back tomorrow. Another stomach bug, I'd said. Just a twenty-four-hour thing, probably.

From the airport, I take a cab to the hospital which is another twenty minutes away. I keep my burgundy suitcase close to my feet when I sit and tight on my chest when I walk. I wonder if the Button Collector is here, lurking, observing. I can't feel his eyes on me in this new place, but perhaps his familiarity will sneak up on me like it always does. I never know when he's there, when he isn't. Now that I think of it, over the weekend I never actually felt the weight of his eyes targeting my back. He must have been here, in Spooner, with his hands locked around Deborah's neck.

The hospital is chaotic but void of emotion, every face bland with exhaustion. I shiver, holding on to my suitcase until I track down Deb's room. Level 4, room 407. Her hallway is behind thick double doors and an imposing desk, though the nurse allows me to step through without a second glance.

The doors lock behind me, and I follow the numbers on the wall leading me straight to room 407. Outside stands a man dressed in black with *POLICE* written across his chest. My attention goes directly to the gun on his belt. Such an easy way to kill someone, with that thing. Why choose a knife? Why thread a needle?

"I'm Jessica Knight, Deborah's niece."

He presses down on the door handle, then stops mid-way. "You need to know that this happened only about sixteen hours ago, so she's still sort of hysterical. If you need me to calm her down, I'm just outside. Call a doctor, as well."

He pushes the door the rest of the way open and motions for me to go inside, and I hold my breath, as if it'll eliminate my urge to vomit.

Aunt Deborah lies still on the thin white mattress, wrapped in a blanket way too light to keep her warm. She looks dead. Her neck is layered with white strips of bandage from ear to ear, her head tilted back on her pillow. Bandages also cover her upper and lower lips, leaving little room for breathing, let alone eating or speaking. IVs are strung from her forearms and wrists.

Stopping at the sound of the door closing behind me, I close my eyes to quickly let my nausea wash over me. The hairs stand up on my arms, crawling up the back of my neck, until I feel my stomach constricting to press the vomit out of me. I take a breath, open my eyes, and swallow the fleeting feeling.

"Deb? It's me, Jessica." I try to keep my voice quiet.

She raises up but winces, throwing herself back onto her pillow and moaning something inaudible.

"Yeah, it's me," I say. I set down my suitcase.

The rings under her eyes are dark, navy blue, purple in the corners from whatever beating she endured. She shakes when she sees me, reaching her frail arm toward me. "*Gesh.*"

Jess.

I pull up a chair and grab her hand, her skin delicate and thin in my grip.

Her words crackle, fractured with grief. Everything she says sounds like it begins with a *sh* sound because of the bandage. I tilt my ear toward her but can still hardly make out her jumbled words through disabled speech.

"I saw the killer."

I want to shout, *Who is it then?* but I try to stay calm for her sake. "Did you tell the police?"

"I kept screaming. I kept screaming, 'Who are you? Why?' But he cut me, and—and I couldn't talk. All I could see when I ripped off the toboggan was the bald head."

I glance behind me to see if the officer might be standing there and feel suddenly isolated when I see only the closed door.

"Deb—"

She takes my hand with both of hers, squeezing, pulling me forward. "I couldn't do anything. You have to tell the police, *Geshica*. Tell them you're next. If you tell them you're next, they'll believe you."

"I will. I'll tell them," I lie.

"Beg them to protect you like they're protecting me, now." She raises her voice as best she can, her grip tightening. "Make them listen to you. They didn't listen to me after Rosa. They didn't believe I was next."

I try to pry out of her hold, but she keeps me in front of her, jolting me, shaking when she shouts, "Tell them, *Geshica*. This is going to be you. It'll be you next. He's going to find me in here, because he knows I'm alive."

A fresh line of red appears across her neck; the wound has opened. She bleeds through her bandage, a large crimson streak growing with each beat of her heart. "Okay, Aunt Deborah, you're bleeding. You need to—"

"I can't stay here. He knows I saw the bald head, the eyes, and now I'm trapped here."

"Deb, lay back." I turn to the door. "I need help in here," I call to the officer outside.

She begins to chant over and over, "Tell them you're next. I can't stay here. I can't stay here. Tell them you're next."

The policeman appears beside the bed, and two nurses race through the door. As they begin to adjust Deb's bandages, she releases me. I grab my suitcase and run out the door before anyone can stop me. She calls after me, but I don't turn back. Even if I wanted to, her words are slurring together, and I know her body is shutting down from the morphine they're giving her. Silence floods the hall again, as I make my way back to the safety of the nurse's station.

It's not until a strong grip lands on my shoulder that I realize my hands are covering my ears. It's the cop.

"It's just me. Just me," he says.

Still covering my ears, I nod to him and follow as he walks me a few paces away so we can speak in private. The officer lets me catch my breath before he talks.

"Did you say anything that triggered her?"

"No. No, she started telling me that I need to tell the police I'm next, because I'm related to her. And she said he's coming back for her. The killer." The words tumble out of my mouth before I can think clearly.

"Right, I heard that. Since you're in town, I'd like for you to go with another officer to the police station. We'd like to talk to you, get anything you can give us about Deborah and your family."

"Shouldn't you be stationed outside her door?" I ask.

"Another officer will be here shortly."

"Oh, you said that already."

"Why don't you wait in the lobby? He'll escort you down to the station. Come get you so you don't have to take a cab."

Come get you. He'll come get you. I rock back and forth on my heels, and the cop offers me a smile, acknowledging his mistake.

"Your aunt will be out for a while, so if I were you, I'd let her rest. It might be best if you come back tomorrow. I'm sure the doctor will call if anything changes."

The waiting room is large and spread out, so I find a quiet corner and wait. Twenty minutes later, an officer with a bushy black beard walks in. Somehow, he knows I'm the victim's niece, walking straight toward my chair. "Jessica Knight?"

"Yes."

He leads me to his car and holds open the door while I crawl inside. The ride to the station is short and silent, so I keep my eyes focused on the clock at the center of the cruiser's dash. It's ten after five when we arrive.

"Would you like to leave your baggage at the front desk?" he asks in a gruff voice.

I almost say no, but my paranoia convinces me that my refusal might raise their suspicion of me, if they have any, so I agree to leave it.

I'm led to an interrogation room that has a wide mirror I can only assume is double sided. I wonder how many other officers are behind it, studying me. I sit facing the officer who is waiting for me. His face seems friendlier than the bearded man who is still at my side. He stands and introduces himself as Chief Lindsay and asks how I'm doing. I lie and say I'm doing well.

"Don't be intimidated by the look of this room. My office is just a little snug, so we moved you in here," he says with a wink.

He sits, but the bearded officer remains standing.

"As you know, the serial killer made his way to Spooner, and I mean" —he laughs to mask his discomfort— "this is a shock for our small town. We barely get a robbery around here."

I shuffle in my hard seat and look down at the scuff marks on the floor, imagining how they got there.

"Sorry." He clears his throat and sits straight up. "That was rude of me. Has anyone told you what happened to your aunt?"

The bearded cop checks his phone then tucks out the door, excusing himself. I shake my head.

"Deborah told us that she was lying in bed, had just turned off the TV, when she heard someone break the glass on her front window. This is not the typical pattern, as you know. The Button Collector normally strikes after people are already asleep. We assume he thinks they're less aggressive that way. Your aunt heard him coming and was prepared to fight back, but he overpowered her. He continued with his usual routine—slit her throat, let her bleed, and tried to sew a button to her lips. She had already dialed 911 on her phone when she heard the glass break, so they were on the line when the attack began."

"Did they hear his voice?"

"Unfortunately not. Only the victim's," says Chief Lindsay. "By the time we got there, she was unconscious, and the killer had fled the scene. She came to in the ambulance, frantic, and woke up and began tearing the thread off her lips, saying nothing but, 'Tell Jessica. Tell Jessica.'"

"Oh, my God."

"Are you alright?"

"I'm fine. Go on."

"EMS took care of her and got her bandaged up."

"He knows where to find. . . everyone."

"You are correct. He's definitely done his research. This time, he seemed like he was in a rush. Perhaps he only assumed your aunt would be asleep, or he didn't see the television on minutes before, but still, he left a clean crime scene."

He had to rush back to Chicago.

"So tell me what you know about your aunt." Chief Lindsay's upper body bounces as he crosses his legs, and he gives me a gentle grin.

Instinctively, I trust him. I feel myself almost involuntarily leaning toward him, reaching out to place my faith in someone.

My right heel taps the floor, but maybe he can't hear it. "She's afraid. I mean, she's been afraid since Rosa, her daughter, was killed by the Collector, so she's really paranoid."

"That would explain why she seemed at least a little bit prepared for him. Her paranoia might've saved her life. Are you two close?"

"Not very close, no, but she's the only family I really speak to. My parents died when I was young, so I lived with a foster family for a while, then a friend, and then I moved for college and we kind of lost contact. But Deborah was the one person I still spoke to once in a while. She called me a lot after Rosa."

Chief Lindsay nods, waiting for me to go on.

"She would call and ask me to come live with her or to tell me that the killer is after me. Or her, actually. Turns out she was right."

"Do you sense that he is after you? I mean, have you seen anything suspicious?"

His question gives me a break to consider how I do feel. The Button Collector doesn't know I'm in here. He can't keep up with me moving this fast. I'm safe to say what I want to say, but I am cautious with my words.

"He's moving down the line, killing random people in my family. I should be next." *And he's watching me.* They'd think I'm crazy.

"Are you scared?" he asks me when I don't continue.

"Yes."

"Now, tell me your relation to all the victims."

"Well, my parents are dead, to start with, but Deborah was my dad's sister. Rosa was her daughter. Um, Martha Pax—she married my grandpa, so that's my dad's dad, but Grandpa died when I was really little. Martha never exactly felt like family, but she lived the closest to me."

"Okay."

"On my mom's side, her brother was my uncle Josh, and he's been killed. My mom's and Josh's sister—the mother of my cousin Robert who was also killed—lives in Alaska."

"She's alive?"

"Yeah. She's so far away, though."

"Too far for the killer to travel, no quick in and out for him."

"Anyway, um, there's Julianne, my great aunt. She was my dad's mom's sister."

"And Martha was your deceased grandpa's. . . ex-wife?"

"Yes."

Chief Lindsay falls silent as he connects the dots, his pupils moving all along my face in his intense focus, only for it to be concluded with the wide-eyed realization that the puzzle of dead people is missing one piece: me.

I nod to him, as if affirming that I am in as much trouble as I thought, and now, as he thinks.

"This is rather alarming, Ms. Knight," he nearly mumbles, rubbing his chin. Readjusting his position to lean over the table, his warm eyes peer into mine, fingers locked in a confident grasp. "Ms. Knight, I'm not going to lie to you, okay?"

I look down.

"You need to take precautions."

"And the rest of my living family members? Besides me and Deborah?"

"We're going to have their local police department meet with them individually to explain what I'm explaining to you, but you're. . . you're more at risk than they are, Ms. Knight. For now, take all precautions you can. If you walk to work, ride. If you sleep with the blinds open, close them."

"But he comes at night and kills them when they're asleep."

"Keep your doors locked at all times. Are you in a house or apartment?"

"Apartment."

"Then you should be a little safer there since there's probably some kind of authorization code or card to enter the building."

"Yeah."

"Tell your neighbors to keep an eye out, still, and I strongly suggest you go to bed after two thirty a.m. every night, because his murders have each happened prior to that time. Do you own a gun?"

"No."

"Then keep a knife by your bed, or a taser, pepper spray, a bat. Anything that you can defend yourself with. We've begun working with the police departments in the cities where your other distant—very distant, and probably not threatened—family members live and will have them assign an officer or detective to each one where resources allow. Just to keep an eye out for anything suspicious. We want you all to be on guard, but you're of the closest relation to the victims, as well as your aunt. The rest of your family. . . well, the ties you had to them are no longer here. Did you tell anyone you were coming to Wisconsin from Chicago, Ms. Knight?"

"No, no one."

"Good. If you do any traveling, keep your whereabouts on the down low. Be as low-key as you can during this time. Now, your aunt gave a description of the person who harmed her. She told us this information while she was still pretty. . . ill, so the details are a little fuzzy. She wasn't speaking very clearly. Nonetheless, Ms. Knight, do you know anyone of short stature who's bald?"

I've asked myself his question a hundred times since my visit with Deb last hour. "No. I really don't."

"Well, like I said, Deborah was pretty hysterical, so her description might not even be accurate."

He must sense the terror stabbing me from my scalp to my toes, because he goes on.

"I'm not saying any of this to scare you but to make you aware of what you can do to protect yourself. If you have any concerns or experience anything suspicious, call your local police department, but please rest assured that we're going to be in contact with them as soon as possible and alert them of the severity of this situation. I'll tell them to make you a priority."

Heat floods my face, and I can feel the sweat budding through my pores under my heavy coat. A lump clogs my throat.

"Ms. Knight, I know this sounds funny, but one last thing before I let you go—if you can help it, try to wear clothes without buttons."

～

It's dark by the time I get to a hotel and am able to check into a room. I'd booked one right in the center of Eau Claire, where people can see me, and I can see them, and no one can get away with anything. The city lights glow loudly below, juxtaposed by a quiet stillness up in my room. Safe or not, I yank the curtains shut.

I take a shower, washing off the remnants of germs from the airplane, the police department, and Aunt Deborah's touch. Then I turn up my room temperature to seventy-four degrees.

Checking my phone, I find I've missed both a call from Ben and a text from John. I open the text. *Hope you're feeling better.* I ignore it and delete Ben's voicemail without listening. The TV is tuned to the local news channel, so I watch it to see what they have to say about Deborah's attempted murder.

"Authorities are claiming that the serial killer, also called the Button Collector, is a small, bald man, based on the description the victim gave."

I learn nothing new from the news, so I turn it off, a little disappointed to know that they have no leads, except that the Button Collector has a problem with my family. But none of them have a connection, at least I don't think. My parent's car accident—was this somehow related? Could they have been the first to be murdered? I shake my head; I don't want to have any nightmares tonight.

It takes an hour for my hair to dry after the shower, but I still tuck it into a brown hat to keep its dampness off my neck. I roll my turtleneck up over my chin, put on a scarf to block even more cold air, and fold up my coat collar. The temperature outside is twenty-seven, not including wind chill, but it's warm and quiet in the cab I climb in outside of the hotel lobby.

"Can you take me to 32 Woods Drive in Spooner?" I ask the driver.

Thirty minutes later, he slows the car and turns off on a dark backroad with one traffic lane full of potholes. I pay the driver, and he speeds away. His red taillights become ominous dots in the distance until I'm left alone on a lonely road covered by draping trees.

Deborah's dirt driveway is blocked from tree trunk to tree trunk with yellow police tape.

The taxi's headlights provided my only source to see as we drove up, but now it's gone, and I have to use my phone's flashlight. I sneak under the police tape and walk down the unlit path to Deborah's cabin. It's nothing but a black silhouette under the looming pines. The outline of her chimney serves as a guide that her bedroom window is also on the left side of the house.

Moonlight reflects off the broken glass on the ground; I can see the sparking fractals from here.

Deb had told me over the phone where she keeps her front door key hidden, in case I ever found myself in Spooner. Really, she had just wanted me to move in. I retrieve the key from the soil in her flowerpot and unlock the dark, wooden door.

The room is clean, quiet, and seems to be untouched by an intruder. The smell of cedar chokes me, reminding me of Rosa's wake, which took place right here. I tune out the scent and close the door behind me. Going left through her den takes me to the short hallway that leads to her bedroom, where I flick on her overhead light. My shoes are carrying dirt, so I remain on the outside of the crime scene. Black plastic covers her shattered window, where more police tape sways in gusts of bitter wind that slips through. Dried blood spots the bed, the carpet, the wooden dresser. The light makes me feel exposed, so I step back into the shadows. I wait to hear movement of some sort, but who am I kidding? The killer is long gone. Authorities have been adamant that he doesn't revisit his crime scenes.

Inside my gut, something twists, and a nauseating feeling settles in my stomach again. I go back the way I came and walk upstairs, flipping on lights as I go.

Deborah's bonus room is a twelve-by-twelve cube, books stacked high to the ceiling and boxes loaded with Rosa's old schoolwork, her bedroom decorations, her clothes. Five months ago, all this stuff had a place downstairs. I shove through it all and make my way to a hollowed-out corner. My dad's college diploma hangs on the wall, crooked, but it's there. His old blazer and ugly Christmas sweater are folded and in a cardboard box. The day I lost my dad, Aunt Deborah lost her brother. She must've taken these things from our house the day everyone came over after the funeral. His old scarves and gloves are in one box, and framed pictures of him and my mom are in another. I get on my knees and open the box of pictures, finding my parents' wedding photographs, moments from our family vacation to Niagara Falls, and one from Halloween. Mom and Dad didn't dress up with me, but I was in a cat costume. I must've been eight or nine years old.

I put down the pictures before I get too emotional and dig deeper inside the box to find an old newspaper buried at the bottom. The edges are faded yellow, and the center is crinkled from an old water stain. Pulling it out, I shake off the dust.

The Portsmouth Journal, published in my hometown three Julys before I was born. The front-page headline reads "Local man accused of embezzlement." And staring back at me is my father.

I skipped out on visiting Deborah again before I left town. My flight was leaving at ten in the morning, and I didn't want to risk upsetting her or her blood pressure again, and I didn't want to risk being angry with her over keeping the contents of that article away from me for all these years. I slept for most of the hour-long flight anyway.

Last night, I studied the article about my dad and conducted a bit of research. The case was settled almost as fast as it was filed; Dad had gone to prison, and the man who accused him of embezzlement, a guy named Castro, got his money back, and two years later, Dad was free, living his life again, and finding out Mom was pregnant with me. It was obviously a big story in my little town at the time, which is probably why Deborah kept this, but I've never heard a thing about it. All I know is that embezzlement sounds like it could be a possible motive for revenge.

Without any trouble, I make it back to my apartment building. On my level, I step out of the elevator and right into Melanie. My exaggerated sigh, as usual, doesn't give her the hint that I'm tired, so she starts jabbing about why she hasn't seen me around the building, and whether I liked her cherry pie. I don't have the heart to tell her that in reality, I forgot all about her stupid pie. I make a mental note to throw it away as soon as I go in my apartment. I fake a smile, tell her I loved it, and slip away before she can ask any more questions.

In the safety of my apartment, I drop my bag at the door and toss the cold pie in the garbage, where it falls with a satisfying thump. The cherry filling splats all over the white trash bag, jarring me with the memory of Deb's bedroom.

"You disgust me," I mutter to the Collector. Just in case he's listening, watching. "Can't she see I don't want her pie?"

"Maybe you should try being more neighborly," a heavy voice responds.

I spin around and knock over a wine glass, which shatters on the floor in my panic. Detective Michael Bradley stands in the light of my living room window, a face I thought I would only recognize in Chief Reed's dark office. He turns to face me, and I go stiff with my hand over my mouth, locking in a scream still clawing to escape.

He sticks his fists in the pockets of his slacks and begins moving toward me. The black coat he's got on makes a light swishing noise with each stride, and I scout to see if there are any guns poking out from underneath it.

"Then you might be grateful for her pie," he says.

"What the hell are you doing here?" I almost shout.

His expression goes flat, his feet stomping to a halt. "Why didn't you tell us you're related to the victims?"

All I can do is look away, flushing, and busy myself by picking up the remnants of the wine glass and throwing it away. Then I go to the kitchen and flip on the water in my sink and let it run to overtake the silence as he waits for me to answer. He's tracked me down, seen my apartment without it being cleaned first, heard me talking to the killer. I shut off the water and enter the living room, wanting to be more intimidating than I am.

"You're lucky you had an alibi, or else you could've been named a suspect for withholding information," he says.

"You and Chief Reed weren't interviewing me that day," I say. "I was there for work getting information from you, not the other way around. My personal life was not relevant to my article." The least I can do is attempt to look comfortable in my own home, so I sit on my sofa and cross my ankles. He remains standing. "And why are you in my apartment? How did you even get in?"

"Spooner PD gave us a call with the information. Told us you need some kind of protection. I've been assigned to you and wanted to be here before you got home in case you had someone else waiting here for you." The undertone to his voice is heavy and knowing.

Knowing I can't deny that. I scoff.

He takes off his coat and throws it over his forearms, then he props up his leg on my coffee table, leaning on his knee. His white button-up is rolled up to his elbows, and his position stretches the fabric. "So let's talk about why you *were* hiding that information."

"How did you get into my apartment?" I ask again.

"You left your door unlocked. Smart move."

"Ugh, God."

I roll my neck back in an attempt to loosen the tension, then, without meaning to, I lock onto Bradley's green eyes. He doesn't blink. He knows people can't lie straight to a person's face. But I have nothing to keep from him. "I didn't hide anything."

Bradley throws his hands up and swipes them through his sandy blond hair before turning his back to me. Tilting his head toward my oil painting on the wall, he takes in the image of a dreary gray skyscraper and straightens the cuffs of his shirt.

"Did it occur to you that you might be the Button Collector's next victim?"

"Are you kidding me?" My answer doesn't satisfy him. "Constantly," I add.

"If that is the case, then did it cross your mind that you probably shouldn't hide any valuable information from the police? We don't know who this guy is or what his motive is, and you—his next potential *victim*—

didn't feel the need to tell the authorities that Martha Pax was your grandmother?"

"Step-grandmother." I stand. "And you didn't take this much consideration with my other family members."

He spins around to face me again, closing the space between us. "The police questioned them, yes, but to be honest, there weren't that many left. The only reason you didn't get special treatment was because we didn't know who you were at the time and just how closely related to the victims you are."

"Well, who am I, then?" *You're the one live person connecting both sides of your family. You're also the person Ben said he'd kill if you told anyone about that night.* The thought dances in my head, but I try to shove it away. Like a stone landing on my chest, I suddenly regret I haven't told anyone about Ben's threats. Ben wouldn't kill my family, though. He'd only be interested in killing me.

"You're the journalist covering the murders of your own relatives. I would think that might be important to disclose. Look, I'm not here to scare you, sweetheart" —he adjusts his shirt sleeves again— "but to a murderer who seems to have a problem with the Knight blood, you sure do look like a fine target."

"Because I'm doing my job and reporting on a murder in the city?" I say, but of course, I know that's not what Bradley meant. It only pissed me off that he called me "sweetheart."

"No." His response is stern and sure. "Serial killers typically thrive off media attention, but this guy isn't leaving any clues, any evidence, any messages to police or the public other than his signature button move. Authorities are saying that attention isn't what he's after. This is a psychopath profiled over and over again by professionals, Ms. Knight, and they're concluding that he has a personal vendetta against your family. And, Ms. Knight, you're nearing the last of them, plus, you're reporting on him—a person who isn't looking to release his identity any time soon. His root is anger. Not attention."

"I'm just a sitting duck, then? I'm just supposed to quit my job, leave Chicago, and plant myself in some rural Alabama town?" I know I don't have to keep reporting on the Collector and giving him the attention he evidently doesn't want, but my raise and promotion are a temptation I'm obviously willing to roll the dice for.

"No." Chuckling, Bradley glances down at his shoes as he moseys toward me. "You can stay right here. We're just going to become really good friends, and based on your attitude, you don't seem to be thrilled by CPD's protection."

His lips curl into a clever smile that thrusts me backward onto the sofa. "So, what—you're just going to move in with me until the killer is found?" I ask.

"You need us, Ms. Knight. As the daughter connecting the two sides of this family, you need us."

Good. He's concluded *that* part. "Well?" I press.

He doesn't answer, but stalks toward the kitchen and surveys the cabinets, the ceiling, even the trash can with the remnants of Melanie's pie. "Not moving in, but I will be patrolling right outside your door. I'll be watching everyone who comes through the building, and I'll be sweeping your apartment and the building every evening after you get home from work. Isn't that what you want?"

"I can sweep my apartment myself."

"You'll be allowing me the pleasure, actually." He flashes me another grin and strolls past me to my windowsill, draping his coat from one arm to the other. "I get that you don't like me being here, so I'll leave soon, but everything aside, I would like to have a conversation with you. To get your take on this case."

I pause and consider how much he already knows. My dad, the embezzlement case, the Button Collector's constant presence that shadows me. When the police find out about all that, I truly will appear to be someone who's hiding something.

"Now?"

"Whenever you'd like."

I begin with a stutter, short of breath, then it comes out. "I think he watches me." Bradley doesn't shift. He nods at me to go on. "I can just feel him watching me. It started after Rosa, my aunt Deborah's daughter, was murdered. That's when I knew it must have something to do with the family."

"Do you think he's watching you right now?" His voice doesn't twist with sarcasm as I expect it to.

"No, it's not—it's not like that. It's only sometimes." I must sound pathetic.

"Are you—"

"It doesn't matter. It's probably only in my head."

"Why didn't you go to anyone about this?"

"Because it's just a feeling," I say. "I can't prove anything."

"So who were you talking to when you walked through the door just a minute ago?"

"My—myself."

He lets the conversation die, shifting his weight, taking his time perfecting the cuffs on his sleeves for a third obnoxious time. "You've got our full attention, now, Ms. Knight."

I almost correct him and ask him to call me Jessica, but I don't want him tasting my name on his tongue.

"It's best if you let us do our job, which is to protect you. We weren't very concerned about the Collector until Pax, but since he's moved through Chicago, we're involved now. I'm truly not meaning to scare you, but you must know that we're concerned about you. In fact, we fully expect that you might be his next target. You've got to do everything you can to stay safe, and you have to let us do our job."

His authority makes my skin prickle with annoyance. Bradley likes to be in control, and he likes it when I try to snub his power.

"Alright, Ms. Knight?"

To keep some level of formality between us, I say, "Thank you. I'll be on guard."

"I will be honest with you; we're having a hard time determining why the killer came to Chicago to kill Pax but leave you."

I sigh at the prolonged conversation, sore from the same trampled curiosities living inside me. "I don't know either."

He bites his bottom lip, then changes the subject. "I'd like to hear more about that feeling you get."

My mind can't bring to surface what he is asking me, the feeling he's referring to. I've lost it in the swamp of all my other emotions. But of course, he's talking about my sense that the Button Collector is watching me. Discussing my wild suspicions won't help anything or anyone. Not until we know a little more about what's going on.

"You said you were leaving."

"Right," he sneers, and my neck turns beet red with embarrassment...or anger. I can't tell which is worse.

I show him to the door.

"Remember, I'll be just outside your window. Here's my card. And my number." The white rectangle appears out of nowhere between his fingers, and I take it without looking. "Call me if you ever feel threatened." I catch the slightest hint of his minty breath, throwing me off guard. I step back an inch and look down at the floor.

"Goodbye," I say.

He holds the moment a second longer, his eyes lingering on me, and then he turns and walks away slowly, without a sound.

The second he's out, I lock the door behind him. I run to my window and drag the shade closed. Next, I pull the curtains in my bedroom and go back to the kitchen.

My knife block is old, barely used, and it sits on my countertop above a bumpy layer of grease that I have been avoiding for weeks. I pull out the biggest one. The blade is heavy, so I lay its weight in my palms, sharp side pointed toward my chest. My reflection shines back from the edge long enough for me to notice the dark rings under my eyes, framed by stringy brunette bangs. I don't like what I see, so I let the knife fall into grip by my side and place it under my pillow and lie down while it's still daylight.

~

I wake from my nap just before five in the afternoon to my phone buzzing with an incoming text. It's John asking me to come into the office for a chat. *Crap*, I think. What could he want? I sigh as I lace up my boots and think about how I will avoid Bradley on my way down.

Once I make it to the street, I cover my face with a scarf and pull my hat low so it might block my face from his view. Detective Bradley's police car is parked on the other side of the road, and, to my dismay, he spots me. Damn, he's efficient. He raises up when he sees me and flicks up a few fingers, but I pretend I don't see him there and hail a cab instead.

Della is in John's office when I arrive, and she takes her time uncrossing her legs to stand, waving goodbye to him even though she works just outside his door. The smell of cigarettes swamps her as she passes me. It's saturated under her clothes, in her hair, between her cleavage, probably lodged there from the night she spent with John.

"Knight, close that door behind you," John commands.

I do, then sit on the edge of the leather chair in front of his desk, unraveling my scarf.

"We need to have a talk, dear." He rests on his desk, not a cigarette in sight, to my surprise. His thinning, silver hair is held firmly in place with grease and doesn't budge when he slouches in his chair.

I swallow, which makes a loud, gurgling noise that I'm positive he can hear. "What is this about, John?"

He pauses, looking down at his hands, the wrinkles around his lips evident and growing deeper as his expression changes. I shake in my seat and hunker down, so he won't notice.

"It's about the Button Collector, dear. Chicago PD called." He waits to gauge my reaction. When I look down, he continues, "They called to inform us about what's going on with the case. Imagine my surprise when they also told us you were out of town. You said you were sick again, Knight. Are you lying? Were you ever actually sick? Is that what your other stomach bug was about too?"

"No, I really did throw up. I was sick before." I definitely almost threw up yesterday too.

"You lied to me and skipped town the other day. What's that about, Knight?"

"I had personal things to take care of. Family things."

"The detective said you might be in danger?"

It's a question, not a statement. Lying to John has always come naturally to me, but today, it's constricting me.

"It's possible that I'm in danger, yes, but since none of this concerned my work, I didn't tell anyone where I was going. The police told me not to tell anyone about my comings and goings."

"Well, I need you to tell me, Knight. Do you plan on leaving town again?"

I shake my head.

"Where did you go? Did you go to that other murder town?"

"I visited my aunt in Spooner."

"The cops think the Button Collector. . . They said he might be after you, Knight. Did you know about this? Are you aware of how serious this is? I mean, you've been leaving town in secret, and this guy is a serial killer. Were you ever going to tell me?"

"I only left once, and no, I wasn't planning to tell you. It's not relevant, and I didn't feel safe saying anything, anyway. The police advised me not to share my personal business anymore because I'll be risking my—my life." My voice quivers as I say that last part.

He angles back in his chair, yanking open his drawer to pull out a cigarette. "I'm giving you a mandatory break from work, Knight. Now, don't tell anyone what this is about" —he slips the cigarette between his thin lips— "and don't argue with me. You gotta keep this on the down-low, like you said. I don't want it to get out that one of my journalists is luring this killer to our neighborhood."

That's exactly what that Spooner PD officer told me—keep things on the down-low, stay out of sight. Become invisible.

"Don't be upset with me, though." John flicks his lighter, sparks a flame, and he holds it to the end of his white stick. "I'm doing this for your own good. You don't need to be writing these eerie stories, and you certainly don't need to be working on a case that might involve you while your family members are—you know. This is tragic for you, yeah?"

"It's been difficult, yes."

He leans over his desk again, folding his arms, sinking his head closer to me. Seems I've made him forget about his cigarette.

"Christ, Knight, why didn't you tell me sooner? Are you sure you're going to be okay?"

No, I never said I was sure. A lump swells in my throat and puts a strain on all my words.

"I couldn't have you feeling sorry for me at the office."

My face falls into my hands, and my shake grows to unmistakable fear. John inches closer, his hand now on my arm. I look up, trying to get some air, and my palms are dotted with black smears from my eyeliner, but John isn't focused on them; he looks only at me. He releases his grip from my arm and sits back down behind his desk.

"I'm worried about you, dear, but I can only feel sorry for you outside of the office, like you said. You know?" He shakes his head and pulls out his chair. "Why didn't you go to the police?"

I use my sleeve to wipe under my eyes just for something to do other than acknowledge his concern.

"I don't know," I say.

His chair scrapes the floor, and he stands, propping himself on the corner of his desk, looking down on me. The smoke from his cigarette swirls too close to my face. It's pure, white, pretty. It knows exactly how to disappear.

"You don't have to talk to me about this," he says. "But how is it that not one of our journalists discovered that you were a part of this family?"

I pull at my collar, adjusting it to mask my discomfort. My action forces a blast of cool air to trickle down my neck and roll down the back of my coat.

"It's a distant relation, because the victims are on both my mom's and dad's side of the family, so police only recently connected everyone to me. It took a while, especially since my parents are dead. The victims weren't close to me. Robert, cousin. Rosa, cousin. Julianne, great aunt. Josh, uncle. Martha, my grandpa's third ex-wife. And Deborah, my aunt. The police only discovered it when they linked me to Deb, and that's their job, so I'm not surprised that no one here has figured it out yet. You know about my parents, and you know I didn't really keep in touch with my family after that. I don't know why my family has been attacked and killed. I don't know who the Button Collector is. I don't know anything."

He brings the cigarette to his lips in a slow bend of the arm and sucks the smoke out of it, watching me. Blowing it out in a gentle exhale, careful to keep it opposite of me, the smoke twirls until it dissipates into more of a fog. "I know, Knight. I know."

We slip into a silent daze.

He takes his time stubbing out his cigarette and avoids looking at me. "You need some place to stay? Hide out?" he asks, his voice chalky with distress.

"I'll be fine. The police are watching my apartment. No one can get in the building without a keycard." I use my thumbs to wipe under the corners of my eyes.

John starts to step behind his desk, reaching for his drawer. "Do you need me to return my key? I will."

"No, no. Just don't let anyone know you have it."

"Sure," he mutters. "Sure. Now, listen, if there's anything I can do. . ."

I shuffle through my brain to think of something he'd be able to do to help me, but nothing can settle the rabid thoughts that are rattling through my mind.

"What did the police say to you?" he questions, despite my unease.

I wipe my face with my coat sleeve to keep snot from dripping down my nose. "They told me I should keep my head low and that I need to avoid the outdoors as much as possible."

"They still don't have any leads?" He puffs on a new cigarette, and I focus on the smoke discharging from his nostrils.

"No."

"And you've got no idea?"

I bite my lip, my gut winding into a tangled knot of discomfort. "I think I might know something, but I haven't told the police." Now that it's off my chest, the knot detangles a little.

John slaps his hands on the table, and I wince. He moves to the back of his desk chair and grabs the top of it. For the moment, I can't tell if he is happy I have a theory, or angry at me for keeping it a secret.

"For God's sake, Jessica, why? Are you trying to get yourself killed?"

The last time he called me by my first name was when I interviewed for this job three years ago. The only other time was later that week when he took me out for a drink.

"I only just found out about this a couple of days ago. I'm working on a theory, and I was going to tell them when I had something concrete."

"When?" He shakes his head at the seat of his chair, pulling it out so he can sit again. "Who is it?" On a casual occasion, John does well handling impatient situations, like when the paper is thirty minutes from going to press and he finds solace in a few additional cigarettes.

They aren't helping him today.

"I think it might be a man my dad embezzled from before I was born. I didn't even know about this until the other day."

"Wouldn't the police have already looked into this guy?"

"Why would they? My parents have been dead for ages. It's a lot of years to still be holding a grudge. I just need some more time to check this guy out."

"So who is he?"

"His name is Davis Castro." I look for any sort or recognition in John's face but there is none.

John doesn't say anything but lays his cigarette in the ashtray, crinkling it until it breaks.

"I'll tell the police soon," I say. "I just didn't really want to until I'm sure. Or at least until I know something more about this guy." If John knows I'm lying, he doesn't question me. I lie to John so often that I doubt he is even suspicious. The truth is, I could've told Detective Bradley about Castro and the embezzlement case, but I just wanted him out of my apartment. With him around, I couldn't think clearly.

"Knight," says John, "go back to your apartment and be safe. Listen to the police."

I gather my scarf and stand to leave. "But what about work? This paper can't run on a handful of journalists, John." Really, I am only concerned about the raise he mentioned a few days ago.

"We've got about six handfuls, Knight, and they all run on my tight clock. When all this is over, we'll talk promotion and raise again." I choose to believe him. "You can work remotely. Don't worry about it, dear. Send me some content every once in a while. Don't worry about your paycheck, alright, Knight? There is no reason you should be worrying about money. And don't touch another Button story."

"Okay. Thank you, John." At least that part is a relief.

"I really am sorry about your family, dear. You stay safe for me, alright?"

"Right." There's nothing else for me to do but thank him for his understanding. I can't even give him a smile. The only thing I can do is get out of sight.

Today, my complimentary newspaper is delivered by *The Chicago Post* people, so I go upstairs and read an article about Aunt Deborah, written by another journalist.

The article doesn't mention me. I'm not of any interest to the public yet. I won't be until I'm dead. I scan the article for anything that might help me make sense of how this is all connected.

ON JANUARY 9, the serial killer known as the Button Collector attacked Deborah Wilson of Spooner, Wisconsin, shortly after 12 a.m. in her Spooner residence.

Authorities at Eau Claire County Sheriff's Office have confirmed that this was an act of the notorious Button Collector due to the nature of the victim's injuries. Wilson suffered a knife wound to her neck and distinctive needle injuries to her lips, and police are confident the Button Collector was the attacker. No DNA was found at the scene.

Wilson, 47, is the only known victim to survive an attack by the Button Collector thus far. The Spooner emergency medical services arrived on the scene at 12:47 a.m. and transported Wilson to the hospital where she is still recovering.

Authorities say Wilson had suffered from a great amount of blood loss and are unsure how long she had been unconscious before arriving on scene.

Chief Lindsay of Spooner Police Department reports, "[Wilson] told us she called 911 when she heard her glass break and claims to have seen the killer before she lost consciousness. Wilson's traumatic injuries and distressed mindset prevent her from saying anything more."

The victim reports the Collector was wearing all black, including a hat and boots. She also claims the man was small and bald. Police are still investigating this case, so details are limited and still unconfirmed at this time.

"Ms. Wilson is still fearful and has been nearly hysterical since the incident," Lindsay says. "We're unsure if she's even aware of what she's saying."

Wilson is not the first in her family to be attacked by this killer. Her 14-year-old daughter Rosa Wilson was brutally murdered five months ago in the same home. Both Rosa and Deborah Wilson suffered from knife wounds to their throats and a button sewn to their lips. In addition, four of Wilson's other distant relatives have been fatally attacked by the Button Collector.

Chicago Police Department (CPD) continues their investigation of the murder of Martha Pax, which occurred in the Gresham neighborhood of Chicago just days prior to Wilson's attack.

Detective Michael Bradley of CPD is quoted saying, "It's unique that Debora Wilson survived this attack. The circumstances of this murderer's actions are getting stranger and stranger the longer his streak goes. These murders are connected, and authorities have identified a link between Pax and the targeted blood-related family. Pax was the third wife of a late family member."

Seeing Bradley's name pisses me off, so I toss the paper down. Plus, I don't want to read the crappy intern's work replacing my very own.

The last time I left my apartment was when John relieved me of my work duties yesterday. In twenty-eight hours, I've had six glasses of wine and a call-in order for Chinese food. When I paid the delivery man a couple of hours ago downstairs, I saw Bradley's police car aimed right at me from the street. I could only imagine the way his chin tilted upward with interest in my direction. He was obvious when he glanced back down once the delivery man walked away with my money. I waited for a minute, standing behind the safety of the double glass doors that were fogged over with ice and tried to make out Bradley's face. No matter how hard I tried, all I could see was his silhouette behind the outline of his steering wheel. But I knew he was watching me too. Especially as the headlights snapped on, glaring at me from across the street as if to taunt me. *I'm watching you, Knight.* Steam arose from my to-go bag, and I held the fire-hot bag to my chest, until the steam started searing my neck. Nothing more was going to come from this, so I lunged at the button for the elevator and rode up to floor 4 without a backward glance in his direction.

Two hours later, Bradley is still out there in the dark, and I can see him watching me. I slip open my blinds but turn off the lights so no one can see inside, including my proposed killer. Despite my annoyance, it is comforting to know that Bradley is there, juxtaposed by the killer peering at me from some corner of Chicago that I can't see.

I close my eyes and count back from ten. Nine.

Eight.

Seven.

On a normal occasion, my countdown would work long enough to make the Button Collector's eyes fall away from me, or at least make me think they do. It doesn't delay Bradley's deliberate stare. His white car remains clouded by mist and dampened with the frozen rain that has been falling all day, pooling on the heat of his engine since he's been idle for so long. If he'd just leave for five minutes to get dinner, maybe I'd be able to use the bathroom without worrying that he's watching. I wonder if he packs his food and pees in a bottle?

The hollow void in my core trickles full of something sharp like ice crystals. I know it isn't Bradley inspecting me right now but *him* again. Bradley can't see me in here from four floors down, but somehow, I know the Collector can.

I count down again. Ten, nine, eight. "Get out of my *head*—"

A *bang bang bang* pounding on my door cuts through the darkness. I drop my mug on my coffee table, and it lands upright in a loud clatter, sloshing the coffee and spilling three large drops over the rim. Leaving the mess behind, I run to grab the kitchen knife from its hiding place under my pillow. In the middle of my sprint, I trip over a lamp cord and fall through my bedroom doorway. A picture frame on my wall rattles; I pause on the floor to let the noise settle and listen for another *bang* on my front door. My elbow stings where the skin is peeled back a little, but it's too dark to tell if I'm bleeding. I push myself up, take the knife, and quickly go check my peephole on the front door.

His body stoops under the weight of a few beers. John is never quite drunk, but never really sober either when he comes to see me. I let him in anyway.

"John."

He stumbles through the door and closes it behind him, then he walks toward me, pressing my back into the wall with some force. John locks me there by placing one hand by my head and holding the other firm on my waist. His boney fingers cut into me.

"I'm sorry for letting you go yesterday, Knight. You do understand, right, Knight?" he mumbles.

"Don't apologize, John. I understand." My grip on the knife loosens.

He leans forward with his eyes closed as if he is going to kiss me but doesn't. Instead, he places his forehead against mine, sighing hot breath into my mouth, and spots the weapon in my hand. The smell of his cigarette smoke slithers straight down my throat. I cough.

"Knight, come on. Why didn't you tell me you were this scared?"

John's hand moves from my waist to my sore elbow, sliding down to my wrist. He hesitates there before taking the knife from my hands. In the thin space between us, he studies the blade, the handle, then lays it on the counter behind me.

"You could've come to stay with me, you know."

"I know, John, but what about Mary?"

"Eh, right. Probably resting at home, now. Treatments always make her ill."

"You should go, John."

"It—it doesn't matter; I told her I'm stayin' at the office tonight, not to expect me." He squeezes my shoulders, moving his hands up to my neck and running them through my hair. "I didn't come here to talk about my wife, Knight. I came here to take care of you."

His five o'clock shadow scuffs my jawline as he brushes his cheeks against mine, and I let him suck on my neck for a short moment then follow as he leads me by the hand into my living room. He twists the knob to turn on my lamp, and I go back to the kitchen and retrieve the knife. Yellow light sparkles on the steel blade, and I now realize how ridiculous I must look to John, carrying around a kitchen utensil under the illusion that it will keep me safe.

Without another word, he takes the knife from my hand and lays it next to my coffee mug, which is still half empty after I dropped it there. I look away as he strips off my shirt. John nudges me down on the coarse cushions of my sofa where we have quick, dry sex. When he is finished and asleep, I pour my seventh glass of wine from the darkest bottle that I usually keep in the back of my cabinet.

~

The second time we slept together, John started calling me by my last name. He said it was because he prefers seeing me at night rather than during the day. He thought it was funny. I wasn't amused. Just after I got my job at the *Post,* I liked that I wasn't John's only extramarital flirtation. He had a wife, which kept us all out of the public eye, and he stayed busy at night with his choice of willing women. When his wife got sick with cancer, he had his pick of willing journalists, most of whom had husbands of their own. The formality was fine with me. It placed just enough distance between us yet held us close enough to keep us satisfied.

John's wife's cancer often keeps her confined to the hospital with treatments and tests, but he's sure to call her every day while she's gone. He is sure to let her know he misses her.

Three years later, here I am, still willing to sleep with John, sipping my coffee while he's asleep on my sofa like it's no big deal. I cramp with the thought that a dying woman is probably more likely to live through next Christmas than I am.

Gray morning light pours into my living room, shining a bright square on the upper half of John's partially clothed body. Some new gray chest hairs have sprouted since I last saw him without his clothes on in the light.

My doorbell rings, and I jolt, sending a drop of burning coffee down my wrist. I look at John and cover him with a blanket so whoever is out there won't see him. Through the peephole, I spy Melanie clutching a crumpled, knit cardigan.

"Hey, Jessica," she says too fast when I open the door. "I'm sorry, I hope I didn't wake you. I was just going through my closet and found this sweater and thought you might like to have it. The cream color would go well with your hair, I thought, so I brought it over."

She knows she didn't wake me; I've got my coffee mug in hand. I give her a forced smile, and I hold out my arm so she can lay the sweater across it.

"Thank you. That was kind of you." But this isn't the type of thing we do. She's lurking for a reason.

"I hope you liked the pie." She must want me to invite her inside, so I step out into the hallway and pull the door almost closed behind me.

"It was good." I keep my eyes trained on Melanie's so she will believe my lie.

She reacts with a smile and tries to lean around me to sneak a glance inside my apartment. She knows I'm hiding something. I turn to block her view and pull the door the rest of the way closed. Stepping in front of her, I narrow the space between us, willing her to go home.

"Oh, you've got company?" She laughs like we are old friends, who we are not.

"No, it's just an uncle. I'll see you around, Melanie."

"Oh, okay." Her features drop, but she keeps smiling. "Well, stay safe. The Button Collector might come back to Chicago. You never know." Her voice is steady and light, but I can't tell if she's being serious or trying to make me chuckle. She pulls a tight smile across her face.

"Of course," I say.

"Have you—have you heard anything more? At the paper?" There it is—the real reason she's here.

"No, nothing more."

When she realizes that is all I am going to give her, she turns back toward her own apartment and tucks inside. I don't mean to, but I slam my door closed when I go back in which wakes John. I pour him a cup of black coffee as he fastens his shirt back up. He guzzles it down, as if he's ready to get out of here. Once he's finished dressing, he clinks the empty mug onto my coffee table and stands to leave.

"Alright, Knight, I'm out of here." He reaches into his shirt pocket and takes out a pack of cigarettes, knocking it on his palm until one jostles out. He immediately pulls it to his lips, and seeing it reminds me of his burnt taste.

He lights it, and his first exhale blows smoke right into my face.

The flavor of a used-up block of coal.

"Stay as long as you'd like," I say. "I won't be going to work today."

He blows another cloud of smoke up at my ceiling. "Wish I could, honey, but the wife will be calling in a few hours. You still okay with me smoking in here, Knight?"

"I don't mind." The smell of smoke will linger in my apartment and remind me of him after he's gone. Maybe when I'm being watched today, it'll make me feel less afraid.

"You shouldn't be alright with that. You've still got pretty lungs." John lets the cigarette dangle between his lips as he zips his fly. "I'll see you soon, Knight. Stay out of trouble. And stay safe." He winks at me, and with that, he leaves.

Melanie's sweater, still draped over my arm, is itchy and woolen. I unravel it and hold it out in front of me. From the collar to the hem, big, brown, glossy buttons are sewn into the fabric. They're disgusting and round, and the thought of someone pulling them off one by one and lacing them to my face consumes me. I dig my nails under the buttons and rip off each one before the Button Collector has the chance. They fall to the floor, grazing my bare feet, and I hate the coolness of them against my skin. The cardigan's hem hangs in shreds, and I am left with nothing but unraveling clumps of loose yarn.

Buttons.

Buttons everywhere.

I gather them into a pile and take them all, along with what is left of the sweater, and dump it in the trash can. Then I head to my bedroom.

In my closet, I yank down my coats. The hangers fly from their rod. All my sweaters, pants, gloves—the buttons must go. If the Collector can't collect anything from my clothes, maybe he'll choose to spare me. But he will come for me. I can only hope he'd clasp my mouth shut with a string of red to match my lipstick.

The hours are slow to drift by, and I keep up with the time by the weather. It snows until one o'clock and rains until seven like it does almost every day. Bradley's presence is constant all morning, but I notice sometime after three he has been replaced by another officer. He is back by eight, and he must have been sitting there for a while because his car is blanketed with a fine dusting of white.

I don't like not knowing who it was sitting there outside of my building this afternoon, keeping an eye on my window, making sure I'm minding the rules. My disdain for Bradley I can at least overrule with trust. He knows my case and how to handle it, no matter his infuriating smirk from behind his foggy windshield. That other guy from earlier I'm convinced knows nothing. Never even met me, probably. The whole reason for this surveillance is to keep me safe, and I flood with rage at the thought that the police might send over someone I haven't had the chance to vet for myself. This won't help me feel safe. At the same time, I'm furious with myself for wanting Bradley to be the only one out there to watch me.

I turn my lights on after I know he's back, but I also close my blinds.

They've been open since John left this morning, and snapping them shut makes me feel secure, closed off from the world again.

My bones warm as I sink into my bathtub beneath the light of my fluorescent bulbs.

Steam coils through the 68-degree air, muddling the mirror, and I think to myself, *If a killer had been here, he might have written me a note on the glass.* I sink in the water until my hairline is soaked with sweat. Instead of getting dressed when I dry off, I wrap myself into the comfort of my thick bathrobe.

I pull my brush through my hair as I move into my living room but stop in my tracks as I reach the doorway. Detective Bradley looks up from my TV and uncrosses his legs, my remote still in his hand. He is not wearing his police uniform, and he looks rather comfortable in his light blue button down and slacks. His upper button is undone, his collar wrinkled. Immediately, my fist curls around my brush. The urge to throw it at him pulses to my fingertips, but I swallow my anger and stuff the brush into my robe pocket.

"Ms. Knight. Good to see you again."

The TV is muted, but he turns it off anyway, taking note of my frustration and laughing at me for backing away. He stretches his arm across the back of my sofa and drops the TV remote onto the cushion.

I straighten my shoulders to form a confident stance but remember that I'm naked underneath and cower instead.

"You have some nerve coming in here without knocking."

Bradley stands and shoves his hands in his pockets, rocking back on his heels. "Yeah. I did knock, actually, but you didn't answer, so I came on inside. You could've been dead in here, you know."

"So you couldn't call?" I say.

"I was just doing my job." He shakes his head and takes a few slow steps closer. "But when I let myself inside, I heard the bath water running so I plopped down here on the sofa to give you some privacy."

A sudden urgency to cover my chest causes me to tighten the belt on my robe just to be sure nothing is exposed.

"Why did you stay if you knew I was okay in here?"

"I saw a man here today." Bradley's jaw shifts, and I freeze.

The thumping behind my ribcage gets so loud I wonder if he can see my sternum vibrating.

"Actually," he says, "I saw him come in here last night."

Dozens of lies come to mind, and I'm not sure which one I'm going to spit out. *He's just an old friend. He's my only surviving uncle. He's a homeless man I give shelter to sometimes.*

But none of these will work, and I know it. Bradley already knows the truth. I never did shut the blinds when John came over. The light was on the whole time. Bradley saw me and John against each other, beside each other, on top of each other.

No, he couldn't have, not from four floors down.

Stuttering isn't going to help my cause, but I offer fractions of explanations anyway. Bradley steps forward, slow but certain.

"I don't need you to justify, Ms. Knight. What I do need to know—despite all the arguments you're going to make with me about your privacy—is who you're sleeping with. Don't mistake my inquiries for being nosy. Your relationships are important right now, especially to the police, so why don't you tell me who that man was last night and why he was getting naked in front of this window? I'm not looking for details;" —Bradley pauses a few inches from my face and leans over my collarbone, his breath hot on my neck when he whispers into my ear— "I saw enough last night."

My face flushes with embarrassment. Of course he could see me. From that angle on the street, I can easily see my TV when I forget to shut it off, much less two pale humans on top of each other.

He spins away and sits back on the sofa.

I tighten my belt and readjust the collar of my robe, braving my shame. "Bradley—"

"Michael. I think we're close enough to be on a first name basis now. Is that okay, Jessica?"

His sarcasm shifts to anger, his brows falling flat. Nothing I can say will ease his tension or weaken his authority over me.

"Yes, that's fine."

"Tell me about him."

"He's nobody. Just a man I meet with occasionally."

Bradley looks away, huffing out a breath of artificial laughter, and closes his eyes for a moment before turning his attention back to me. "That's a little strange, Jessica."

"From the outside, Michael, yes, it is. So I'm going to ask you to stay out of my sex life. It'll be a lot less strange for the both of us."

"How long have you two been sleeping together?"

I avoid looking at him, and instead bend down and briefly pick at a scab on my ankle from where the blade caught it the last time I shaved. "A few years."

The shock that I expected to see in his reaction is nothing but a respectful nod. "You two must be serious."

"We're casual. It's none of your business, really. He and I are very private, and I would like to keep it that way."

"I just need his name."

"He's not involved. This is. . . a *non*-issue. He has nothing to do with anything."

"I'm going to have to find him, and when I do, we're also going to have to bring him in for questioning."

"What?" I say. "Why?"

"Because he's deeply involved with you, and it's going on record. You might as well tell me who he is now so I won't waste my time or yours. You might want to give him a head's up, as well. I don't want to catch him with his pants down again."

"I would really rather keep him out of all this. What if I stop seeing him for a few months?"

Michael's nostrils flare open, then shrivel back down to size.

"Besides, I've found someone who might have a motive for killing my family," I continue. Shifting attention away from John and back to the murder case is my saving grace, and it minimizes the sting of Bradley realizing how much of a whore I seem.

I wander toward my travel bag, which is still sitting by the door, packed full of my stuff, and Michael follows me. I fish out the folded newspaper, but he snatches it from my hand before I can object.

"What is this?" He scans the headlines.

"Read the headline. Then flip to A3. Nearly thirty years ago, my dad embezzled money from a man named Davis Castro. I think he may be involved in the killings."

Bradley finds the story and takes a seat at my breakfast nook. Moments pass as he reads in silence without so much as a glance in my direction. While his attention is elsewhere, I sit across from him and study his hands. The rough calluses on his palms suggest physical activity, remnants of rigor he must have to go through for his job. Despite that, his nails are clean, and his skin is unscarred. By the look of his tight sleeves and thick forearms, it's clear the calluses came from a gym.

"How long have you had this newspaper?"

"I—I found it in Deborah's attic while I was in Spooner. I didn't know about any of this until then. No one ever told me." I sneak a peek at his narrowed eyes to gauge whether he believes me.

He folds the paper and lets it fall onto his lap. "You know what you should've done the second you found this?"

The shadows from my kitchen light keep half of his face dark, but he can't hide his glare.

"You should've brought this to me immediately, you know that." He stands with a force so strong the chair scratches my floor when he leaps up. He slaps the paper on the edge of the table near my elbow, and I feel the breeze from the force of it. It sends a blast of cold racing down my chest, competing with the drops of sweat that are already there.

I hardly notice anything other than the dark blue veins pulsing on the side of Bradley's neck.

"Immediately," he repeats.

"Shouldn't you have already known about this?" The edge in my voice is undeniable.

"Chicago PD? No, we just opened this case, Jessica. I'm pretty sure no one has looked for any connections that far back; your parents have been dead for nearly fifteen years. Our investigation was the Pax murder, and we did our job, figured out who was responsible, and, like Reed said, never anticipated finding this Collector killer. That is, until Spooner called us and explained who exactly you were. The PD's job now is to try and find this guy so you don't die. Do you understand that? My job now is to make sure you're staying alive, and for some reason, you want to buck on that."

"Well, sorry, then." I cross my arms.

"*Sorry*?" he scoffs. "You're sorry? You've been a recluse about this case the moment CPD came into the picture, and it's starting to concern me. You deliberately kept this information from me for over an entire day. That's an entire day we could've been researching this potential lead."

"Well, forgive me for not running straight into the arms of Detective Bradley after my aunt was almost killed, and after I'd just gotten back from the airport, and after I'd just been given an extended leave of absence from my job, and now, after I'm being interrogated for withholding my family's information about something that was already dropped." I stand, balanced on a scale of confidence and frustration. "You can get out of my apartment and stop watching me with my clothes off though my window, okay? Why don't *you* go start researching this Castro guy now and just leave me alone?"

He looks at me for a moment but doesn't speak. Finally, he makes his decision and, in two mere strides, he yanks his jacket from my sofa and stomps out the door, slamming it hard behind him.

The sound reverberates in my head, and the pinch in my gut—it's a sharpness that I hardly recognize. It's been years since I've felt this level of anger at anyone, and now, the abrupt silence leaves me with nothing but my shame.

8

I shredded the newspaper after Bradley left my place yesterday. If CPD needs it, they can find it in an archive online. Having it in my apartment felt like a bad omen, like I was somehow asking for trouble. It almost felt like it was the Button Collector himself.

Despite the police's insistence that I stay locked in my apartment, I defy their orders and decide to go out to breakfast. Before I leave, though, I peer out my window and confirm exactly what I expected: no cruiser, no Bradley, not even some fill-in cop today.

Looks like the only person I'll be trying to sneak past this morning is the Collector.

I open my door and step into the hallway where I bump into someone blocking my way.

Suddenly, I am chest-to-chest with Ben, and the surprise knocks the air out of me. My gasp startles both of us as I scamper against the wall, looking at his hands to see they are empty of any knife, needle, or weapon.

"Oh, I didn't mean to scare you," he says, placing his hand on my door frame, but I cave to make the space between us bigger. I grasp at the wall to have something to hold onto, to prop me up and disguise the fear that weakens my knees. My eyes make their way up to Ben's white face. He hasn't had a shower today; his hair is flat and oily, speckled with white flakes of dandruff.

The cold, hallway air steals my breath, and I can't catch it back.

"Ben," I gasp, "what are you doing here?" I inch backward, and he follows, keeping the gap between us small, tight.

"I heard you took a leave from work, that you're involved with—"

"No. No, I'm not. Please forget what you heard."

He presses me a step further, but I brace myself against the doorway and start to wonder if Melanie has heard us. My chest tightens, adrenaline numbing me from the neck down. I glance behind Ben's head to see if she might come out and silently pray for once that she's home, listening to my distress. An abandoned hallway surrounds us on either side.

"Are you safe, Jessica?" he asks. "The rumors at the office are true, aren't they? You're part of that family that's being murdered?"

"Where did you hear that, Ben?" My voice shrivels with a stress I haven't felt since our first date. I stiffen with panic, wishing I had remembered to grab my knife. But Ben's harmless. *Isn't he?*

"From John's office," he said.

"Were you eavesdropping?"

"I was passing by. It's nothing, Jessica, please—"

"You heard our conversation?" My words crack more under some kind of weight; I can't control the shiver that develops under my skin, a reaction to having Ben stand this close to me.

His voice softens to a whisper. "Most of it."

I feel the hairs on the back of my neck prickle. Despite the chill spreading over my skin, sweat acquires under my bra and I'm suddenly suffocating.

I let my arms fall away from the door frame, but when I do, Ben takes another step toward me, so I reach out to lock my fingers there again.

"I'm part of the targeted family, yes, but please stay out of my business."

He closes his mouth and pinches his lips, glancing down at mine briefly. I'm suddenly self-conscious of my red lipstick, thinking I've drawn too much attention to myself. He leans in like he's going to kiss me or smell my hair or put his cheek on mine.

"Wait," I exclaim. I push past him and look down the hall. Left. Right. Still, there is no one else out here. I look toward Melanie's door, sealed tight. Besides, she would never let a stranger into our building. "How did you get in here?"

Could he be the. . .

No, just get out of here ASAP.

With a discreet sweep of his hand against his front pocket, I get my answer. I can make out the outline of a rectangle tucked away in there. A keycard.

"You have a card? Where did you get that card?"

He doesn't respond, but it doesn't matter, I already know the answer to my question. "You broke into John's desk and stole this."

His eyes are dark; I'm unable to make out even his pupil, but I make him look at me, challenging his hollow black eyes. They stare right back, piercing into me.

"Jessica." The way he utters my name, deep and possessive, sounds more like an angry hiss. "Are you sleeping with John?"

My breath catches in my throat. "What?"

"You're sleeping with John, aren't you?"

"Why would you ever say that?"

The lines on his face, on his forehead and around his eyes, wrinkle with a dangerous emotion. "I knew it. I didn't believe it at first, but it's true, isn't it?"

"I'm not sleeping with John." Heat rushes into my cheeks, so I look down to avoid his accusatory glare. John and I kept our relationship hidden for years, and now all this? Two confrontations within two days?

"You're a liar." He creeps closer.

Chest-to-chest again, the thumping in my rib cage beats up to my throat. Ben can probably smell the alcohol on my breath, so I try to bend away from him, thinking he might like the smell and try to kiss me again. I dive my fingers into his front pocket and grab the keycard, and in one swift motion, I stuff it down into the pocket of my jeans. I twist behind me to check the handle of my apartment door. Locked. Good. Then I shove past Ben to the freedom of the hallway. I convince myself Ben wouldn't dare try to break into my apartment after I leave, so without a backward glance, I charge down the hallway. I have nothing in there for him to steal, anyway.

I take the stairs; the elevator would be too enclosed, and I hear Ben's footsteps puttering behind me the whole way. Once I reach the ground floor, I shove the door open, and I am hit by cold rain that pelts against my coat and hood, absorbing into my boots, but I keep moving. When I reach the sidewalk, I increase my stride, wondering if Bradley is somehow watching this situation unfold. Ben follows, picking up his pace to match mine. I don't slow down until I am sure that we are far enough away from my building that Ben won't double back and try to sneak inside.

I stop under an awning a few blocks away and turn toward him, taking note of the desperation in his face and the fact that he has trailed me all the way out here. Ben's heavy breathing comes out in spurts of grunts and irritated moans. His shoulders droop from disappointment, and I can tell he wants to say more but doesn't.

"Do not follow me anymore. Stop calling me, and never come to my apartment ever again. Understand?"

"Jessica—"

"No, Ben. Leave me alone and don't mention anything to anyone about my situation, okay? This is stalking. You're stalking me, and it's not fair to me. Not to mention it makes you look bad. This could bring you into this murder investigation, especially if you start making assumptions about my personal life. It makes you look suspicious, maybe even guilty. Alright? Stay away from me."

I don't wait for his response but instead turn to leave, scanning my surroundings to search for the safety of Bradley's car but don't find it. I silently will for him to realize I have escaped from my apartment, to flash his lights, to tell me I'm okay even though I can't locate even a hint of safety.

Bradley's probably too angry with me to offer his protection anymore. They might have even removed him from my case.

Instead of succumbing to that heavy feeling in my chest when I think of Bradley's absence, I try to remind myself of how pissed he made me last night.

I march into *The Chicago Post* office building and take the elevator to the seventh floor, tucking my hair into my coat and hoping no one will notice me on my pit stop to breakfast.

The other journalists don't pay me any attention; they're all consumed by their computer screens. Della isn't sitting at her desk outside of John's office. I stand and wait a moment, then when she doesn't appear, I make my way around and peek through John's door. It's cracked open just enough for me to catch a whiff of a fresh cigarette. The room is dark, and from here, I can't tell if he is in there.

I go in anyway. A half-smoked cigarette smolders on his ashtray, his chair pushed all the way back against the window. With Della gone from her desk and the chaotic state of John's office, I know this scene all too well. This buys me at least a few minutes before they're through having sex in the bathroom. I open his left drawer and put his keycard to my building back where it belongs—under a stack of unpaid bills, a carton of cigarettes, and tucked behind his box of emergency matches. Somehow, Ben knew exactly where to find this key. With this new level of stalking, there's no telling what else he's discovered about me. My thoughts shift to Bradley again, and I wonder how he would handle Ben if he knew the truth. If Bradley knew about all this, he'd tell me to come clean about what exactly happened between me and Ben. I am not going to do that; it would only complicate things.

I pull a sticky note from his desk and write, *Hide my keycard for my safety. Can't explain now,* and slap it on his carton of cigs.

The drawer slams louder than I mean for it to, and it rattles a circular, golden frame that sits next to John's brass desk lamp. His wife's face smiles from inside. She is beautiful here, her eyes and flesh so full of life before cancer took her over. Still with white teeth, still with lush, brown hair that's graying only at the roots. Cancer is such an ugly disease.

I leave John's office before my guilt has the opportunity to eat at me. For years, I've blamed both my immaturities and my indiscretions on not growing up with parents. No one taught me it was best not to sleep around. No one taught me that it was a poor decision to trade favors with my landlord in exchange for discounted rent by a hundred dollars. No one warned me that it was risky to let men buy me drinks at bars.

These are things I learned for myself.

I leave the door cracked how I found it and hide my face in my collar until I'm back on the street.

The paint on the restaurant window that says *Blueberry Pancakes, Breakfast All Day Long!* is chipping at the corners. Rain drips from where the paint is peeled up on the other side of the glass pane. It bothers me, the inconsistent dribbling that doesn't quite match the rainfall. I look away until a waiter approaches my sticky tableside.

"Just coffee," I say, before he can speak. My appetite left when Ben did.

The waiter returns with a chipped white mug and splashes a steady black stream into it. He doesn't speak, and I motion him away. When he rounds the corner and is out of sight, I unlock my purse and dig around looking for Bradley's business card. I keep my eyes on the handful of people around me until the card's corners stab my fingertips, so I fish it out and place it on the table in the shadow of my mug.

Detective Michael Bradley, Chicago Police Department. I finger the foil blue lettering and contemplate my next move.

His office number is printed on the front, but on the back, he's written the word *private* with a different number scrawled in black ink. His sloppy scribble is smeared a bit, like what I'd expect from him. Maybe I'm overanalyzing, taking too much time lingering on each pen stroke. His writing seems hurried, frantic even, reflecting in the zero he didn't fill in completely. I bet he hates having an assignment like mine. I can picture the way his chest must have heaved with a sigh as he wrote his number on this card. I must be miserable to patrol.

Unraveling my scarf releases the heat that has been sweltering on my neck, made sweatier with the embarrassment I feel when I think of actually calling Bradley. He gave me his personal information for a situation where I might need him, and that thought makes me flush even more.

I slip the card back inside my purse, sip at my coffee, then take the card back out again. His name—*Detective Michael Bradley*—is in bold. If I call him, what would I say? I ask myself that question over and over again, trying to come up with anything just to hear him on the other line. Maybe it's advice I'm seeking, even though I don't want to tell him about Ben, or maybe it's anger I want to express to him for not patrolling me this morning like he'd promised.

Our last conversation swirls on repeat in my brain. He had told me last night that we were on a first name basis now. I cross my legs, wondering what he'd thought of my naked body.

Did he think it was ugly or pretty? Were my thighs slim or too thick for his taste? Red hot heat burns my skin. He probably had binoculars in his patrol car, and I picture him zeroing in on my undressed body. I had basically just given him access to free porn. What man with a pulse wouldn't have looked at that?

My thoughts turn to John, and my shame shifts to remorse. At twenty-three, when John and I had met, I had jumped at the opportunity to sleep with him. I had thought I was special, but I realized quickly that he had a propensity for most women, and then I quickly became content with the secrecy. When his wife got sick with cancer, he couldn't get out much anymore, so he started sleeping with the journalists on our floor. We all knew, and we were all aware that we'd done it with him at least once, twice, habitually, but none of us cared. Most of my coworkers had husbands and lives outside of the office. The only exception was me.

"Married women are better secret keepers," John had told me once. And it made a secret keeper out of me, too.

John trusted that I wouldn't tell anyone about us, even though I wasn't married. Perhaps he understood that I was not so different from him. I was only interested in the sex for what it was.

Disclosing my relationship with John to Bradley is a hard no. Bradley would never understand it. I stare at his name on his business card, flipping it from front to back. The only reasonable excuse to call Bradley would be to apologize for getting mad last night, but I can't bring myself to reach for my cell phone. With the Collector still lurking somewhere in the shadows, Bradley's presence and promise of protection would make me feel better. This morning, I felt that old familiar gaze of the Collector watching me; it grabbed me as soon as my feet touched the floor, as if he were waiting for me. While I've learned to ignore it, I can't help but ask myself the question: could he have followed me to breakfast? I'm not sure. I've become numb to his stare. If the Collector is hiding somewhere and watching me from afar, if he does have a red laser dot pointing over my heart, then Bradley should be there to intervene. My blood would be on Bradley's hands if something went wrong, but I wouldn't want him to pay the price for me banishing him from my apartment either. It would serve him right for letting me slip away from my apartment today, but I am not that vindictive.

"I suppose this seat's not taken." His voice breaks my train of thought.

Bradley is standing over my coffee, then slides onto the bench of my dirty booth without my permission. He slips out of his black winter coat to reveal his neatly pressed police uniform, and he brushes drops of rain from his forehead. I watch him adjust his position as he gets comfortable opposite of me.

He flashes me a grin.

I uncross my legs, then recross them, as if my body demands I respond to his presence, but I can't even figure out whether I'm annoyed he's popped up out of nowhere, or pleased he kept his word.

"What are you doing here?" I ask.

He stretches his arm across the back of the booth and keeps that grin on his face, glancing out the foggy window to his right.

I shrug. "Hello?"

He brings his arm back down, placing it with his other one on the table. Meeting my gaze, he reaches across the table, wraps his hand around my mug of coffee, and pulls it to him. He tips it toward his face and looks inside before sliding it back to me.

"No cream? Sugar?" he asks.

"I couldn't afford lattes as a college student, so no. I got used to it with no sugar."

Bradley summons a waitress. "Coffee and cream," he tells her.

"Why are you here?" I ask again once she's gone.

Bradley takes a breath and leans back against the cool, red plastic of the booth. He has the face of a man who deserves two kids and a wife who cooks for him. A nine-to-five, then off to the gym it is. Maybe off to the bar with a few guys from the office.

If I uncrossed my legs, our shoes would probably brush against each other's, so I stay still.

Tiny water droplets dot his edge of the table, and he takes his time wiping them. "Come on," he says. "You know why I'm here."

"I know. I'm being followed everywhere I turn."

He leans over the table. "I'm getting paid to follow you. It's my job to keep you safe. To keep the Collector off your back, if he's still here like you say, and, well, like we might assume."

"You're not doing a very good job, then."

"I'm not here to argue, Jessica."

"Don't call me Jessica."

The waitress returns with Bradley's coffee and a small bowl of creamers.

"Alright." He pauses, eyes moving between my chin or my lips. I can't tell. Bradley taps on his mug of coffee, letting his gaze fall to the table. "Ms. Knight, I'm here to drive you down to the station. When you're through with your coffee, of course," he adds. Drawing two creams from the bowl with effortless skill, he peels back their lids and pours them into his mug without so much as a splash.

"We can leave now," I tell him.

He brings the mug to his mouth with a wide bend of his elbow. "You walked all this way in the rain, Ms. Knight. Finish your coffee first."

I glance out the window and spot his squad car parked on the street. I hadn't noticed it when I first took a seat, but I'm suddenly sure it has been there the whole time.

Bradley—he's good at his job, but he's not the only one who hovers around me. If he didn't want me to know he's been tracking me, I wouldn't have. I can't help but feel a little comforted underneath all my frustration.

I apologize to him for leaving my apartment without informing anyone and thank him for not abandoning his post. A flicker of a genuine smile begins to form on his softening expression. "You thought I'd give up on you that quickly? I'm better at my job than that."

I expect him to follow up his sentence with my name. *Jessica. I'm better at my job than that, Jessica.*

"So has the murderer had his eyes on you again?" he asks.

"He's always there, Bradley."

He nods a little, then takes out his wallet and slips a ten-dollar bill under his mug and stands, motioning for me to do the same. He pulls his coat over his uniform and offers me his hand.

"I still go by Michael."

$\sim$

At CPD's Fuller Park station, I'm led to a conference room with a dark oval table with eight uncomfortable-looking chairs around it. Bradley pulls one out for me at the tip of the oval, and he and another man I've never seen take a seat on either side of me.

"Jessica Knight, this is Sergeant Lockheed. He's over the detectives," Bradley says.

Lockheed shakes my hand. "Nice to meet you. Chief Reed mentioned that you stopped by to ask him a few questions for an article about the Collector a while back." He's taller than Bradley, more muscular, and he appears to be around fifteen years older. His salt and pepper hair reflects years of Chicago PD stress, but his mustache is still dark, growing all the way down to his chin.

"Yes, I did," I say. I didn't expect him to come down so hard on me.

"You didn't tell him you were related to Martha Pax." It's more like a statement than a question.

I shake out of my coat, which provides some relief from both the heat of this room and Lockheed's hard expression that bears down on me. "It—it wasn't relevant to my article."

"But it was something that should've been brought up," he says, as if he's waiting for me to agree with him. "I imagine it's also against some sort of protocol at your work to be reporting on an article so personal to you."

"Well, I've been given personal leave from work since my editor realized the situation." I try to steer the conversation in another direction. "Detective Bradley told me you've got information about Davis Castro?"

"Yes," says Lockheed. "We contacted the man your dad embezzled from." The way he says it is almost degrading. "Castro was in Portsmouth working for your dad's company at age twenty-seven. Almost twenty-nine years ago, after the trials, it came to fruition that your father was undeniably guilty. In fact, he didn't even fight the charges."

Bradley interrupts in an effort to smooth things over. "You had no idea this happened until a few days ago, right?" he asks me.

I nod and focus my attention back on Lockheed. He continues, "Your father was put in prison for two years, and Castro moved his family to California. Eight years ago, he moved to Hawaii and hasn't been back to the continental United States since."

"My parents never told me my dad spent time in prison."

Bradley says, "You were a kid after the fact. That's understandable." But his words don't make me feel better.

"It's clear that this Castro guy had nothing to do with these murders," Lockheed says. "While he might have had a motive all those years ago, it wouldn't make sense to rehash everything now. He's got two kids out there, a wife. When he left Portsmouth, he left the entire embezzlement case behind and hightailed it out of there with his settlement to live in tropical paradise." Lockheed almost laughs.

"So it's not him," I say.

"No," Bradley says. "It's not Davis Castro. Like Sergeant said, he hasn't traveled outside of Hawaii for some time."

"We're back to the beginning then. No leads? No names?" This isn't Lockheed's fault, but I can't help but direct my frustration toward him.

Lockheed closes his eyes and pats the table, as if withholding his aggravation. "Not exactly. Now, listen for a minute. Detective Bradley mentioned you feel as though you're being watched by the Button Collector."

I look to Bradley, and he shifts in his seat, nodding down to his lap. My face blushes red, while my cheeks simmer from the heat creeping up from my neck. Nothing I say could reduce my humiliation or the impression of me that Bradley has painted for Lockheed.

Sergeant Lockheed remains silent. Motionless. Waiting for me to make the first move.

My life, a game of chess. Who can steal the queen and tip over the king first? "It's true. I sometimes feel like I'm being watched."

"Detective Bradley said you feel that way most of the time and that you think it's the serial killer. Can you explain why you think it's the killer?"

"No, no. Okay." I brush my hair behind my ears. "This isn't what it seems. I promise I am not crazy. I don't *know* anything; it's only just a feeling."

"Do you ever talk to the person who you think is watching you? Do you think he can hear you?"

"I'd really rather not—"

"Jess—" Bradley begins but catches himself. "Ms. Knight, anything you suspect about the killer and your safety automatically becomes a part of this investigation. Like it or not, you are a part of this as one of the last living, close relatives of the victims. It's nothing to be ashamed of, but it's something to be taken care of."

"I'm not ashamed. I'm just saying it's not as important as you're making it out to be. It's only a—"

"A feeling," Lockheed finishes. "Right. But nonetheless, it's something." He glances at Bradley, who tilts his head just slightly enough for me to notice. "Can you tell us *when* he's watching you?"

I'm trapped, pinned under pointed stares from both Lockheed and Bradley. In the silence, I hear the dim buzzing of the lights that flicker overhead.

"In the morning, before I go to work. Sometimes when I leave work. In the evenings. It's not all the time."

"Is there anyone you can think of who might have a reason or an interest in stalking you? Think of anyone, even if you believe that they might not be the killer."

If I hesitate for too long, they'll know I'm lying. "No," I reply, keeping my eyes locked on Lockheed.

Sergeant Lockheed's mouth contorts into an unreadable position, and he leans up to the table, as though he's considering something more. I stiffen, assuming they both see right through me.

"Ms. Knight," he says, "we'd like to get you some help. We want to send you to someone who you can talk to about this *feeling*."

I turn toward Bradley because surely he can't be on board with this, but he won't look at me. Lockheed can't understand my "feeling," that it's personal. It's nothing that could help CPD solve the case.

Bradley doesn't budge in his chair, a sure sign that he's not going to take my side. I worry that maybe Bradley could have been the one who suggested I need professional help. After my antics at my apartment, I wonder if they're on to something, that maybe it would help to have someone to pour my heart out to.

Still, betrayal burns in the space between me and Bradley.

He finally acknowledges me and looks down into my eyes that are hot with tears. "It might help to talk to a professional. Maybe a psychologist could help."

I stand and grab my coat, but I don't bother to put it on. Maybe I should deny the entire thing, claim that every instance I felt the Collector watching me was nothing more than déjà vu. It was all a mistake, and I never had any feeling at all. But that would make everything worse. Plus, Bradley's already formed his opinion of me, and he thinks I need mental help. Denying anything would make me look like I'm covering something up, and the truth is I would be. I'd be doing nothing but digging a hole full of lies, and eventually, Lockheed would bury me in them.

At last, I find my words, and they come out riddled with contempt. "Mental help? You think I need a doctor because I feel like someone is watching me? So I might feel like I'm being watched by the person who's murdering my family members one by one. That doesn't classify me as crazy. It just means I'm scared I'm going to be his next victim."

Lockheed holds up his hand to cut me off. "Which is why—"

"If you think I'm so paranoid that I need psychiatric help, then stop making me feel like I'm a person of interest in this investigation. Use your time and resources to find whoever *is* doing this."

"A person under your amount of stress can sometimes start to—"

I push my chair back to leave and bolt out the door before they can stop me. Bradley must have taken me through twelve different turns and gone up a few floors to get to that conference room, and by the fifth dead end, I'm lost.

Bradley finds me out of breath against a wall. "Can you wait a minute?"

"I'm capable of finding my own way out of here."

He takes one step closer. "That's not what I asked. Where are you going?"

"Home. I don't need a psychologist." Turning my back to him, I dart down another hallway and find an elevator at the end. When the doors open, I press the button for the ground floor and turn to see that Bradley hasn't budged out there in the hall.

With a sigh, I ditch the safety of my escape and step out of the elevator. "You know, I don't appreciate the assumption you made about me."

His shoulders straighten, as if he's satisfied I'm poking at him, ready to take me on. I hate that about him, always ready for a fight.

"I didn't make one," he says.

"Please. The second I told you about how I think the Collector watches me, you suggested to your boss I go talk to someone about it." Marching toward him, I point down the hall in some direction Lockheed might be lurking. "You didn't believe anything about anything. You just think I'm going insane. Didn't you tell me I was supposed to trust you?"

He takes a step forward, nose to nose with me in the center of this tight hallway. "Yes, but my job doesn't require me to trust *you*. I'm a detective. I'm supposed to question you, and I'm supposed to be suspicious of your paranoia. I get paid for it, remember? So I can call you crazy if I damn well please."

A door down the hallway cracks open, and a head pops out, inspecting the shouting.

I lower my tone, eyeing the man as he slips back behind the door. "I don't believe this."

"Well, I don't know what to believe." Bradley slams his hand against the wall, and a dozen picture frames of officers in uniforms rattle.

"You're not the one who wakes up every day not knowing if it'll be your last time," I spit.

I turn my back to him and walk right back to the elevator, but before I leave, I notice the handgun on his belt appears bulkier clipped to his side. It's been there for the entire investigation, but it feels more ominous now, and I don't like the way it seems to gleam at me. I imagine what it would feel like if it were pressed against my skull, its cool barrel digging a cold ring on my forehead before I'm blown away. I would almost prefer that over waiting to see how long it is before the Collector can get to me.

I would bet that Bradley has shot and killed someone. It's evident in the way he carries the gun with such confidence. With it firmly locked on his side, he seems to have little awareness it's even there at all, but with great acknowledgement of the power it holds. He's killed someone. Why can't he pull the trigger on the Collector? Why can't he find him?

"I don't want your protection anymore," I tell him once I'm back at the elevator. His face sinks into soggy disbelief. I gulp down a knot in my throat.

"I'm requesting another detective. Please tell that to Lockheed."

I turn, jam my fingers against the down button, and don't look up at Bradley when I enter the elevator. As the doors close, I catch a glimpse of him in my peripheral, unsurprised to see he's still there.

For three days, no one from CPD calls. No patrol cars park outside my apartment, either. I assume that they have decided to just forget about the entire case. There have been no new murders, and it seems that all the buzz about the Collector has slowed down.

Yesterday, I had a visitor. I was surprised when I peered through my peephole to find a familiar face knocking on my door. Jane was a journalist from the office, one of the new girls, young and pretty, hasn't quite found her beat in the industry yet. Smart, also. Someone John wouldn't dare touch. Yet. Her blonde hair was in a ponytail, too bouncy for a job like this one.

"Hi," I said too fast, "what are you doing here?"

She pointed to Melanie's door. "Hi. Um, the lady across the hall let me in. I told her I worked with you. You remember me, right?"

She asked me for a quote for a story she was writing and thought that I, as a survivor of the Knight family, might have something helpful for her. Not a chance. I turned her down as quickly as I could by telling her I wasn't related, then I slammed my door in her face.

The Button Collector stories have dwindled in the newspaper. Just recently, it was my profile article headlining the front page of the paper, and now, the update of the killer—or lack thereof—is a column buried on the inside, but it's still one of the top headlines on national news. It's good online clickbait too.

Serial killer Button Collector on the move from Chicago, according to police.

Authorities have few leads on national case.

The Button Collector: Where is he headed next?

Another headline, the worst of them all: "*The Button Collector isn't finished yet," officials say.*

I haven't given in and clicked the links. It's best I don't know which police departments are saying those things, whether they're the PDs from Robert's town, Deb's town, Josh's town. One thing is for sure— they seem to be taking it more seriously than Chicago PD, who started by just easing residents' minds until the Collector "passes through."

On the move from Chicago, according to police.

Maybe those writers documented quotes out of context before Chicago police told them Jessica Knight might be the magnet keeping the killer here. I've been known to do that too, make it sound catchier than it really is. Either way, I've at least convinced Bradley that the Collector probably isn't leaving Chicago. Not as long as I'm here. He's the one who said, after all, that since Spooner PD called them, it's Fuller Park's job now to chase leads, find the killer, and keep me safe.

Seems if I died, everything would be easier for everyone.

Every morning, every afternoon, every evening, I still hear about the Collector on TV. The anchors continue to claim he's not a threat to the general public, yet in the same breath they also report that he should be considered armed and dangerous, but only to the immediate and extended members of the targeted family.

They still talk about the attempted murder of my aunt Deborah, though her airtime seems to be waning. Still, no one on any major network makes any promises about finding the Collector, and they can't make any predictions about where he's going next. Neither does the local evening news.

Ever since Martha Pax was murdered, their storyline has been the same. Over and over they report, "Members of the targeted family have made their relation known to authorities, as well as provided their personal information to police so they may take all necessary precautions to keep individuals safe." Way to broadcast those details to the killer, blowing the covers of people like Bradley who are trying to lay low. No wonder he hasn't struck again. Now he'll never get caught, should he aim again for someone who isn't me. To the killer's benefit, I'm unprotected now and have been for the last three days.

Beyond Rosa, Uncle Josh, and Martha Pax, I barely have any family left. Definitely not enough to warrant all of the continued media attention.

I called Deborah after Jane left my place, and it rang almost all the way to voicemail before she answered. Her voice was hoarse, still raw from her injuries. I imagine she has also had at least a few nights of screaming at anything that made a noise outside her house.

"Aunt Deborah, how are things?" My voice trailed off, but I caught myself just in time from almost asking *how are things... after?*

"They're escorting me in and out of the hospital. They're everywhere. They won't leave me alone, Jessica."

"Who're they?"

"Nurses, doctors, the Spooner PD people. Every time they check up on me, they take my gun away, or my knife, or my tennis racket." I silently commended them for removing her gun. God only knows what she might do with that.

"Are you healing well from your injuries?" The moment I asked, I regretted not calling Spooner PD for a check-up instead of Deborah.

"They let me out for good. I'm home now, but some lady moved her stuff in my house. They think I'm going crazy, Jessica. They think I'm a lunatic. They keep saying they're going to take me to a home if I don't stop... stop doing this."

"What lady?"

"The woman who Doctor Allen is making stay with me."

"They want to take you to a home?" I asked but quickly wished I hadn't; a psychiatric unit is exactly where she belongs.

The conversation only reminded me of what Sergeant Lockheed talked to me about, which made me think of Bradley, and I got a twisting feeling in my stomach. I made up a quick lie in order to hang up the phone. The truth was, I couldn't stand to listen any more about how crazy Aunt Deb has become; it all steered back to the Collector's eyes on me and the awful way that Bradley does not believe me. Hearing that he and Sergeant Lockheed think I am just as crazy as Deb scared me more than angered me, though. I don't want to turn out like Deborah, wrapped in a blanket pointing a gun at the door all night—I cannot become her. And I think some nights I am.

On my fourth night alone, I peer out through my curtains and see again there is no patrol car parked down on the street. I've not heard anything from John, either.

The road is wet with melting snow that was scraped against the curb into piles before the sun rose this morning. It has seeped onto the sidewalks, and on a damp day like today, my alley is probably covered by a thin sheet of ice. While Chicago is having the storm laid over it all day, I imagine CPD leaving me behind and moving on to new cases, new investigations, new women whose families are being killed.

With Bradley and Sergeant Lockheed admitting they had no leads, I realize today the only one thinking anything crazy was me. Now, though, they've probably given up on me and my bizarre feelings. The Collector has still managed to stay under authorities' radar after all this time. I worry that if the case becomes too stagnant, CPD will forget I was ever in danger.

I snap my curtains closed and go into my bedroom. The past few days, I've been leaving the knife under my pillow, and tonight in my restless attempt to go to sleep early, I wake up to a searing, fire-hot pain. I grab my pillow as a shield, clutching it to my chest in fear, until I realize I cut myself with my own knife, which sliced straight down my forearm. I was dreaming of the Button Collector. He was picking through my apartment, taking his time collecting all my buttons. In my groggy state, my first thought is *he's here for me.*

But it's just a nightmare. Nothing more than a nightmare.

"Ten, nine, eight," I begin counting, screaming through the pain. Scared. Even more scared when I notice the bright red numbers flashing on the alarm clock next to my bed. Prime time for the Button Collector: 1:27 in the morning. Once I summon the nerve to get out of bed to clean my wound, I throw the covers back, and by accident, the knife tumbles to the floor with a loud bounce. I leave it there as I run toward the bathroom. My blurry vision is cleared up in a few blinks when I see my arm. It isn't a large gash, only a few inches long, not too deep, but my blood spills from it, seeping out both sides of the cut. I wrap a white bandage around my self-imposed stab wound, dig through the cabinet behind my mirror, and pop a couple ibuprofen pills.

Trudging back to bed, trying to go to sleep again—it's no use. An hour and a couple shots of tequila later, I rewrap my bandages and search for the dusty knife I had abandoned near my bed. I find it pretty quickly sticking out from under a mess of bloody sheets piled on the floor. The pills and alcohol fog my memory; I don't remember making that pile last hour, but I do know I need the knife to make me feel safe after my nightmare. It's no use. I know I will never get back to sleep.

It's pitch-black outside at 2:38 when I begin pulling on my sweater and coat. The alcohol and medication mixture hasn't really worn off by now, but I'll manage. I let the layers of fabric fall over my wrist, covering the knife's handle which is glued to my grip. A hat could make me too unrecognizable to the killer, so I put on a scarf and leather gloves, then step into my snow boots.

I slip the blade up my sleeve. It's hidden now, I tell myself.

My apartment door clicks locked behind me, and, while I'm waiting for the elevator to arrive, I wonder why I even locked the door. I close my eyes and take a deep breath. If I want to find the Collector, maybe I should leave him an easy entrance.

Melanie's footsteps patter toward me, drawing me out of my daze. She stands beside me to wait for the elevator, dressed in a black waterproof coat, the kind with fur that lines the hood. I catch the faint scent of her lavender shampoo, then finger the tip of the knife to calm me. It must have shifted; I catch sight of the blade peeking out beneath my sleeve. I shrivel into my fleece, pulling up the blade before Melanie can spot it.

She flicks her tired eyes at me before fixing her gaze upon the elevator doors. She rests her weight from one leg to the other as she waits for the doors to open.

"Hey, Jessica."

I nod to her, smile. She must be on her way to the early morning shift at Highway Diner. After I'd opted out of babysitting her daughter the first few weeks Melanie got the waitressing job, she left me alone about it, but I'm still careful to avoid the topic, lest she ask me again.

"Did that, um, journalist pop by your place yesterday? She was just standing outside the front doors asking if I happened to know you. I was skeptical, you know. I didn't really want to let her in, especially since the Collector is still out there."

My wounded forearm burns with fresh pain. "Yeah, she came by."

Melanie yawns, then looks at me, but I stay focused on the doors.

"So that girl is someone you know from the paper?"

"Yeah, I know her."

"Well, she told me about you—you know, about how you're related to that family, and I just want to say that I can't believe you didn't tell me in the first place. I thought we were friends." She turns her body to face me, and I want to turn the other way, but I stay still, concentrating on keeping my breathing calm and even. If I move even a little bit, the knife might slip too low, and she'll see it. The elevator dings as it travels up the floors of the building. I shuffle in my coat, unsure of how much longer I can ignore the pain from my scrunched shoulder, which is twisted funny to keep my weapon hidden. I think I can feel blood seeping through my bandage.

"Jessica," she continues, "I have a daughter, and with you as probably one of the targets, we are at a huge risk. That Button killer could very possibly come within five feet of my door looking for you. My daughter and I could get hurt in the process, and we don't deserve to feel terrorized in our own home. You should have told me, Jessica. I don't appreciate that you didn't at least warn me that you were a part of this."

"I'm not related, Melanie." *And we are not friends.*

The elevator opens, and we both step in. She waits for me to press the first-floor button, but I don't move. The knife in one sleeve, my seeping injury in my other, I'm locked in place like concrete.

"I'm going to have to ask you not to associate with me or my daughter anymore." She lets out an exasperated breath and shakes her head, keeping her eyes trained on the ceiling, avoiding mine. "I'm sorry, Jessica, but it's just too dangerous." She finally presses the button for the ground floor and the doors close.

I've only met her daughter a handful of times in the few years I've lived in this building, and I've never even been to her apartment. I have certainly never given Melanie any reason to believe that we were anything other than two women who live on the same hall. She's the one that tries to come up with any excuse to make conversation.

"I'm sorry to hear that," I say.

"It's okay. No hard feelings, this is just temporary. Just know I can't have my daughter in danger. She's with the babysitter right now, and I've told her about our situation here, so if you see a red-haired college student in the halls, please do not speak to her."

Situation. People say that word around me like they're trying to hide its severity.

"And, Jessica, since all this is going on, I just have to ask you what in the world you're doing at this hour? It's almost three in the morning. You're scaring me, a little bit."

"Just going to the office early." I throw my gaze in her direction, locking on her eyes so she might believe me. "It's press day at the paper. Have to make sure everything is going smoothly."

"At three in the morning?"

"That's when our delivery trucks get there on release day."

She nods and cocks her head to the side.

When we reach the bottom floor, she bolts out of the elevator and out of the building before I'm even across the lobby.

Outside under the streetlamp, I see the snow has stopped falling, so the air is clear, dark, and icy cold. I wait until Melanie rounds a corner before I head in the opposite direction.

I walk for a block until I feel his eyes land on me.

Ten. Nine.

No. No more counting. I need to keep feeling him. The Button Collector is out here. His stare is a hidden energy that pushes me forward, driving me away from the safety of my building. I want to run as far away as I can, which I know will only lure him closer and closer until he's almost on my back. The streets are empty at this hour, quiet and frozen. I duck into an alley a quarter mile away from home. It is empty, with the exception of some huge metal garbage cans and a few overflowing dumpsters.

I slide the blade from under my sleeve, my forearm throbbing under the bandage.

I know you're here. "I know you're here."

I know you're watching. "I know you're watching."

But between the tight brick walls and depth of the darkness, I can't see anyone. I wait, turning in slow circles all around, examining the edge of the roofs above me and the closed, curtained windows along the looming brick walls. I reveal my knife, not to taunt him, but to show him that I am not afraid. No one is in sight, but I know that's exactly what he wants.

My breath looks like smoke snaking out of my nose and through my lips, and my thoughts go straight to John, and the stale smell of his cigarettes.

The bitter air bites at my lungs and stabs the inside of my chest. I resist pulling my scarf over my mouth because if the Collector is out there, I want him to see me. Words start plummeting out of me again—*come here, come here, come here*—until I don't know whether I'm thinking them in my head or screaming them out loud or carving them into my skin with the knife in my hand. I squeeze my eyes shut, hoping the Collector might appear before me when I open them.

The same vacant space surrounds me when I stop circling. Both ends of the alley are clear of any people, but still, I keep my guard up, turning, twisting, searching for the Button Collector because I know he's searching for me too.

Something metal rattles behind me, but the ground is clear of any debris. There's no wind, only a subtle breeze, so it must have been some type of animal. A person would've made a bigger noise. A footstep or shuffle of pants, but there's no one hiding in the clearing in front of me. My eyes flood with tears—from the wind, from my fear, I'm not sure.

I spin around to check the other side of the alley, and I gasp in the cold air at the sight of a dark silhouette about twenty yards away. The air burns my throat, and I gag on it, coughing until my throat is moist again and I have breath back in my lungs. I throw myself back a few feet and resist the yearning to run away no matter how hard it pulls. I swallow, trying to breathe through my nose, and take a few slow steps toward him. I hide the knife behind my leg. All my noise and vulnerability doesn't faze the person at the other end of the alley. He stands there like he's not threatened.

Sharp needles of fear prickle down my body. From the other end of the alley, I face his tall figure head on, remembering Deborah telling me the Button Collector was short and bald, but this man is different. Tall, lanky with a mess of tangled hair outlining his profile. Deborah must have gotten it all wrong. Maybe she doesn't know what she saw. Could the media have gotten it wrong too? They took note based on Deb's description, but the cops insist she is delusional.

Because this—*this*—is the Button Collector.

My hand tightens around the knife, my fingers cramping from the hard handle. He stands without moving, facing me, watching me.

Watching me.

And this time, I'm watching him too, moments away from seeing the face of the person whose stare is always locked on me. His eyes are invisible but heavy. Always invisible. The skin of my palm pinches from my unbreakable grip on the knife. I hold it flat to my thigh.

It's real, I keep thinking. *You're real.* He has to be the one who stalks me, who watches me every day. He's here, after all, at 3 a.m. in this backstreet.

My fear switches to an odd level of satisfaction when I think about Bradley telling me it's his job to be suspicious about me, so much so that he felt the need to question my mental health.

This is real. My feeling was real. Is this him?

But Bradley's not here now. I'm alone, all at once, alone and aware that Bradley's not here, and for the first time, I regret refusing his protection.

I move forward, the knife hot on my palm. "You've got me," I shout to the Collector. "I'm here. Do what you want."

His breath sends a cloud of fog into the darkness. I watch it streak across the moonlight.

Oh, my God, what have I done?

He must have seen my knife in the reflection of the light; it's obvious what I'm here to do. What *am* I here to do? Kill the Button Collector? My plan doesn't seem so viable anymore. I'm going to get myself murdered, and for what? Just to prove something to Bradley? To Lockheed?

Now that I've seen him, I should run. It's not too late. I can just go back the way I came. That's the problem, though. He knows which direction I came from. Worse, he knows where I live. The Button Collector knows everything about me.

What do I do?

Bradley's business card flashes through my mind, but I can't remember the number he scribbled on the back for emergencies. Why can't I remember? It's too late. I don't even have my phone.

I rotate the knife handle in my fingers and see the man's head tilt. Positioning my feet to charge at him with my knife, I take my offensive stance. He bows a little, reaching for his side, and something in my chest plummets when I notice his arms coming together before his silhouette, holding the handle of a gun.

I heave myself in the opposite direction, crashing into the concrete abdomen of another person. A bloodcurdling scream erupts from my body, and before I can see who it is I'm against, I am being thrust behind him with a single shove. My face slaps hard against the damp pavement, my knees soaking with melted snow water. I lose my grip on my knife, and it falls, clinking next to me on the ground. It bounces a few times before it lands just out of my reach. I scurry upright, and make a grab for it, but I can't get to it from here; just above me, a broad-shouldered woman is positioned to cover me. Her gun is drawn and aimed straight at the Collector. Her hair is cut straight across her ears in a bowl style, so I wonder for a split second whether it's a woman at all.

She jolts, firing three bullets in quick succession. Shell casings rain past my face, one burning my ear as it grazes over. The crack of noise resonates in the alley and lights up the dark even after I duck into the black of my coat. Another shot plows through, bursting from a different direction, and a brief moment of stillness clogs my vision and holds me down. All around me, muffled vibrations reverberate on the ground. Blue and white lights flash against the wet pavement, then the noises come to fruition, and I realize the alley has become a tunnel of urgent voices and running feet.

A dozen pairs of police boots rush past me and the lady with the gun.

She cups her ear and says, "He's headed east down ninety-third. Wearing a coat. About my height, give or take. Male." Then she yanks me up by my wounded forearm, her thick, red bangs sweeping across her eyebrows. I wince and grab my arm.

On the street, a police car squeals to a stop, blocking the entrance to the alleyway. Two men in uniform jump out, both holding their guns, both speaking into some sort of walkie talkie on their shoulder.

The woman grabs the nape of my neck and guides me to the hood of the police car. "What's going on?" I say, my voice cracking.

She locks her gun back into the holster on her belt and addresses the other men. "Get Johnston moving west. We need eyes on all these streets. And call Fuller Park. Get Lockheed down here, now." The woman holds out her hand to me, then takes it back before I have time to shake it. "Susan Welch. Chicago Police Violent Crimes."

"Jessica Knight."

"I know who you are."

"How do you—I mean, what's going on?"

"We followed you down to this block, got the team heavy on your trail."

I spot my knife lying close to the dumpster, dark and thin on the ground, still too far to get to from here. "How did you know—how did—" Nothing I say comes out clearly. Each syllable runs into the other, my words blurring together.

"Jessica, don't be alarmed. You've been under our protection for days now."

"What?"

"We've been watching you. It is our job to take care of you, to make sure no one is doing anything suspicious around you."

"I haven't left my apartment."

"Which is a good thing."

"Why haven't I seen you? I've been looking."

"We're good at our jobs." She smirks. "Better than the other guys they had looking after you."

"Lockheed?"

"Can barely solve a normal case, much less a national one. So they called us and put me on you."

"You've been outside my building?"

"If you didn't know we were there, the Collector didn't either. If he can be invisible, so can we."

A man's voice mutters through Welch's walkie talkie, *Lost him. Got guys spreading out.*

Can't find a shell.

"Listen, Jessica," she says, turning the knob to silence it, "I've been concerned with this case since the Button Collector came to the city to murder Martha Pax."

I try to swallow, but my mouth is too dry to produce any saliva.

"Mostly, I'm concerned about why you're still alive. He was here yet he didn't kill you. Why is that do you think? It's not right. He spared you for a reason. The Collector went from Chicago to Spooner, and he didn't get you mixed in the crossfire. You think that guy was him?" She motions back to the alley.

This doesn't follow the Button Collector's pattern. Everything is the exact opposite—his hair, height, and *gun*. Not his typical knife and needle.

"Yeah, it must have been him," I say, trying to convince myself now.

Her nose scrunches up as she looks behind her. "We'll find him. Listen" —she waves me over to the driver's side of the car— "I'm sure Lockheed told you that the chance of you being his next victim is very high."

"Detective Michael Bradley told me, but then my aunt Deborah was nearly killed."

The gun on Welch's side isn't as big as Bradley's, but she wears it bolder even though she must be six feet tall. "Bradley's the guy who sent me to you. He trusts me, that's why he asked me, but God, they're sloppy over there."

I keep hanging on her comments about the Fuller Park Police Department. Sloppy? Can't solve a case? Bradley might have been cocky, but he wasn't bad at his job. In fact, he probably wouldn't have let me wander all the way out to this alley in the middle of the night and almost get shot. He'd have stopped me the second I stepped out my front door.

A white car pulls into the alley, and I recognize it from Bradley's squad. Blue lights swirl, but the siren stays off. Lockheed steps out alone.

Welch meets Lockheed between the two cars, and I try to listen as they start discussing details and names I've never heard. Sirens echo in the distance. The entire block will be closed off soon, I assume. At the other end of the alley, where the Collector stood, several officers scout the place where the shots were fired. Behind me, Welch and Lockheed turn their backs to me as she points down the road, giving me a minute to slip back into the alley and retrieve my knife.

It'll stick out of my sleeve again, so I can't keep it there.

I grab it and stuff the handle in my inside coat pocket just before a deep voice calls me from behind.

"Ms. Knight."

He waits for me to walk toward him and Welch. "Sergeant Lockheed. Hello."

Welch grins, and Lockheed pulls out a pen and starts scribbling on her notepad. "I need you to tell me what you were doing out here, and don't leave anything out. Try to remember what you saw, and anything that stands out about this guy."

The other end of the alley is empty and seems far away, or maybe it is just blurring with my tears and the hostile wind.

"Oh, okay," I say through shattering teeth. My muscles shiver, keeping my body hunched over, to my advantage making me appear vulnerable.

"Does this have anything to do with the discussion you and I had the other day?" he says. Welch's wide mouth twitches as she tries to hide a smug smile. I pretend not to notice.

"You made me doubt myself. All I did was try to prove my feelings were real, and they are. Look where that got me. I was almost shot."

"There was no need to put yourself and others in danger just to prove yourself."

"The Collector just exposed himself, so at least we know he's here."

Lockheed glares hard, a classic trait of being too stubborn, refusing to acknowledge that anyone other than he could be right. "You've been warned numerous times to be discreet, so if you don't follow our instructions, you could die, Ms. Knight. It seems very obvious now that you might be the one he's really after. Do you understand that? We are trying to protect you, but you seem to be extremely resistant, and this time you put one of CPVC's people at risk."

Welch nods. "He's taunting you, the Collector." She crosses her masculine arms over her flat chest, her pistol a black lump on her uniform.

"Take her to the safehouse," he commands Welch. Lockheed then looks to me. "You'll be safe with her."

He walks back to his car and calls someone, and I think, *It must be Bradley. He's calling to tell him what just happened.* I crane my neck in an attempt to hear better, but the next thing I know, I'm being pulled away.

Susan Welch directs me to her car and guides me into the backseat, another officer piling into the passenger's seat next to her. Relief spills through my pores as soon as the door closes, despite the chatter that is still coming through their walkie talkies. I no longer sense the Collector's gaze on my back.

Or whoever's gaze it was.

The man in the alley. . . could that have been him? Were my eyes deceiving me? Who else would have been out there, prepared for me with a gun, if not the Button Collector?

Welch and the officer drive me to my apartment, explaining on the way that I am to pack a bag, essentials only, and that I'm to leave all weapons at home. Welch tells me that as if she already knows I'm carrying my kitchen knife in my pocket. They also explain that I'll have Welch walk me inside while the other officer waits to stand guard at the front entrance to my building. By tomorrow morning, there will be another officer assigned to stay at my apartment.

"A safehouse?" I ask. "Where is it? How long will I have to be there?"

Both officers sigh, and Welch says, "Not sure, Knight. Pack like you're taking a winter vacation."

We park at my building five minutes later without a fuss. No blue lights or sirens indicate my arrival, but I can still see the swirling glow of both red and blue lights from the emergency responders reflecting in the foggy air from where they are still parked a few blocks away.

"Let's be quick," Welch says, opening her car door.

I lead her inside and up the elevator and into my apartment. My heart thuds against the knife hidden in my coat.

She closes my apartment door behind us, then looks out the peephole. I fly into my bedroom and, while she's distracted by my possessions in my living room, place the knife inside my nightstand drawer. I notice my phone on my pillow. I was intentional in leaving it here when I left, didn't want the option to cry out for help. My rage begins to build on top of all my other emotions when I see the notification there. The screen glows 12:02 a.m. *Missed call: Ben.*

I must have missed it when I was barely asleep, and the sound of the vibration hadn't awoken me. There is nothing from John, still no word from Bradley either.

My duffel bag from the Spooner trip is crammed under my bed, still packed from my last Button Collector adventure. I pick out a few clean pairs of underwear from my dresser and shove them inside, wondering how long I'm going to be gone. A week's worth will have to do, and if it doesn't then that will give me an excuse to come back home.

I make my way into the bathroom for the essentials that Welch stressed, avoiding my face in the mirror.

She knocks on my door jamb. "We ready?"

"Almost."

I throw my red lipstick in my bag and close the blinds in the living room. Then we leave, but I have no idea where we are going.

The safe house is about thirty minutes north, into the city a little deeper. It's a skinny, brick townhouse, with curtained windows that remind me of my own. Welch escorts me through a heavy looking door which she deadbolts behind us. Inside, the water-stained walls are cream colored and bare except for the security cameras that are hidden along the crown molding. Welch points them out, and I take note that they are scattered in every corner, placed on every mantle, and tucked between every book. It is clear that I will not have any privacy here.

"We use the townhouse for times like this," Welch tells me. "There are several others throughout Chicago."

I want to ask how many other times like this there have been, but I'm too overwhelmed by the sharp scent of musky books and damp cardboard that it traps my words inside me.

Welch's boots stomp against the bubbling laminate floors as I follow her into a bedroom that faces the street.

"This is where I'm going to spend most of my time, but you feel free to do whatever you want as long as it's under this roof." She motions to the kitchen. "There's plenty of food in the cabinets, but don't forget to check the expiration date. Fridge is broken, but there's warm soda."

"How long are we here, though?"

Welch pauses half-bent while putting down her big, black suitcase that she dragged in from the car. "For however long it takes, Jessica." She arches an eyebrow, high, pulling up a smirk, as well.

"You were already packed?"

"We were going to be taking you here today regardless. You just sped up the process. Or slowed it down. However you want to look at it. I suggest you get up to our bedroom and go to sleep. It's almost five a.m., and you've already had a trying night."

A trying night. A trying Knight. There's no difference.

"Why were you going to take me here today?" I feel like I just got kidnapped by Chicago Police Crime... whatever these people are called. I can't help but imagine how they had been planning to come to my apartment, snatch me up against my will, and stuff me in here like a criminal in a detention center, awaiting a trial. A sentence for my future. Maybe I'm overthinking it.

"I've been on this case since the beginning," she said, "and I knew you were related to Martha Pax since she died. Pulled an all-nighter that night, you know. I'd been wondering why the heck you were alive this whole time."

"You made that connection before Bradley's—er, Lockheed's—people did."

"Yeah, well, they're just a police department," she says.

"Aren't you?"

"No. My people and I investigate violent crimes, and Pax's murder was nothing less than that. The Collector's been on my radar since he went feral on your family. My investigation of Pax revealed she had a little granddaughter in my city."

"Step-granddaughter."

"Tomato, tomahto. And you're wrong about Fuller Park."

"What do you mean?" I ask.

"They didn't make the connection that you were related to the victims. They'd never look that far into it. They were informed by Spooner PD, remember?"

Of course I remember. "Oh," is all I can drive out.

She shows me to our room upstairs. We're sharing, she exclaims. I peek through the doorway and to my dismay, it's nothing but two twin mattresses and a narrow window. I take the one that's not by the door—a command of Welch's—so I'm stuck against the wall with the cracks and a view of the spotty mold in the ceiling.

"I'll be downstairs if you need anything." She pats the doorway on her way out.

~

Yeah, she's sleeping like a baby.

The jagged edges of her voice wakes me, but my head is too fogged for full consciousness. I have no idea what time it is, or how long I have been sleeping, but it can't be more than an hour because it is still dark, though the night is starting to lighten with dawn.

She's got it on the floor charging. Hold on, let me get it.

The cord clicks and dangles by my bed.

I put the new one there. She'll figure it out in the morning.

I hear Welch leave the room.

Everything around me is dark, so I wait for my eyes to adjust to the dim light before I get out of bed. I run my hand down my phone charger all the way to the end, and my cell is gone, replaced by a thick square that is definitely not my iPhone. My foot dangles off the mattress and scrapes against the cold floor. Fragments of Welch's conversation start to make sense.

She must have taken my phone and given me a new one. I pick it up, and the screen lights into a picture of a purple field with a single tree in the center. Lovely wallpaper. The contact page has only a handful of numbers. Susan Welch's is there, and so is Sergeant Lockheed's; I notice a few other officers and detectives listed, but they are all people that I've not been introduced to.

I set the phone on my mattress and creep down to the last step of the staircase. I tiptoe past the living room sofa and toward the other bedroom, which has been turned into a makeshift office. Welch sits at a desk with a computer, talking on the phone. The crooked clock hanging on the wall above a frayed sofa says it's a little after six.

Since she's distracted by her call, I sneak past the office doorway and place my back against the wall, pressing my ear against it. Her raspy voice comes through crystal clear.

"I'm looking at it right now, and I'm only seeing a few calls in, a few out." The volume on the other side of her conversation is too low for me to hear.

"They're to the aunt up in Wisconsin, a couple to someone named John. She's got dozens from a man named Ben. These are mostly missed calls or incoming."

I hear her fingernail tapping on my phone screen as she stands from her chair. Her heavy footsteps pace from one end of the office to the other, dull then loud, far away then close.

"Her text history is pretty basic. There're some messages from John that say, 'hope you're feeling better' and 'can you come into the office for a minute?'"

Welch hums, and I press closer, wondering what she's hearing on the other line.

"I'll talk to her when she's awake. Meanwhile, have Tuffin contact both John and Ben. I've sent their contact numbers to you, and I'll have someone come by and take the phone when it's light out. And hey, check this Ben guy first. Run a background on him. The way it looks, Knight's been avoiding him. She's gotten eleven calls from him this week, none outgoing, but one incoming from around midnight tonight. Has anyone from Fuller Park been tracking her?"

I lean in.

"Of course he was. Still is, probably. Call Detective Bradley. Keep him in the loop."

Welch waits a moment, and I hear her put both my cell and hers on the table. She sighs a wheezy breath and begins to pace again. Her footsteps clack louder. Louder. Closer, until she's facing me.

"Jessica." In an instant, her attention goes to my bandaged forearm. Speckles of brown have seeped through, likely from the hours my pulse ran high with fear and adrenaline, when I felt the wound seeping warmth. I can still kind of feel the significant spike to my blood pressure. "What's this?" She takes my wrist and holds up my arm.

"I cut myself accidentally."

"This is pretty big for an accident."

"I was afraid of sleeping in my apartment, so I kept a knife under my pillow, and it cut me. The Spooner police officer told me I need to keep a weapon near me for my own protection."

Welch nods, concentrating on my face, and drops my arm. "Serial killers can smell blood from miles away, you know."

She smiles but turns around before I know whether she's joking or if she means this as a warning. Either way, I stay quiet and stand in the doorway of her office room while she picks up my cell phone from her desk. She walks me into the living room and plops down on the sofa.

"You must've heard me talking to my boss."

"I did."

"Then you know we need to have a discussion about the two men you've been talking to on your phone."

"They're nobodies."

She pats the cushion beside her. "Who is John?"

Yellow light spills in from the office, and it's just enough for me to see the wiry lines that form the shape of a parenthesis around Welch's mouth. I gently sit on the edge of the sofa next to her.

"He's my boss at *The Chicago Post*. I'm a journalist. Those messages are about having me come into the office so he could tell me I should take a break from work for a while. The Spooner people informed him about my situation. Or Chicago PD people. I can't remember." I rub my face and think for a second that I can actually smell the blood on my arm. "The other text was from when I got sick and had to miss a few days at work. It is nothing more than him hoping I would start to feel better. John has nothing to do with anything."

I told Bradley that too. I hope this time somebody buys it.

Welch bends over and rests her elbows on her knees. "I trust you, Jessica. The first thing you need to know about me is that I trust you. Otherwise, I wouldn't be here. You're the Button Collector's target; I've told you that, so you're first on my list to keep safe. But I have to have one of my guys call in John for questioning. I wouldn't be doing my job if I didn't. If nothing else, it's just a precaution to see if his story matches up with what you're telling me. Everyone in your life at this point should be considered a suspect. I don't think you're lying to me if that's what you're wondering."

"Then why are you having my phone checked?"

"We have to look at an extended list of your phone records, and we need it in case someone else is tracking it. It's not because I don't trust you. I'm doing this for your safety. We got a warrant to do so."

Wow. "It doesn't feel safe here. There aren't even any officers parked outside."

"The station is six blocks away. We can't have back-up hanging around outside or we'll be too obvious. And this is a very safe place, Jessica."

"Bradley was tracking me this whole time?"

"Yes. Again, just protocol for a situation like this one. Just doing what he was told."

He knew where I was even when I thought he wasn't there. Something heavy in my body lifts, like. . . like relief. I wonder if he's still tracking me.

"So tell me about Ben. Why so many calls? Why haven't you returned any?"

"Ben is a guy I work with."

"You're friends?"

"Not really. He likes me, but I don't like him."

She squints, casting temporary shadows to form across her face. "Are you involved with anyone romantically?"

I shift myself to face her so the light will be on my back. "No."

"Why don't you like Ben?"

My heartbeat thuds, and I can feel it on the surface of my arm wound. I rub my bandage to tame the heat. "He's just—he's clingy. We just don't feel the same way about each other."

Welch reaches for her small notepad and a tiny pen that disappears in her large hand as she scribbles. Upside down, I read the list she makes.

Ben:
Clingy
Works with J
"He calls a lot and stops by sometimes."

Welch glances up. "You could say he's an unwanted visitor?"

"Yes."

Calls a lot. Unwanted.

"That's all I need." She stands, gliding to the kitchen to pour a cup of coffee. Holding up the pot, she offers me a cup. I shake my head.

"I don't want you worrying, Jessica. You're in good hands."

I push myself up and spin into the light of her office. "Better than with Lockheed and Bradley?"

She slides the coffee pot back onto its heater. "I don't mean to sound like they weren't doing a good job with you, Jess. I'm just better at what I do. I'm more informed on this serial killer, this investigation. Do you trust that?"

Walking back to me, her arm bows around her waist, as if she's still wearing all her police gear. I go back to the sofa and plop down. She seems less intimidating in her black pants and black shirt, half tucked in. She holds my gaze as she takes the seat beside me.

"Yes."

At the same time, we lean against the back of the sofa, which emits the strong odor of mildew. Welch gulps her coffee like a man—big sips, loud and slurping, and she seems to like it best when it's steaming hot. The hotter the better.

"Why aren't you asleep?" she asks.

I shuffle in my pajama pants and tee shirt, inching closer to the arm of the sofa. "Would you sleep if you were me?"

"Honey, I'd be in a temporary coma right now if I knew someone like me was down here keeping watch." She points to herself with her thumb.

"Have you updated Bradley?" I ask.

"I'm sure Lockheed told him. Needs all the distractions he can get."

"What do you mean?"

She breathes in another sip. "Bradley's had a rough year. No kids. Wife left. The divorce brought him down for a while. I hate making light of this investigation, but it's kept him busy. I'm not trying to say he's happier now, 'cause, you know. But since he took on the Collector case, he seems more like his old self."

Married? My first reaction is to scream at her. Second, I want to scream at myself, embarrassed for being so harsh with him. "Aren't you the one taking the case from him?" I ask.

The flat grin she had a moment ago has fallen into a shocked scowl. "No, Jessica, you are."

I t's funny how in a skinny house with cold walls and cracked windows I can sleep just fine. My dreams are no longer dark and bloody, filled with my fears of the Button Collector but of being alone in my own apartment and seeing him now that I know what he looks like.

If that was him in the alley.

My subconscious thoughts have painted a calm picture of an apartment that's whiter than my own, too bright for me to remain unseen. In the dream, I'm afraid I won't be able to hide.

The bandage in my dream still covers my arm but only over the big vein on the underside of my elbow. I've had my blood taken a couple times in that spot because it's easy to locate. Bleeds a lot. I don't remember the pain of the Collector's needle piercing my skin in this dream. I only know it happened, and I was thankful the needle got my arm instead of my face.

Every morning—all three that I've been in the townhouse—I wake up thinking about Ben. I'm not sure whether it stems from my own thoughts or whether it was planted there by Welch's investigation. Behind my eyelids in the warm seconds before I fully wake, the blackness of sleep feels fuzzy and swells around me until it is pierced by the Chicago sunrise that beats through the cracks in the thin curtains. And that's when I see Ben. That's when I realize I'm trickling back into my bleak reality of living in the safe house.

My vision of him is always the same. He's standing at the end of a dark tunnel, tall, his outline thick. His arms are extended toward me, but I can never tell what he is holding. It looks kind of like he's pointing a gun. Just before I can be sure of anything, my eyes open and my vision is lost.

This morning, it's because Welch is saying his name. "I'd like you to come to the station. Gotta talk to you about Ben."

"What about him?"

"We're onto something, but don't get your hopes up."

No matter what time I look over at Welch's side of the room each morning, her bed is untouched. I wonder if she ever sleeps. Welch is meticulously neat, which makes me a little uncomfortable. She keeps her toothpaste, toothbrush, and contact lenses in the bathroom on the first level and lines them up on the countertop from longest to shortest, but the bathroom itself looks completely unused. There is not even a single droplet of water left behind.

Welch hands me my new phone and motions me toward the door. I check to see if I've missed any calls or texts, even though it hasn't made a single noise since she gave it to me.

"It's for emergency use only. Use it if you're in trouble," she tells me, noting my disappointment.

Today, I'm bundled up and tucked into a black BMW she calls her own. It must have been dropped off some time after we got here because she hasn't left the townhouse once.

Welch speeds through traffic, honking the entire way, but never utters a word. She tilts her chin down to focus and presses the gas hard, weaving through the lanes with expertise until we arrive at Chicago Police Violent Crimes a few red lights away. She tells me that Ben was brought in for questioning yesterday morning, and so far, he hasn't been released. I scan the parking lot looking for his car, but I realize that authorities probably surprised him and brought him in handcuffs in the back of a squad car. That thought makes me shiver. I ask her if Lockheed would be here as she's putting the car in park.

"No. We've got Ben, and Lockheed's interrogating John today, asking him a few questions."

"So you and Fuller Park work together on cases?" I ask.

"Let me break it down for you, Jess." She cuts the engine to the BMW. "Chicago PD, the sheriff's office, and us—CPVC—we initially investigated the Pax murder, and, only recently, Fuller Park took you on to protect because they're over your neighborhood. Right? Then you went and told Bradley to go away, and I had my opportunity to get my hands dirty in this case with someone the killer actually wants to collect." She chuckles at the last part. I ignore it. "You could say Lockheed recruited me to protect you, as if I needed recruiting. Or permission. Guess he knew this case needed some investigators who specialize in violent crimes. Maybe like a premonition." Another chuckle, but this time, she nudges her elbow at my arm, padded with my coat and sweater. "Anyway, I've been investigating for a while. Just got the honor of taking you under my wing."

I sink into the scarf around my neck. "I'm your only connection to Fuller Park, then."

"No, we've worked together on a handful of cases in the past. You just got Fuller involved, and then you got lucky and snagged me right when you needed me most, it turned out."

Welch winks at me, grins, then opens her car door to step out. I get out of the car, my mind gravitating back to John in an interrogation room.

Bradley will interview him. Welch doesn't tell me that, but I know he'll recognize John as the man who spent the night with me, and he'll want to take him from Lockheed to dig for every detail about him.

As we are walking through the parking lot, I pause. "Can I make a phone call?" Welch comes to a stop and turns to face me. "I just want to call Detective Michael Bradley."

Her nostrils widen with an exhale, and she waves me forward to start walking again, her strides too long for me to keep up with. "In the lobby. Make it quick. What's this about?"

"I want to explain those text messages to him. The ones from John."

She opens the front door for me and ushers me inside before continuing into the lobby.

Though I pretend I don't see it, her disparaging glare is hard to miss.

I pluck my new phone along with Bradley's card out of my purse and punch in his number. I check to make sure Welch isn't watching me before adding him to my contact list in case I ever need him. He answers on the second ring.

"Is this Detective Michael Bradley?" I ask, though I know his voice well enough to know it's him.

His grin stretches through the line. "This must be Jessica."

"Yeah, I'm calling because of John."

"John. . . the man you're sleeping with?"

I press the phone hard to my ear and turn my back to the lobby. "Please don't say that out loud."

"I knew I would hear from you eventually."

"Can you do me a favor and not mention that? It'll just complicate things, and he shouldn't even be considered as a suspect because he was at work when my aunt Deborah was attacked in Spooner. Bradley, he sleeps with everyone—all the journalists at the office, not just me. Please use some discretion and keep that quiet or he'll lose his job. I'm serious, please."

Through the phone, I hear Bradley's chair squeak as he adjusts his weight, and I imagine him leaning back. "Lockheed told me to bring him in for questioning about some text messages. I already read them."

"He was just hoping I was feeling better because I called in sick, and the others were because he needed me to come into the office . . . because he'd heard about my family being killed. He wanted to give me a break from work, that's all."

I can see him now, propped over his desk, slow breaths, green eyes blinking deep in thought. I imagine the look of his broad shoulders and the masculine boost they get from his bullet proof vest.

It's the little things like that which make me wonder why Bradley and his ex-wife divorced. Was she too overbearing? Could she have wanted a man a little softer around the edges?

No. His wife probably began feeling unloved, taken for granted, forgotten under stacks of paperwork, under Lockheed, under CPD. That's what I tell myself every time I take his card out of my purse and consider locking my bedroom door and calling him. He was the problem in their marriage. She just didn't have the patience for him.

My heart skips a beat when he lowers his voice, his tone sincere. "I know, Jessica. I'll go easy on him. Alright?"

On the other side of the lobby, glass doors separate me from where Welch is standing at the entrance of a hallway, snapping her fingers at me to hurry.

"Thank you," I tell him, not ready to hang up just yet.

"No problem. I hope you're staying safe."

An apology bubbles up in my throat, but Welch rolls her eyes then snaps her fingers again. I can't get the words out properly. "Bradley, I—"

"Don't, Jessica. It's okay. Just stay safe."

To my surprise, Welch didn't take me to see Ben. Instead, she hands me off to another man in uniform. He tells me they've already taken Ben into custody and that he denied he was the Button Collector. Due to a lack of evidence linking him to any involvement, they're releasing him this afternoon.

"We kept him as long as we could, but the only thing we had was some grainy street footage from a security camera on Ninety-Third Street that revealed a man of similar stature walking somewhat near the crime scene," the man explains. "We can't be certain that it was him, and of course he denied that it was. We also searched for the weapon and tested for gun residue on his hands. We found nothing. We searched both his home and his car. If Ben is the Collector, he must've dumped his coat and gotten rid of the gun. As of now, that's the assumption we're working with because we can't find either item. We also can't charge him with any crime. He's claiming that he never left his house that night. He did admit, though, to working closely with you."

Welch adds, "We have been able to keep him this long on circumstantial evidence, but it's not enough anymore. We got all we could out of him. And we're still waiting to get a report from Lockheed about John."

As Welch directs me to a kitchen on some other level of the building, I find myself walking close to her, as if Ben has been released within these walls and is out searching for me. He's far more dangerous in my mind now more than ever. I'm certain he is also angrier at me now more than ever too.

Welch pours herself a cup of coffee. She doesn't offer me any until she takes her first sip, but I turn her down, anyway.

She backs against the counter, bringing the mug to her chin. "You said the man who shot at you was the Button Collector."

I take a few awkward steps and make my way to a chair at a fold-out round table. I remember we had some like this at the family reunion, where I last saw Robert. "I didn't get a good look at him. It was dark."

"Well, Lord knows I didn't either. From a distance, I could only see the outline of his shape." Her coffee is still steaming and curls up by her lips. It annoys me to listen to the gulping sound she makes when she swallows. "But you said you were certain. You are confident that it must've been him, right?"

"I'm not sure, anymore," I say. "Is this what you meant earlier by 'we're onto something'?"

"Yeah, as a matter of fact." Her voice tightens and picks up a scruffy undertone like I've noted it does when she gets aggravated. "We're onto Ben even if he isn't the nation's favorite serial killer, okay?"

"Okay."

"The man from the alley was tall and had wild hair. Can you confirm that?"

Welch would know that liars avoid the eyes, so I hold my gaze steady with hers. Plus, it would be useless to lie about what I saw—she saw him too, and we both know the description and behavior was not that of the Button Collector.

"Yes. Tall and had hair," I say.

"Your aunt claimed the man who attacked her was short and bald." She steps closer to me, towering over me from afar. "Which means the man who shot at you, whether or not it was Ben, was also not the Button Collector."

Every detail about Ben lunges at me—his freakish height, his crazy hair, how willing he was to steal my keycard from John's desk just to get close to me.

My entire body shudders, and Welch pulls out a chair to sit beside me.

"What?" Her face lifts with genuine concern, but I don't want to say any more.

"Nothing." I swallow. "Nothing."

"Can you think of any reason that Ben would have a motive to kill you?"

I look across the table and stare at her coffee mug. The steam rises, and I watch as it hits the freckles on her neck. "Not that I can think of. Like I said, he was interested in me, but I didn't like him like that. But that's not really a new thing. It's been going on this way for years."

"People snap, Jessica."

She stands, pushes the chair in, and I have no choice but to follow.

She drives us back to the townhouse, my head pinned against the window the entire way. When the backdoor is closed behind us, I ask her if I can call Bradley again to see how his interview went with John.

"It wasn't an interview," she says, yanking the key out of the dead-bolt. "It was an interrogation."

I pause with my foot on the first step to go upstairs. "I'm a journalist. We do interviews," I mutter under my breath.

I reach my room and close the door for at least the illusion of some privacy. Then I dial Bradley and he answers quickly. "Bradley speaking."

"It's me again," I say, hunched against the cold windowsill, hoping Welch isn't hovering outside the door.

"Calling twice in one day?" He chuckles.

"I just wanted to know how it went today with John."

"He smokes too much, Jessica." When I don't respond, he continues, "He's clean, though. You're right about his alibi. Nonetheless, you've made a good choice to cut off ties with him. For now, at least. Don't make him a priority."

I move to my bed and find myself peering out my window, wondering what Bradley is doing right now, where he is in the office. If I couldn't hear phones ringing in the background, I'd assume he was parked outside the townhouse watching me from his squad car on the street. "I never have," I say.

"Do better than John. He's married, you know."

His words rip a hole open inside my chest, inside my heart. It feels like it's oozing from the center, a tear no surgeon could repair. My vision prickles with black dots, so I stand up but then sit right back down again.

"I know," I say. "Does anyone else know that. . . we're. . ."

Bradley lowers his voice. "No. I'm the one who ran the background check, did all the dirty work." Then, like an afterthought, he adds even quieter, "I kept it out of the case file."

Out of the case file. "Isn't that. . . That's illegal. You can't do that, can you?"

"Let's just say I pretended not to see it." I assume "it" means us having sex in my apartment that one night.

I almost run downstairs and ask Welch to escort me to Bradley just so I can wrap my arms around him. My desire to laugh with relief almost comes out, and just like that, I want to call Bradley my confidant in this case.

"Thank you. Wow. I don't know what to say."

"You said you're not going to be involved with him. I'm choosing to trust your word." He says it with the same hard authority he displayed the first time I met him in the chief's office.

I nod, even though he can't see me. The moment of sentiment silences me. There's so little I can say without sounding weak or desperate for him to be here watching over me instead of Welch.

"Just so you know, John sleeps with every girl in the office. It's not just me." I try to return Bradley's authoritative tone.

"Stop talking. You're not helping yourself."

My jaw tightens. "I'm not a whore."

"Let's keep it that way, then, and forget about John. He's just an old pervert, and now you know he won't be considered a suspect anymore. He checked out."

"Okay, fine," I say, and I can't tell if it comes out too firmly or just soft enough. "Good."

After a long pause, he says, "We'll talk later. I have to go."

When I first began working at the newspaper, Ben had actually caught my eye. In a good way. Three years ago, he had shorter hair, and he'd often lean over from behind his computer to flash a crooked smile at me. After a week of flirting, he approached my desk. I'd smiled up at him and stopped my typing.

He'd asked me out in a way that wasn't even a question. His confidence turned me on, and his voice took on a seductive drawl.

That Saturday night, Ben took me to a musical at the theater, and I spent most of the show wondering whether he'd invite me back to his place or if I'd have him up to mine for wine. We ate dinner by candle-light at a nice place on the water.

Staying in Chicago after college inspired me to try a new thought process, especially after I'd landed my job at the paper. I'd slept with John twice by then, which was fine for me, but I wanted to try my hand at this new relationship. I considered my new job to be my fresh start. I remember thinking, *Maybe I won't have to be alone anymore.*

Upon accepting Ben's offer for a date, I decided on a whim that I would shift to relationships rather than one-night stands. I'd also had that thought earlier that morning as I was getting dressed in my land-lord's bedroom.

My fresh start didn't last long. I'd gotten back to my routine rather quickly: men, drink, then work again. It was only a month after my date with Ben that I'd felt a sweet familiarity in John's invitation to take me for a drink once more. I'd felt relief the next morning when he let himself out of my apartment before I'd woken up, as he had those other times.

I think back to my dinner with Ben. At first, his questions had begun with light curiosity, asking the usual things. Where did you grow up? What about your parents? I'm sorry to hear that. How long have you been in the city?

The innocence of his inquiries had turned dark too fast, amplifying to intense demands, triggering my fear of being alone with him. He demanded to know why *I* hadn't asked *him* out sooner. When I didn't answer his questions about my sex life, he became angry. "Are you afraid of me now?" he'd challenged me.

"That's it, isn't it?" he'd repeated, his voice getting more intense as he drove me back home. "You're afraid of me now." I'd jumped as he slammed his hand on the steering wheel and closed my eyes as his speed kept increasing. "I knew I'd put you off. Shouldn't've asked you those questions. Does that really *scare* you, Jessica?" I had not answered him, which only made it worse.

He had followed me up to my apartment without permission, so I'd stood behind him in the elevator, feeling both threatened and intimidated. At my door, I had lied and told him I didn't want to wake my roommate who had to go to work the next morning.

Before I knew it, his hands were all over me, and my head was pounding against my own door from his kiss. I'd pushed him away, but I was no match for his strength.

I shudder as I remember how he had grabbed me by my neck and yanked me closer with both hands.

"If you ever tell anyone about this, I'll kill you. I know where you live, I know where you work; I know everything about you."

He left me in the hallway, collapsed into a heap on the floor, as he sped away.

That following Monday, I'd called in sick and didn't go back to work until Wednesday. Ben ignored me at first, then, through the research I conducted at my desk, I'd discovered that Ben had been temporarily suspended from work for harassing another journalist who had ended up quitting during her ordeal. The suspension had been hush-hush and eliminated from his work records following a twenty-four-month probation which required him to behave appropriately. That probation had ended six weeks before I had gotten hired. I was terrified to learn how hard he'd worked to stay in the office.

I ended up reaching out to that other journalist who confirmed my suspicions. "It was rejection that pushed him over the edge."

"Did he threaten you?" I'd asked her over the phone.

She told me that he hadn't, at least not directly. He'd only gotten angry with her for turning him down, but she said that was bad enough.

So I kept my mouth shut. I didn't tell anyone about the night I had rejected him, but despite that, he's been staying close by to make sure, trying for another chance ever since.

Could Ben have thought I told someone about that night? Why else would he be the one pointing a gun at me? If I explained to Welch what had happened between us that night, she and her team would take him to jail, probably. But if they released him again, he'd kill me just like he promised he would. It feels like a lose-lose for me. It couldn't hurt to tell someone now. Now that he's a suspect.

The bed that Welch has been sleeping in is still made perfectly each day before I wake up. I think I've been here two weeks now, though the time inside this townhouse collides into one never-ending day of light and darkness, sleep and consciousness. A dusting of snow came through the city and melted, and a new storm blew in last night. Cars on the street haven't moved under the heavy ice and seldom do I see new tire tracks on the road that cuts through this sketchy neighborhood.

I catch Welch downstairs as she moves from the kitchen into her office, holding a cup of coffee.

"Yes?" she says calmly. Her breath smells stale but rich, mixed with the scent of black caffeine.

"Can you fill me in on what's going on with my case? I'm lost. I'm not in my house, I'm not with people I know, and I'm not sure I can take this any longer. I mean, I'm turning my underwear inside out because the washer in this place is broken. If the Collector wants me badly enough, he'll find me just as easily here as he would anywhere else."

Welch eyes me from head to toe, lingering for a moment on the thick, pink scar on my forearm. "Come sit." She nods toward the couch.

I move in the direction she points me, but I don't sit down. "No. You need to sit," she says.

Fine. I shrink back against the sofa cushions and wait for her to start talking. Welch's muscles flex, bulging under her blue collared shirt and black uniform pants. The gun on her hip is steady, tight, secure.

"If it weren't for me and the people at CPVC, you'd have been lying in that wet alley until you bled out of your chest, alright? I told you I trust you, and if you can't trust me then you've got to figure out how to come to terms with me. I'm not your enemy, Jessica. I'm trying to protect you from the killer."

She wheezes, breathing heavily out of her flared nostrils. We hold each other's gaze, and neither of us looks away. She's close enough for me to see the age spots on her cheek.

"Do you still feel him watching you?" Veins on her temples engorge, spider-webbing in such a way that reaches across her forehead. "Do you?" she questions again.

I snap my gaze away from hers and shift my attention to the fog that has built up outside the window.

"You don't," she says, "because I brought you here."

Just because the Button Collector doesn't know I'm here yet, I think.

The sound of Welch's boots stomping away on the bare floor smashes my last nerve. She makes her way into her office and slams the door behind her. The living room goes silent. Before I allow myself time to think about what I'm doing, I realize that I'm staring down at Bradley's name on my contact list, my thumb hovering just over the call button.

But before I can make the call, my mind flashes to the narrow hallway in my apartment building. The thought of Ben makes everything fall dark. My neck stings in remembrance of his grip. It still chokes me when I remember the way his hot breath felt as it spilled into my ear or the way the dampness of his lips felt sweeping across mine.

If you tell anyone, I'll kill you.

The townhouse is always cold, but there is an extra chill in the air caused by the half-foot of fresh snow outside. Welch doesn't suggest turning up the heat or starting the fireplace. The bedroom upstairs is the coldest room in the house, while Welch's office downstairs is the warmest. She stays comfortable as she works arched over her computer, taking up space in her small chamber.

Today, she tells me that she's stuck at her desk "working on a smaller case while things are stagnant for a minute."

I leave her to her work but keep her door cracked behind me, making a point to be noisy as my feet clatter up the stairs. I grab my coat from the edge of my mattress and slip it on as quietly as I can. It's still damp from this morning when I attempted to go for a walk outside to enjoy the snow. Welch didn't approve and forced me back inside.

The zipper comes up to my chin, and my beanie covers my eyebrows. I keep my hair down instead of wearing a scarf.

One less thing I can get choked with.

I can't let my morbid thoughts continue.

I slither down the stairs, pressing my snow boots to my belly.

Through the crack I left in Welch's office door, I can see her back to me, engrossed in her work, so I make my way to the backdoor in the kitchen. She clicks away at her keypad and rolls her chair out of my sight. I wait for a moment, expecting to see her burnt red hair as she throws open the door to bust me, but she doesn't, so I push forward with my plan.

The backdoor squeals under its rusted hinges, and I freeze but hear nothing from Welch's office. Cold air sweeps through my legs and flows through the kitchen. Welch's door blows open a couple of inches, but she is still focused on her screens.

I snatch my purse from the counter and pinch the back door closed. Before my boots are on, snow has already melted into the tips of my socks, making my feet cold and wet, but once I reach the freedom of the street, I don't feel it anymore. Instead, my cheeks take the brunt of the frigid cold.

Behind me, the safehouse is quiet, boarded up, untouched from the outside. CPVC is a few blocks away, but I am unafraid that they will catch me. I reason that I'm probably unrecognizable to them in my winter clothes, hiding under my layers. A thread from my coat pocket tickles my hands, dangling there from the morning I ripped all the buttons off my clothing.

And then, he's here again. He watches me walk, watches me from some place up high; his piercing scrutiny of me stabs at me no matter how fast I dart between the streets. My gut clenches. Ben should be at work right now. Unless John fired him, setting him free, releasing him onto this road with me. These invisible eyes are not those of Ben, though. They're too clever, too beady to be his. If not him, then who? My mind is playing tricks on me. Of course it had to have been Ben in the alley. But was it Ben who has been watching me all this time, or was it merely a coincidence that placed Ben on my path with his gun? He must've known I was there. How would he know without watching me? How would the Collector watch me while Ben's at work? Maybe I am crazy. Maybe Lockheed was right, and no one is stalking me, and all the wine I've been drinking to cope with my exhaustion these last few months—years, really—has finally gone to my head.

I turn around and check one more time to be sure that the street behind me is still. When I don't see Welch flailing after me, I step onto the salted road and hop into a cab.

The driver goes twenty minutes south to my storage unit. When I moved to Chicago, I brought my parents belongings that were left to me in their will, and I stuffed them into a unit. Eight months ago, I visited the unit and shuffled through a box of old photo albums. One of the albums held Robert's middle-school picture, his young features so different than that of the young man's face they kept flashing across the TV screen.

Yes, it's the same person, I thought. My memory of Robert's youth was fogged by the chaos of what happened to him: my cousin, brutally murdered.

The taxi dumps me into the snow that I crunch through all the way to unit 474. My boots stomp holes in the thin layer of ice, and with each print I make, I wonder how someone could commit a crime leaving no evidence, especially in a snow-covered city like Chicago. After I'm finished in my own unit, I'll make a lap around the two other buildings in case I need to deny being here for any reason, in case they find my footprinted path leading to my unit.

472. 473.

474.

That's the number they rented to me, a half-sized unit because I didn't need anything bigger than that. I had sold most of my parents' bigger items before college just to get by.

Approaching the silver sliding door, I start to dig into my purse for the smallest key on my keyring. I feel around through the sharp metal, and just as I pull out the keyring and graze my fingers over the unmistakable smoothness of an unused key, it falls from my grip and bounces onto the frozen ground below. The padlock on the sliding door ... *is snapped.*

A hot flash spreads over my cold body. The lock dangles from its hook, its openness insulting my ignorance, but emphasizing my vulnerability.

I back away from the lock, though no one could be behind that door; my footprints are the only ones here, and no shrapnel from the broken padlock lies on the snow.

The door, pulled shut, is swiped clean where there was once dust and dried mud caked around the handle. Stepping closer, I see the impressions around the handle where the wipes were made—large and narrow, belonging to a glove.

I pick off the lock. Its exterior is unbruised, barely scratched from years of going untouched; then I tuck it in my pocket, reaching down to slide the door up. The growl it makes when it opens pierces the silence as a pale light sheds on the damp, lumpy boxes and wooden tables that are housed there.

I plow through the towers of disheveled cardboard and dive straight to the back corner.

Someone was here. And that reality replaces my fear with a critical demand to know who was here and when. I imagine the killer eyeing me from afar. I didn't feel him in the taxi, but here, his presence grows thick around my body. Like I'm already in a casket just waiting for the lid to close, hugging the air out of my lungs. *This*—this is my imagination.

My dad's gun case is already sprawled out on the table, unbuckled, cracked open to reveal what I already know. It's empty.

I set my purse down and gather the long, black rifle case in my arms. I had already come up with the lie I planned on telling the taxi driver. It's an old telescope of my dad's, I would say. Winter is the best time for stargazing, I would add. I'm going to take it to the country this weekend and look for the nebula in Orion.

If Welch asked, I would tell her a different version of the truth if she ended up finding it. I'd say I simply wanted my dad's gun. I wouldn't need any more explanation than that because I know she would never permit me to keep it in my possession. I would have to let her have it…at least for a little while. I just wanted it in the house, but it's gone now, stolen by the hands of someone who didn't want anything in the storage unit except this.

I place the case back on the table and put my purse back over my shoulder. My dad used to say, "There're a few rules about guns you need to know. First, don't ever leave the safety off; you need to always keep it locked in case an accident happens. Never point a gun at someone, loaded or unloaded, because there are a number of things that could go wrong if you forget you've got a bullet in the chamber. Also" —he'd scrub the barrel with a cloth each time he explained this to me— "never leave your fingerprints on the gun. You've always gotta wipe it off because the oil from your fingertips is bad for it."

Then he would make his very last point. He'd place the rifle back on the shelf, and my kid eyes would stare up at it.

"Never leave your gun by a door. If someone breaks in, that's the first thing they'll pick up if they see it. Can't have someone shooting you with your own gun."

I'd remembered his words when I rented the unit, and I'd stuffed the rifle in the back corner under the cover of a sheet. And now it's gone. The bullets in the alley shooting were confirmed by the police to have come from a handgun, not a rifle. Why steal it with no purpose of using it?

The Collector wouldn't know where I had hidden my father's gun all those years ago, so I examine the rest of the space, looking for any clue as to who else could have been here. My thoughts land on Ben. *Impossible,* I think. *How did he know about my storage unit?*

Peeling sheets up from the floor, I reveal the old boxes of photo albums and refrigerator magnets and broken coffee mugs. All untouched. *How could the Collector know?*

But he watches me. He follows me. Of course he would know. He'd have seen me come here the week of the first murder, perhaps observing my response to it.

I turn back to the front of the unit and study the vantage point that the thief would have seen when he slid open the door. My organizational skills have always been lacking, but in this small space, I was determined to try and keep some kind of order. I had arranged a few old tables so they laid a pathway and stacked the boxes as neatly as I could. Toward the back corner there was just enough space to conceal the rifle. No one could have seen it from the doorway, which meant only one thing. Whoever had come for the gun had known where it was hiding.

In my haste to grab the rifle, I had not noticed that some of the boxes had been disturbed.

The sheets I had covering the tables are scrunched and wrinkled where someone has brushed against them, pulling them nearly to the floor as they crept toward the gun. How had I also missed the fact that drawers on my parents' dresser are pulled part-way open?

The further back I go, the shadows grow long and dark. Whoever was in here must have stumbled, bringing down a floor lamp. Shattered glass sparkles all over the concrete floor, and cracks under my boots with every step.

Any glimmer of hope that I had about retrieving the gun disappears. Standing here alone, being here in this unit—it was a bad idea. My back tingles with a chill that sends me running out of the unit.

I jerk the door down behind me, placing the broken lock just how I found it, then trace my own footprints back to the road and take my phone out of my purse. I call a taxi to pick me up, certain Welch has realized by now that I am missing. She's probably tracking my calls from her office in the safehouse. By chance she hasn't, I call Bradley as I stand by the side of the road.

"Hello?"

"Bradley, it's me. Something's happened."

He goes silent, but only for a moment. I hear him jostling around as his tone deepens.

"Jessica, what's going on?" His attitude stays professional, polished. The familiarity of his authoritative nature comforts me, helps me stay level-headed.

"Someone broke into my storage unit in Crestwood."

I hear him gathering his car keys and click his holster onto his belt. "Give me an address."

A car speeds by on the road, so I turn my back to avoid the breeze and step into a brown puddle of slushy snow. "No, don't come here. It's a waste of time. I don't think this was recent."

His keys go silent.

"Ben," I say, "the guy who Welch's people held for a couple of days—he told me three years ago he'd kill me."

"Why didn't you tell anyone?" He slams down the keys on his desk so loud that my phone vibrates. "Why did he say that?"

"I went on a date with him, and he's been obsessed with me ever since. On our date, he went crazy and thought I was rejecting him since I didn't invite him up to my apartment, I guess. He—he was the one in the alley. I'm almost sure of it; I just didn't tell anyone yet. I'd know him anywhere."

"Where are you?"

"I called a taxi. I'm going back to the safehouse." I turn back to face the road again, searching the gray highway for a yellow cab.

"Does Welch know you're gone?"

My sigh gives him the answer, and he groans. I picture him rubbing his face in annoyance.

"I'm going to find Ben, and I'm going to send people to get you at the storage unit right now. Do not move," he says. "Is Ben the one who broke in?"

"I don't know." I give him the address to unit 474, and he shouts to someone in the office. "Bradley, the only thing that was stolen was a rifle."

"A gun was stolen?"

"Yeah, the lock was broken on the unit, and the gun case was open and laying out." A taxi veers off the highway and I jump in.

"I'm already in a cab," I tell Bradley.

"Then go. Don't wait on my guys. Get back to Welch. Why did Ben threaten you?"

"Because I didn't like him. He said if I ever told anyone about that night then he'd kill me."

"Have you told anyone?"

"Not till now."

"Just get back to Welch. Keep your phone on."

Bradley hangs up, and the driver turns onto the highway. "Please hurry," I say to him. "I'm in a rush."

In twenty minutes, I have the driver drop me off a dozen townhouses down from the safehouse. Throwing open the car door, I charge out and tumble into a thin maple tree planted on the sidewalk. My hands scrape against the bark, peeling up my skin, but I push myself off and hurry to the salted path. The sun has set behind the row of roofs, but the streetlamps aren't on yet.

I feel vibrations against my arm from the phone tucked inside my purse, and I jump at its unfamiliar ring.

Detective Michael Bradley flashes on the screen.

My muscles release the tension I held the entire ride back to the city. It's barely been half an hour. If he's already arrested Ben, he wouldn't have been able to call so fast. If he didn't arrest Ben, then maybe I've got more time to make sense of all of this to Bradley.

"Bradley?"

A cracking wind blasts through on his end, masking his voice. His words tumble out; it sounds like he's running, but by the next instant, the background noise goes mute, and I hear his car door slam shut and his engine roar to life.

"Ben isn't at home, Jessica. He's on his way to you."

I look to the safehouse. On the outside it seems the same as I left it—undisturbed, empty, deserted, disguised as an abandoned townhome.

"What?" I breathe into the phone.

He shouts at me to get to the nearest station, but the only words I keep hearing are *He's on his way to you.*

Bradley's engine revs, and I hear his sirens start to blare. His breath is quick and dense. "His door was unlocked, and I found a half-empty box of bullets on his table beside a picture of you."

My staff photograph from work flashes behind my eyelids, the same picture that prints in the paper every week. Ben isn't the Button Collector; he doesn't care about the time or the cover of darkness. He's going to kill me *now.*

"Oh, my God."

"Are you home?" Bradley yells through the line.

Dozens of scenes flash together in a single vision: Ben's every phone call, stealing John's keycard, his reaction when he found out I was sleeping with John.

Bradley yells again, "Are you home, Jessica?"

"Ugh, my God, Bradley."

"Where are you?"

"He knows about John," I say.

Bradley's car shifts gears, horsepower roaring through the phone. He blows a huff of frustration that sounds like static.

"Don't go in that house until I get there. He's either there already or he's on his way. How would he know you're sleeping with John?"

"He must have guessed or overheard a conversation or something." I break into a run down the slick sidewalk, and despite Bradley's warning, I head straight to the townhouse, too disarrayed to stay still.

Bradley hears me, demands that I stop. He tells me not to step foot inside, but I end the call and drop the phone in my purse.

The stairs leading to the front door are hidden under a pile of unblemished snow. Around the corner, the ground blurs past me as I sprint to the other side of the house and to the backdoor where I'd left from earlier. Looking for Ben's prints in the slush—I have no time. I have to get inside. As I round the corner, everything Bradley told me is confirmed. The backdoor is wide open, swinging by its hinges in the wind. I fling it aside, race through the doorway, and skid to a dead stop just inside the kitchen. My body stops so suddenly in its tracks that my purse skims off my arm and lands with a loud thud as it falls against the laminate floor. Where my purse lands, the items from inside tumble out and spread across the floor, all the way to a pair of motionless legs in the living room. My tube of red lipstick slides to a stop by her right foot.

"Susan?" I say.

Her feet are turned into each other. I walk closer and more of her lifeless body becomes visible. Welch's arms are spread over the floor, front side down, mouth hanging open. A line of blood has trickled down her temple, not yet dry.

I tear through the kitchen to get to her, disregarding my safety. But before I can reach the living room, I collide into a hard body, solid as a brick wall on my face. All I see is black, a disheveled appearance. I bounce off of his dark chest, and my skull slams backward into the cabinet. I collapse next to his boots, paralyzed by a sharp pain searing up my neck until it reaches the back of my eyes.

He doesn't budge.

White lights take the form of tiny, dancing dots that disappear when I open my eyes. I reach to touch my wound, and my fingers graze a circle of pain on my skull.

I stumble to my feet, my forehead throbbing from having struck his chin.

"I expected you to be home when I let myself inside." His words pierce my ears, and I feel my heart pounding toward my injury.

Ben's shape comes into focus, his outline the same as the one I saw in the alley. It's so obvious to me now. The same handgun is held solid in his grip. Like the last nail in a coffin, I make the fuzzy conclusion that he's not the man who stole my father's rifle. *He's not the Collector,* my brain whispers. Or did I say it out loud?

I brace onto the wall for support. "What did you do to her?" I ask.

He inches closer, but I slink up the wall. Ben's face closes in on mine, mirroring my movements as I try to see if Welch is breathing.

"I always knew you were afraid of me. You lied to me when you said you weren't."

"I didn't tell anyone about what you said," I murmur.

"You slept with John but won't even return my calls?" His wild hair tickles my nose, and I think again, *This isn't the Button Collector. This is a whole other maniac.*

"What kind of whore sleeps with her boss but won't call me back after the first date? We work together, Jessica. You don't even speak to me in the office."

He wraps his hand around my neck, his palm moist and tight, and pulls me up eye-level, pressing me against the wall.

"Why would you take John and not me?" he says.

He moves his hand up my throat, stopping at my jawline, clenching my mouth shut.

I suck in a breath through my nose and readjust my position so I can breathe, and Ben loses his grip, his hands slipping from his sweat.

"It was you in the alley," I push out.

Ben stands back and wipes his hands on his dark jeans. I shrink down the wall again and catch my breath now that my airways are open. Unamused, he croaks out a sarcastic laugh. He studies the gun gripped tightly in his palm, as if he's trying to decide what to do next.

I wheeze, and a mixture of tears and snot spurt from my face. Ben's hands find my neck again, but this time he squeezes harder. My vision clouds, my hearing disintegrating. I blink, seeping into unconsciousness. Sliding deeper into his grip, my knees go limp, so Ben grabs me by the side of my head and clutches a handful of my hair. He throws me into the living room. My boots catch on Welch's ankles, and I slam into the floor, landing face down just like she did. My senses prickle back to life as I gasp for air.

"You shouldn't have gone looking for trouble that night," he says.

Rolling to my back, a discomfort in my tailbone stops me half-way. The scent of blood seeps into my nose, then its sharp flavor lands on my tongue. Warm fluid floods my cheek.

Ben brushes his hair out of his face with the same hand that holds the gun, and a tortured sob explodes from somewhere deep inside his chest.

"You never listen," he whines.

He points the gun at me, takes his stance, plants his aim. *This is it.*

Desperate to stall him, to give Bradley enough time to get here and help, I pull up a little and rest my weight against the shattered remains of the coffee table. "How did you know?" I try to ask.

"I waited so long for you, Jessica. And I got tired of waiting, and waiting, and finally, *finally,* I had you alone in that alley."

I stay down. If he shoots me, I'll end up here, anyway. If I get up, he'll just push me down again.

The phone in my purse rings, taunting me with its jingle. Ben hears it too. *Bradley.*

"The police are on their way," I tell him, praying I'm not just being hopeful.

Ben's eyes go dim and flat, scrunched under his drawn brows. Light from the streetlamps outside the front windows reflect against the paleness in his face and reveal tears that streak down his cheeks.

We both look down at his gun.

The rule I always forgot was the one my father explained to me each time I picked up his rifle: he insisted that I was never to put my finger on the trigger until I was ready to pull it. But that's where Ben's fingers are resting now.

Ben thrusts the gun toward me, pointing it at my stomach, my heart, my brain. He flails around, but he keeps his grip tight around the gun's handle. It's only a matter of time.

Welch's body is only feet away from me. Her gun, still in the holster on her belt, is on my side of her. If Ben looks away, I could seize the opportunity to grab it. "The police know you're here," I say.

His gun wobbles in his shaking hands.

I scoot closer to Welch but disguise my movements with sounds of my pain, and the writhing that goes along with it. He thinks he's hurt me.

"They don't know anything," he taunts.

"Yes, they do." I flop over to my side, allowing a deliberate scream to escape me.

"Then why can't they find your killer?" he demands.

I stretch my fingertips toward Welch's holster; it's still just out of reach. Hesitating, I restrict myself from moving any closer.

"He's not my killer." Blood spits from my mouth, leaving dark red droplets that splatter the floor. "I'm still alive."

"It doesn't matter if they come for me because you'll be dead by the time they get here," he growls.

"Are you him? Are you the Collector?"

His lips quiver, forming a slimy scowl. "No, Jessica. But I'm your collector."

"You're not the one who watches me. You aren't smart enough to not get caught."

Ben bends his free arm over his face to wipe his tears, then lowers the gun. He screams into his sleeve, but the sound that comes out erupts into an earsplitting noise that echoes through the small room.

My chance presents itself.

I heave myself to Welch's side and snap her handgun loose. The safety clicks off, and I fall flat on my back, fumbling for the trigger. When I regain my composure and cock the gun, I point it in Ben's direction.

He pounces on top of me, propelling the weapon free from my hold. His weight crunches my sternum and pinches my lungs. I kick my legs, but he's on his knees, pinning my forearms to the floor. Welch's gun lands in my peripheral, just beside me. I thrust my waist to buck him off, but he straddles me tighter. His ribs close in on mine as he leans over me.

Ben pulls my coat open and yanks up my shirt with the barrel of his gun.

He's going to gut me. He's going to shoot me with a bullet and dig through my gut.

I scream, throwing my legs high behind his back and wrestling between his thighs, thrashing for a release.

My bra snaps against my skin from his attempt to rip it off me. He grabs it a second time and gets a solid grip right between my breasts. It tears in two and partially reveals my chest.

Welch's gun landed by her ankle, and it's closer to me now as a result of my fight for freedom.

Ben slits through my pants zipper, and the copper button flies across the room, landing out of sight. He traces his fingers down my torso, but when he does, his knees lose their grip, freeing me just enough that I start to feel my blood flooding back through my veins. A brief twinge of pain slithers the length of the scar on my arm, but a new chill of cold beneath my waist draws me back to Ben; he's yanked my pants down to my hips. I drift upward as he edges down my body, and I reach for Welch's gun.

It rattles against the hardwoods, and Ben locks eyes on it.

All movement stops under a tingling silence. He leans up, raises his gun just as I manage to pull Welch's from the floor.

I steady the cool metal in my grip and hold it to his nose.

An explosion booms through the air, reverberating between the walls. Yellow light strikes at Ben's back. The shrill fire of a shot cuts through my ear, banishing everything around me.

A buzzing swarms my brain at the direct closeness of the blast.

Welch's gun is still firm in my control. I haven't fired, so I keep my eyes closed and await the pain in my shoulder or chest or wherever he shot me, waiting for Ben to plow through my wound and slash me open.

But there's no pain, only the weight of Ben's body folding over top of me. He falls, his eyes violent and wide, staring right through mine.

I drop the pistol. At the same time, Ben's gun clatters out of his clutch.

And then I see him. Standing in the shadow of the kitchen, Bradley hovers in firing position.

I shove Ben's head off my neck and call for Bradley. He gets to me in two leaps and drags Ben's heavy body off me while I pull my shirt back down to cover my exposed breasts.

I bring myself to my feet and gather my clothes back together while Bradley plants two fingers on Ben's wrist for a moment. I take off my coat and throw it on the sofa.

"He's dead."

Somehow, beneath a puddle of blood under my tongue, I find a way to speak. "Check Welch. She was like that when I got here."

Instead, he steps to me and cups my face. "Are you okay?" He sponges away my blood with his jacket sleeve. "Your lip is cut."

"Fine," is all I can manage. I point again to Welch. Just then, I hear sirens echoing down the street.

Bradley hesitates and lets go of me, calling someone on his phone and bending down to Welch. After a second, he says into the phone, "She's alive."

I stand over Ben, my chest red from his blood. Still warm from his body, the dark fluid spreads through the fabric of my sweater. I swipe my fingers across my collarbone. They come back smeared with streaks of red, but I can't tell if it's from my lip or from the bullet hole in Ben.

Behind me, Bradley relays into his radio a list of everything that's happened: There's a dead man at the CPVC townhouse. There's an officer down and unconscious. There's a victim of an attempted murder. A stolen rifle. A verbal threat from the man now dead.

And no, it wasn't the serial killer.

12

My lip will heal without stitches, the nurse in the ER says. Other than that, I should be sore, and the soreness will intensify over the next three days. The CAT scan came back fine, and I rejected their offer to schedule a meeting with a therapist.

Before the ER released me to the Fuller Park station for the night, they put me behind a white curtain on a white bed in a white room. Bradley told me he wanted to stay with me, but I knew he was aching to get back to the office and investigate the details of what happened at the safehouse. I shooed him away and changed into the white tee shirt they gave me as a replacement for my sweater that was drenched with the first and fatal drops of Ben's blood.

After an extensive search, my father's rifle was not found at his house, which I learned from Bradley when he came to pick me up from the hospital several hours later. Neither was the coat he wore the night in the alley, but it doesn't really matter after what happened tonight. If Ben had survived, he'd be locked up for a whole host of crimes ranging from breaking and entering to sexual assault, then topped off with two attempted murders.

Lockheed met his team at Ben's house to inspect the hidden wall safe Ben apparently had, which he left open. They were able to establish that Ben was the one in the alley, and my confession to Bradley about how he said he'd wanted to kill me concluded their questions about motive. With the first attempted murder against me solved, they can focus on the fact that they still have no leads to the other killer who is still after me. That also still leaves the mystery of my father's stolen rifle.

Bradley continues the conversation about the investigation this morning, waking me up from a cot where I slept in the basement of Fuller Park after I left the hospital. Dressed in his full gear, he finishes his explanation by giving me some good news.

"Your things have been collected from the safehouse. You can go back to your apartment now. Turns out, Ben was a major threat to you, Jessica. You've been wandering around this city on borrowed time with him and the Collector on your back. But now that he's gone and we can rule him out in the other case, we can go back to focusing on the actual serial killer."

"But the killer's still going to know where I am, my schedule, my life. He's still going to watch me. At least at the safehouse, he lost track of me."

"Somehow, Ben didn't, though."

"Think they were corresponding?"

"It's likely, yeah. We're investigating right now, so until we know more, we can't speak too much on that. You'll be safe at your place again, though. As safe as you have been for the past several months. As safe as you were at the townhome, apparently."

I lie back down on the thin cot pillow. "I had no idea, Bradley. I mean, I knew Ben was crazy, but I didn't think he would. . ."

"I know."

"What about Susan?"

"Severe concussion. They're keeping her under observation in the hospital for a couple of days to keep an eye on her. She's sleeping, mostly."

"He's not the Button Collector," I reiterate.

Bradley scoops up a chair and swings it to my bedside. He sits next to me and gathers my limp hand into his strong ones. I half expect the familiar cool sensation of John's wedding ring rubbing against me but feel only Michael Bradley's warmth. With him sitting here so close to me, I can't help but notice the scruff from his unshaven beard that stretches from ear to ear.

He rubs his thumb over mine. "We've kept you alive this long. The Collector can't go on much longer."

"He won't be through until he runs out of family to kill."

"Who's left besides you?" Bradley asks.

"That's just it. The connecting link, remember? I'm the only one he even wants."

I pull away, expecting him to let go of my hand, but his fingers clench harder, zoning me back in.

"Jessica." He stares down at me, opening his mouth and then closing it.

"What, Bradley?" I sit up and throw my legs over the side of the bed. We let go of each other's hands, but neither of us breaks our gaze.

"You went looking for your dad's gun in that storage unit."

"Did you tell them that's why I went?"

"They made the assumption since you didn't say otherwise."

I wait for him to continue, void of filler words anymore.

"They're concerned about that. That you went to get a gun without telling Welch, without telling anyone you were leaving, let alone going to get a weapon."

"How do they know I wasn't going to get something else?"

"Why else would you be there behind everyone's back?"

"What am I supposed to say to them? All I wanted was to have a gun since a serial killer is after me. That's not a crazy-person thing to do," I say.

Bradley waits for me to keep talking.

139

"I don't think that's weird," I continue.

He nods, his eyes dropping toward my bare feet. "It's not. But Lockheed still doesn't believe that the Collector watches you."

"But I told him it was Ben who was stalking me the whole time. Probably. Doesn't he believe *that* at least? Whether or not it was his freaking eyes on me the whole time?"

"It's not enough for him. It was all very circumstantial. And really, Jessica" —he freezes, breathes, swallows— "was it Ben all that time? How can either of us be sure?"

The bags under my eyes puff in tune with my heartbeat. Ben stalked me, I know that for sure, but I also know the killer still sees me. The Button Collector was always the one on my back. I know that, but I need Lockheed to believe it too.

Bradley bends his chest over his knees and comes within inches from my face, dawning a grave expression. "You have to lie to them."

"What?"

He looks over his shoulder and comes closer to me. I lean back a little, even though I like his close proximity. "Lie to them," he almost whispers. "Lockheed is convinced you were going there for that gun. Convince him otherwise. He thinks you're not well mentally, that. . . that this whole thing has driven you insane. The best thing you can do for yourself right now is lie to Lockheed and tell him that gun is not what you were there for."

"How am I supposed to do that?"

"Just do it. Say anything. I'll back you up, Jessica."

I lean closer to his face. "Why do you want to help me?"

"Because you're not insane, and they think you are."

They've thought I was insane since I made the mistake to admit that I feel the killer's eyes on me. My quest to get my father's gun made their suspicions worse. Of course it did.

"How do you know me like this?" I whisper back to him.

"I don't," he says. "But I know the situation."

Situation.

I put my shoes on, and Bradley takes me through a maze of hallways and elevators again, and before I know it, we've arrived in Lockheed's office. The muscles in my thighs tense, calves tightening with every step. My lower back is tender from the battle with Ben and my hard landings yesterday.

I sit in Lockheed's chair at the front of his desk, and my tailbone stings under a fresh bruise.

"Ms. Knight, good to see you again. Not so much under these circumstances, but I'm glad to hear you're okay. That was quite a scare."

"It was," I say, then clear my throat. "It was."

Bradley sits in the chair beside me, all the gear on his belt clanking until he's settled. He says, "We need you to give Sergeant Lockheed the description of your dad's gun that was stolen from your storage unit."

Lockheed rubs his mustache, then slaps down a notepad and picks out a pen from a cup on his desk. "First, Ms. Knight, tell me why you went to the storage unit. According to Chicago Police Violent Crimes, specifically according to Welch, you weren't supposed to leave the safehouse. You knew you'd be in danger, but you went anyway. Is that true?"

This is already starting to sound like an interrogation. "I'm in danger everywhere I go."

In my peripheral, I catch Bradley looking in my direction but when our eyes meet, he veers his glance to his shoes. My bottom lip pulls with every word, constricted from the beginning of a scab, and when I speak, I taste blood.

"For the sake of your safety, we're not associating your name with this attempted murder, regarding media attention. If the Collector is after you, and since we know it's not Ben, we don't want the killer thinking someone else almost got you first. The less attention on you, the better."

"What will you tell the press?" I ask.

"It's being reported as nothing more than a breaking and entering. The case is still under investigation, so we—and CPVC—can't legally grant the media any information. We also don't want the public to know the intruder was your co-worker. By the time his name is allowed to be released, it'll be old news. The whole thing should have been un-disclosed given the breaking and entering was in an 'abandoned' townhouse, but since Ben was shot and killed, it hit the news."

I nod.

"So tell me why you went to the storage unit. What were you going for?"

Blood sours the tip of my tongue. "I went to get a box of photo albums."

"If I send some men to that unit, would they find a box of albums?" he asks. His goateed chin tilts down as he looks from his paper to my timid eyes.

"Yeah. Yes, why—"

"So you didn't bring the box back with you?"

"No." I double take at Bradley, who chews on the inside of his cheek. "I—I got distracted by the empty gun case I saw and left. I went to get the box of albums and the rifle case was lying on a table. It was open, and the gun was gone. So I called Bradley, and he told me to leave. I forgot the photo albums."

"That's when you told him about Ben's threat to kill you, when you called him at the storage units?"

"Yeah, that's when I told him."

"Why did you keep that information from us when we asked if you knew anyone who might be a threat to your life?"

"Ben said he'd kill me if I told anyone. I was scared."

Bradley contorts in his seat. "She felt she couldn't tell anyone, Sergeant. That's understandable." He looks at me and continues, his voice quieter, "We've dealt with that before from other women. Nothing unusual."

Lockheed sends him a sharp eye and lingers there before moving on to me again. "Describe the rifle to me, Ms. Knight."

"Um, it was a Remington 770, 243 caliber. There was a scratch on the wood under the barrel from where I dropped it as a kid."

"You played with your dad's gun as a kid?"

"He let me shoot it once. I grew up in a place called Portsmouth, a very small town. Guns were okay there."

Lockheed hums a quick, flat tone, not once looking up from his pad. "It's peculiar that you left a safehouse without telling anyone. You have a habit of putting yourself in danger, Ms. Knight. I want you to know that I believe you carry some of the blame for Ben's obsession. You're not a very difficult target. As hungry as he was for you, you made it pretty easy on him." Now, he peers into me, stabbing my pupils with his hot knife of an observation.

"It's as though the killer doesn't exist to you," he says.

It's over. Because I've never seen the Button Collector. I've never touched him or heard his voice or found evidence of his existence. To me, the only part of him that exists is the weight of his stare on my body all the time.

I clear my throat, turning my gaze between him and Bradley. "Do you—do you think it's me? You think I'm the killer or something?"

"Well, we know it's not Ben," Lockheed says.

I can't help but gasp, though I try to hold it in. I thought he would at least try to deny my inquiry.

"The evidence that we have collected exonerates him, and now that he's dead, we've dropped him as a suspect."

"So we're back at square one with the Collector investigation?"

"I wouldn't say that, no." Crossing his large arms over the table, Lockheed sighs, making a whistle through his mustache. "Spooner PD contacted us about your aunt. She's been put in an asylum."

So they finally took her, I think.

Blood seeps out of my young scab, creating a wet line between my lips. I wipe it away, but Lockheed hands me a tissue anyway, and I watch my blood soaking through a corner of it. I didn't realize my wound was so noticeable.

"Were you not aware of that?" he asks.

"She and I don't really stay in contact." I dab the tissue at my mouth.

"CPD is concerned for your health, Ms. Knight. We believe mental illness could run in your family and could have something to do with your current situation."

The tissue falls from my grip and glides into my lap. "I'm not crazy. I'm not going insane. Bradley, tell him I'm not going crazy."

He holds up his hand to calm me. "Sergeant, I think she's just a little overwhelmed."

"I know the killer is watching me. You have to believe me. Ben tried to kill me, and now you're calling *me* a murderer?"

"No one said that," Bradley says.

Lockheed starts waving away my complaint. "We know, we know. I believe that Ben tried to kill you. Your story about him checks out. He was guilty of shooting at you that night in the alley. We finally found shell casings there that matched his handgun which was recovered from the safehouse, plus your claim that identified him and his violent threat to you helped support our conclusion."

"He literally held a gun to my head."

"I've just got a few questions to ask you, Ms. Knight."

"No, I'm not answering your degrading questions." I stand to leave, and Bradley mutters something to Lockheed. Jerking open the door, I walk in silence with Bradley following behind me. When I don't make the correct turn in the hall, he whistles at me and points in the right direction, waiting for me to pass by him before he trails behind me.

After the ambulance arrived last night to take me to the hospital, the only item of mine I'd brought with me was my purse. I had stuffed it under my cot once I'd gotten to the police station last night.

I take it out when I arrive at the cot and slam it on top of the paper-thin mattress. My stomach spasms, and I near an outburst of tears that threaten to flow, burning the underside of my eyelids. I give up trying to fight it.

"Jessica." Bradley spins me around by my shoulder. "I believe you. I understand. Let me drive you home."

"Which home?"

"Yours."

"Remind me why that's suddenly okay again?"

"Because Welch isn't here, and because I say so. You're mine again, okay?"

～

First, we go to the safehouse so I can pack the rest of my belongings. I run through the yellow police tape on the backdoor and straight upstairs, through the scene of the crime without looking down.

Last weeks' worth of dirty panties and foul-smelling shirts are piled into a pyramid in the corner of my room. While Bradley waits downstairs, I brush my teeth, careful not to tear my scab, and shove my clothes and toiletries into my duffel bag, storing Welch's contacts, comb, and toothbrush separately.

Downstairs, the crime scene is still laid out before me. I can't help but see it. Ben's blood has dried brown on the living room rug. The coffee table is pushed out of alignment with the sofa, where cushions are scattered across the floor, something I hadn't noticed yesterday.

Aside from that one room, the safehouse appears just the same as it was before.

Bradley drives me to my apartment next. He carries my bag to the fourth floor, and inside my home, everything is exactly as I left it weeks ago.

My TV remote sits on the side table, my candle is still dusty on my dining room table, and icy snow is there again piling up outside my windowsill.

Bradley drops my bag to the floor, and I walk to my window to draw a smiley face in the frost with my middle finger. Two dots and a curvy line.

"Are you going to be okay here by yourself?"

I wipe the glass. "Thanks for dropping me off. I'm fine."

"I can stay if you—"

"No, it's okay. You've done enough."

We stand at separate ends of the room, me by the cold window and him near the dining table. I dread how quiet my apartment will be when he leaves, how motionless everything will feel. What will I do? I could dig out some wine, but I'd only get myself drunk. I could take a bath, but I might fall asleep in the water. I could let Bradley stay, but I know what I'd do if he didn't leave.

"Isn't it too coincidental that two people were trying to kill me at the same time?" I say.

"Yes, and we're thinking about that."

It's the same old thing I've been hearing for the past day: *There's nothing about Ben that ties him to the Button Collector. He's got alibis for each murder. He doesn't match the description.*

"So what do I need to do now? Now that Welch isn't here?" I ask.

"Lockheed is figuring it out as we speak. Meanwhile, he'll have patrol cars around your place like before."

What about you? "Should I return my temporary phone Welch gave me?"

With a regretful nod, he walks to me, and I take the phone from my purse and hand it over. "I'll give it back to CPVC," he says. "Did they give you your personal cell?"

"Last night, yeah."

Bradley turns to the door, and I follow him there to open it. "I've still got your card," I say, "with your number."

"You can call me anytime you feel like you need to. I'll be in contact with you soon." I think he can see the dissatisfaction in my eyes, because he says, "You're still under protection, so you're not alone. You're safe with us. Like before."

"What happened to Lockheed today, Bradley? It's like he turned on me."

"Don't get ahead of yourself. It was just protocol."

Bradley looks at me a moment longer then throws his coat over his shoulder and heads out. "Just so you know, Jessica," he calls, "I'm still on your side."

I smile at him, and I can only imagine how ridiculous my face looks today—snow white against my tangled brown strands of hair, purple rings under my eyes, and dried up red lipstick on my lips, trying to reflect a hint of happiness.

My door lock makes a loud click as the bolt slides into place.

The room is cold and empty. Empty as my father's gun case. Hollow as the bullet that entered Ben's back.

He's wrapped in a bag right now, lying in a morgue. I should give John a call and warn him of Ben's death before the authorities call corporate, but I'll stay quiet—the police will make it known soon enough. Sitting on the sofa, my scent bellows from the cushions, reminding me of the dust from the sofa in the safehouse. It's been weeks since I've been surrounded by my own things. Weeks since I haven't been under the thumb of someone bigger than me.

Weeks since I've been alone with only my kitchen knife in the view of the Button Collector.

Susan Welch, Room 177, second floor.

The nurse says, "Her concussion is healing nicely so we're releasing her tomorrow. Just keep your voice low, and don't turn on any lights."

I crack open the door and skim through. Welch lays on the hospital bed on her side with a pillow over her head. She wriggles under her thin cover.

"For the love of God, close the door quietly," she mumbles.

Instead, I don't press it all the way closed to not make any noise. "Susan?"

"Jessica, is that you?"

The blinds are shut, encasing the room in a sleepy, gray twilight, even though it's morning. I tiptoe so my shoes won't make loud claps on the shiny floor.

"Yes, it's me." I sit on the side of her bed, the pillow still covering half her face.

She opens one eye, and her lid hangs barely above her iris. The red of her hair has turned a bronzy brown in this lighting, and her bangs frizz from the pillow.

"What are you doing here?"

"I came to bring you some of your things from the safehouse. Your toothbrush and contacts."

"Well, I don't need my contacts because I haven't been able to open my eyes since your obsessive, wannabe boyfriend knocked me out, and the hospital already provided a toothbrush for me." She sighs, her lid falling over her eye. "Thank you. Just put it on the table."

Behind me, I lay the Ziplock bag from my pocket onto her food tray. "So they explained everything," I say.

"Yeah, I got the scoop."

"Can I apologize, Susan?"

"You mean for undermining me and nearly getting me killed? I'm expecting your apology any minute now."

Welch pulls the covers high above her flat breasts and removes the pillow from her face.

She stretches out and pushes herself up into a sitting position.

"And you know," she says, "you aren't the only one in danger. When we're doing our jobs to protect you, we expect you to respect the fact that we're also putting ourselves in danger. Okay? So don't forget that when you decide to do something stupid, you're risking my life too."

She grabs her head and hunches over, grunting from the pain. "I'm sorry, Susan. I—"

"Stop." She holds up her hand. "It's fine." Leaning back on the pillow, she closes her eyes again, and I cower into my sweater.

Vases of flowers sit on a table by the dark window; gifts from the police station, I suppose. The petals have already wilted from the lack of light, longing to be back in the refrigerator from which they came.

"They said your gun was stolen," Welch says.

"It was, and they're assuming it was the killer, but they think—" A lump forms in my throat, so I stand and seek the safety of darkness tucked in the shadows in case I begin to cry again. "They think I have something to do with the murders since I went to the unit and didn't tell anyone. They think I'm going crazy."

"Well, Jessica, you don't do a great job of presenting yourself as sane. Look," she sighs, "I don't think you're the killer, but come on, stop being an idiot. You do this to yourself. What proof do they have?"

I breeze back to her bedside. "None. Only suspicion, but they think I'm insane."

"Then you're fine. Just stop putting yourself in positions that actually make you look crazy."

"So you believe I'm not ill? They thought I was going to get the gun for some specific reason, but I told them all I wanted was a photo album, that's all."

"Is that the truth? Did you actually go to that storage unit for a picture album? Because they have reason to believe that you went for the gun."

"I know. And yes, it's the truth."

"Then you should've come to me."

"I know." I turn my back to her and play with a few cords dangling from her monitor. "But no one knows for certain if it was the Collector who stole the gun."

"It wasn't Ben, that's for sure. Like I've said—what, fifty times now?—Ben isn't the Button Collector. But now that he's gone and gotten himself executed, we know the person who stole your gun was probably the killer. He knew you'd be looking for it."

"But I wasn't," I lie. Looking back on it, I never would've gotten away with sneaking my father's rifle into the safehouse behind Welch's back.

"Doesn't matter now," she says.

"The killer uses a knife," I add.

"Yeah, but maybe he doesn't want you using a gun."

She has a point, sharp as a tack. There are no connections in my brain that attach the Button Collector to my dad's gun, to wanting to steal it. No one knew it was there except me, anyway, and what's the purpose of having a gun if you aren't going to shoot it?

To keep Jessica Knight from having it. The invisible words are all over Welch's pasty skin.

"Fuller Park," she says, trailing off. "I told you they don't know what they're doing."

"Bradley said it's only protocol."

"Suspicion is protocol. Accusations aren't."

I sit on her bed again, and she rolls away from me, getting comfortable before inching her way back to me.

"Are you coming back on the case?" I ask. "They might listen to you because you don't think I'm going insane; you don't think I'm involved with the murders."

"Can't. They won't allow me to after a physically harming incident. I'm going to be assigned to a new case."

The sharp tip of grief slices into me, and once again, I scarf down the knot in my throat that makes me feel the need to cry. "So you're off my case for good?"

"Let's be honest, Jessica, you never were that fond of me, anyway."

I recall the night she jumped in front of Ben's gun to protect me. But I realize now it wasn't because she cared about me at all. She was only interested in the investigation and was doing her job. I don't matter to her.

You don't matter to me, I keep telling myself to fill the silence in my thoughts. "Besides," she says, "you'll get someone new."

"From where?" I ask, already knowing the answer.

"CPVC put Lockheed in charge of the investigation. Don't worry, we're still going to be involved, but Bradley's going to be your guy again. That is, if you don't request someone else." She presses her back into her pillow and rests her eyes again.

Outside my apartment building's front door, a man with a camera around his neck and press pass rushes up to me. I reach into my purse, so he'll maybe think I'm too busy snagging my keys to have a conversation, or if I'm lucky, that maybe I've got a weapon in there, but he doesn't hesitate to approach me.

"Excuse me, Jessica Knight?"

"I'm sorry, I'm not speaking to any press."

He holds up a pen and pad in a process that I know all too well. "I'm with *Chicago Daily*, and we're doing a story on the Button Collector, and rumor has it you're one of the closest relatives of some of the victims. The last of the few surviving ones, that is. Can you confirm or deny this?"

"I'm not willing to speak about this, sir."

I take out my keycard, but he steps in front of me.

"I've contacted *The Chicago Post* where you work, and the editor said the same thing. Nonetheless, a young writer there told me it's suspected you're a surviving member of the family."

I scan the card, and the door unlocks, closing behind me and trapping the reporter outside. Once I reach my apartment, I lock the door and slide down to the floor. To my surprise, I find John parked on my sofa, waiting for me. He's got his legs crossed, and he is flipping the channels on my TV like he owns it.

I stand and set my purse on the dining table loudly, thinking he might acknowledge me.

"What are you doing here? Did that reporter outside see you?"

He clicks off the television and bends over his knees, winking at me. "Good to see you too, Knight." His voice, scruffy as ever.

I run past him to the window, wading through the cloud of his fresh cigarette smoke. No patrol cars loiter outside my building, but I spot the reporter walking down the street, rounding the corner away from me.

"Knight, let me get you a cup of coffee." He grunts, pushing himself off the sofa and sauntering into my kitchen. A slight limp from old age slows him down.

"What are you doing here?" I ask again once he returns. I plop down on the sofa, taking a hot mug from John's outstretched hand. He sits close and puts his arm around me.

"It's been a while. They questioned me, you know, a few days ago. You alright, Knight? What happened to your lip?"

I take in a sliver of black coffee, recalling the variety of sounds Welch made with her coffee intakes. John's breath is warm against my profile, laced with the memory of our first night together. I lean into him a little more, absorbing the sense of comfort that his embrace provides.

"Yeah, I'm fine. I just bit it accidentally."

"The case is still unsolved?"

I nod.

"Does anyone know about this?"

This? The two of us. Despite the comfort John brings, it's Bradley who delivers safety.

But the closer John gets, the further Bradley feels. "No," I lie.

"Knight." John leans over me, taking my mug and placing it on the coffee table. "I've got some bad news."

There's a certain element of numbness that dulls my anxiety about surprises. I attempt to lash my best look that doesn't quite represent how unphased I am at the news he's going to share.

"Ben is dead, dear."

I turn away from John and make my way back to the window, trying to act how I think I would if this were the first time I was hearing this. Would I cry? Be relieved? Make nothing of it? I increase my breathing and count to a slow ten before exhaling a full, heavy sigh.

"Dead?"

"He was killed by some cop 'cause he broke into a house or something. Tried to rape a girl. Can you believe that? Tried to rape her."

"I kind of can, yes."

John walks over to where I'm standing, turning me so we face each other.

"Who killed him?" I ask.

He hands me back my cup of coffee and wraps his hands around mine, on the mug, pulling it to his mouth. I feed him a soft sip, then take one myself.

"I don't know. No names released. The editor in me tried to get them, though. They even said they aren't releasing the info about Ben's violence. Privacy reasons, or something to that nature."

I look down.

"You okay? I mean, I know Ben used to harass you here and there, but can you believe he's dead?" he says.

"It must have been horrible," I say, "how he died. Gruesome. Violent."

"That unlucky girl."

"What have you heard about her?"

John hacks on a cough that's dampened by his COPD. "Nothing. Guess the survivors aren't important if the rapist is the one to die."

John goes back to the sofa, but I stay where I am, staring out the window and listening to the wind whistling against it. Cold, outside air creeps through the glass and into my sweater, so I move back to the couch and snuggle up to John again.

"Who told you?" I say.

"I got a call yesterday from corporate right as I was leaving the office. They said a cop from one of these police stations around here broke the news."

"Hm."

"He told me not to go around spreading gossip for reasons that had to do with the serial killer who's associated with one of my journalists." John pinches the point of my chin, looks from there up to my hairline. *Pretty little thing,* he'd once whispered years ago. "You're still not safe, are you, dear?"

"No," I whisper to match the memory.

"I want you back at the office. With Ben gone, we could use the help, and with you being here" —he gestures to each corner of my apartment, not realizing that I haven't been here for the past few weeks— "you need something to do. Come back to work, love."

I place my hand on his thigh. "Oh, John."

"Please. You've been so quiet lately." He picks a cigarette out of his front shirt pocket and lights it up, puffing on the end of the stick. "It'll keep you busy, get your mind off things. I'm telling you, Knight, you'll go crazy cooped up here all hours of the day."

Crazy.

"My wife—" he says, whooshing out a circle of white smoke, "she starts getting a little claustrophobic when she's got to stay in the hospital too long. I don't want you feeling that way."

"I understand it."

"I know you do, Knight. Say, how's that aunt of yours?"

I make something up about how she's recovered but moved into a friend's house. And I keep lying, spitting out things about her that aren't true, about how the attack on her life swayed her to start taking yoga classes, something she's always wanted to do but never had the time for. John just nods, keeps inhaling his nicotine. I tell him that she's also thinking about backpacking through Europe and opening her own seamstress business and selling her baked goods. Making up stories gives me some distance from the killer and allows me a moment of brief imagination that I am living a life other than my own. John believes me, then he doesn't. I can tell the second that his mind changes, because his face changes too. He believes I'm lying. He's heard my rambling when I've had too much to drink, and he's soothed me while I've gone on and on about my perfect childhood, my parents, going off to college, and now, my flawless aunt Deborah.

He offers me a sad half-smile: *Don't kid yourself, sweetheart.*

I blink at him: *I'll try.* "Why do you worry about me, John?"

He drops his cigarette into his cup of coffee and traces the collar of my sweater, which makes me think of Ben's grip on my neck. I shiver, but John mistakes that for an invitation. His fingers trail down to my waist, and he nudges the hem of my shirt to raise it a few inches.

"You've not got anyone else worrying about you."

"You didn't even care for Della this much when her mother died." I shrug away from him, and my shirt falls, covering my waist again.

"She has a husband to help her cope with the loss."

He crawls closer, but I hold a finger up to his lips. "Don't, John. Not now. It's dangerous for you."

"No one saw me come in, love."

"It's just not a good time."

John's breath is hot, smelling of coffee and cigarettes. The heat of it fills the air around me with his massive sigh, but his discontent is brief. Though no one is patrolling me, and despite his desperate need to sleep with someone while his sick wife is resting at home, he knows I'm right. Besides, he has plenty of other options.

"Is it because of Ben?" he asks me.

And it is. It is because of Ben. "Yes." But I continue, hoping to explain what else it's about. "If the police found out about us, you and I would be outed to the public."

I picture the headline on our very own newspaper: *Editor Caught Sleeping with Button Collector's Target.* The realization sends John deep into the nook of the sofa.

"They'd put you all over the news for having an affair with me, the journalist associated with the Button Collector." I start rambling again, lost in my own head, lost in my empty words. "They'd name you a suspect, and you'd lose your job, and Mary—Mary would find out, and she's so sick, John. She's so sick."

"I'm sorry, Knight." His knee shakes up and down. "You're right. We'll be more careful, love. Alright, Knight? We'll be careful, dear."

He stands without bothering to fix his crumpled shirt and takes his coat off the back of one of my dining room chairs. I hadn't even seen it when I'd come inside, and I hadn't seen his scarf or leather gloves either.

"When you're ready to come back to the office, your desk is exactly how you left it," he tells me.

I take my coffee mug to the kitchen and help John into his coat, feeling his shoulder bones through the fabric. His old age has thinned his skin and softened his muscles. I try on one of the gloves, then he taps me on the forehead to bring my attention to him as he pulls off the glove finger by finger.

In the tense space between our bodies, I say, "Thank you."

"G'night, Knight." With a cold peck on my cheek, he lets himself out.

I cover my nose and mouth with my hand and breathe in the scent left from his glove.

Della looks at me funny when I return to the office, maybe because rumor has finally gotten around that I'm the last of the nearly extinct family. She glares at my long coat, at my red lipstick, then spins in her chair to a filing cabinet against the wall as if releasing me from her judgment.

John's office is empty, so I go settle in at my desk, and it's exactly how I left it, just as John told me it would be. Ben's desk sits empty, an ominous sore that everyone tries not to look directly at. Clicking the power button on my computer and waiting for it to boot, I count the journalists, designers, and marketers strolling past his old space and pretending to read files or something on their phones. They make room between themselves and the desk like Ben is still sitting there with one leg spread out, overtaking the aisle, forcing an invisible radius in which no one may enter. And then when they pass by me with my head low and my limbs tucked into my coat, they swerve to stay out of my way too.

Ben and I, dead and alive, criminal and victim, both accidentally pushing people away.

The one thing we have in common.

My email is full of subject lines that say, *Brief Question* and *Evening News* and *Button Collector Inquiry* and even *Ms. Knight, a moment plz?*

I trash all the emails without opening any of them; they can't write stories on me if I keep ignoring them. The only one I do open is from John, a short list of some assignments he's come across, six new stories he wants me to work on for the business section of the paper. He's keeping me away from crime pieces, my usual cup of tea, and giving me things more suitable for a beginner.

I start with a story that requires me to research a new business development on the east side of town. There are two new bakeries, a pizzeria, and a few boutiques opening. My college newspaper internship trained me to always try for in-person interviews so I can also snap a picture for the story and so I can get a more genuine feel for the person I'm talking to. Phone interviews are easier, though, so I spend the morning at my desk.

By one o'clock, John still hasn't shown, so I duck over to Della's desk to ask where he is. "Left before you got here. Something about his wife in the hospital." She rolls away from me to end the conversation.

On my lunch break, I go to a little soup place a few blocks down, and before I bring the first spoonful to my mouth, my phone dings in my purse. I'm taken aback at the sound of the notification because the last time I got a *ding!* it was from the phone Welch gave me. For a moment, I hesitate, allowing myself a moment to hope it might be her telling me she's coming back to the case, and she and Bradley will be working together this time. It's been a while since I've wished for anything, and this scenario would provide a mild break in my hopelessness.

But the text is not from her. It's from Bradley.

Jessica—just wanted to let you know one of our departments identified Ben's coat behind a tire shop last night. It was the one he wore when he shot at you and Welch (we found the gun residue on it). Just wanted to let you know we 100% confirmed it was him in the alley. Will be in contact soon. Stay alive. MB.

An abundance of emotion shakes in my fingertips. I want to write a hundred things, but nothing seems right. I type, then delete *Thank you; Can we meet up? I miss you; Come back to me;* and *You saved my life. You killed Ben.*

I read his message over and over again, staring at each word until my soup stops steaming and the ice in my glass of water has melted into small chips. No appropriate response comes to mind, so I close my phone, eat half of the cold the soup, and get back to the office.

John is there when I arrive, and he's shuffling back and forth between his office and Ben's desk with a small cardboard box.

I set my purse down against the leg of my desk. "You're back."

"Been at the hospital all morning."

"Is she okay?"

John sighs, plopping onto Ben's chair and giving me time to notice his puffy, red hospital eyes. I've never seen John cry, but I've seen the aftermath, the cursing at cancer, the silence of fear.

"What are you doing over there?" I ask to change the subject.

He closes Ben's desk drawer with a softened *tap* and scoops up staples and a few pens and pencils that fall right back through his fingers.

"I should have seen it, Knight." John walks to me, leaning in close to keep other people from hearing him whisper, "You know, he was excused one other time with another journalist who quit because of him. He should've been fired right then."

I sit down, remembering how John's glove felt encasing my hand a few nights ago. "Did his family not come to clean out his desk?"

"Yes. Made 'em do it over the weekend." He rattles a cardboard box in which he pushes all the staples and drops in a few pens and pencils. "They left all the pointy items."

John slinks back into his office and closes his door, locking himself inside with Ben's dangerous office supplies, and I pull out my phone and click on Bradley's text again.

Stay alive. MB.

I type back, *Thanks for the update.*

A moment later, my phone buzzes: *May I come over tonight? Assuming you aren't busy with another's company. I'd like to talk.*

I type out a quick *Sure,* and press send before I can change my mind.

By dark, I can't decide between making a pot of coffee for Bradley and me or picking out a bottle of wine. Neither suffice. So I busy myself by throwing my dirty clothes into the hamper and straightening the rug in the living area, blowing hot air onto the window then shining it clean.

On the frosted street, Bradley's squad car hasn't arrived yet, so I text him and ask if we can go out to talk instead.

I'll meet you at the coffee shop around the corner, I say.

No, he responds, *don't leave your building. Meet me at my car when you see it and not a second sooner. I'll drive us someplace else if you want.*

I do as he says and wait in the lobby of my building, eyeing the chair outside the doors where I sat in early January and watched the rain beat on the red petals of a winter flower. The plant has since broken under the weight of the snow and ice.

Then again, so have I.

In my scarf and snow coat, no one would be able to see my burgundy sweater, but I use my reflection in the window to swipe on my red lipstick that matches it anyway.

I look down the sidewalk but can't see anything beyond that dying flower because of the dark. By now, John has been home for hours and Ben, on a normal evening, would've called me at least three times by now.

The Button Collector doesn't see me when I walk outside and slip into Bradley's cozy car; it's like the Collector missed it, like I was too quick. I can feel how alone I am with Bradley. It's just the two of us—no killers—in his dark car when we pull away from the curb. Bradley's driving is smoother than Welch's. His car blasts through the layers of salt on the asphalt, making soft turns and quick accelerations. The ride is silent, filled only by the humming engine and a mutual understanding that we will wait to talk until we're seated at the coffee shop.

But he passes right by it.

"That was the shop, Bradley, you missed it. Turn around."

The car shifts gears, whirring a higher pitch, and the beginning of a grin twitches on his profile. "If I'm suspecting correctly, you haven't eaten well recently."

I look down at my stomach, but I'm three layers of clothing thick, impossible for him to estimate me as skinnier.

"I'm a detective. Knowing that is my job," he explains when I don't respond.

Thinking back to the past few days, I don't recall seeing his squad car outside my building, but he's right; I've only ordered take-out since I've seen Bradley last.

"I've got a decent place in mind, good food," he says.

He parks us at a small restaurant just outside the city center, and I follow him inside. A hostess with a low ponytail and black pantsuit seats us at a corner booth with a round table, lit by a single candle in a bubble of glass. She hands us two menus, and Bradley opens his like he's been here a hundred times. I imagine it's been with women dressed nicer than I am right now. As if I won't be here long, I keep my coat on.

I slide my menu away, and he sets his on top of mine. "I'm not hungry for something like this," I say. My coarse coat fabric rubs together, too loud and big for this small area.

"I'll order for you."

"I want to start talking, like you wanted to do."

A dark haired waiter stops at our table, but before he can greet us,

Bradley holds up two fingers and orders us both water. "Unless," he says, gesturing to me, "you'd like something stronger."

I shake my head, hoping he or the waiter can't tell that I would rather be at home with something definitely stronger. The waiter nods and leaves us alone.

"You said you wanted to talk," I say.

"I did. How about we eat first? Wouldn't want you to lose your appetite."

"You think I'm going to lose my appetite because of something you want to talk about?"

"Depends. What do you think of me?"

The question is so quick and small that I almost skim right over it, but he tilts his head, imploring me to answer. My hypothetical text responses come back to me: *I miss you. Thank you for saving my life.* But I pile the thought under a new mound of irritation.

"This isn't a date," I say.

"No." He rests back in the booth and chuckles. "No, this isn't a date."

"Then what are we doing here? I mean, look at this place."

The waiter comes back with our waters, and Bradley tells him the Sicilian pasta dish is what we'll have. Once the waiter leaves, Bradley continues, "Lockheed wanted to make sure you were going to be okay with my protection again. He wants me on your case as your full-time guardian."

"Does he want that because he thinks I'm going insane now? Like my aunt Deborah is?"

"He wants me to do it because I've been with you before."

I wait for him to apologize for the way it sounded. But he goes on instead, "So let's talk. Welch is off the case, and you've got nobody else. Your day-to-day gets more and more dangerous with every hour that passes without any known movement from the Collector, Jessica. You need someone, and if it's not me on you at all times, it's going to be someone else. Lockheed's already got a few other officers in mind."

"You said I would be safe at my house."

"I said you'd be as safe as you had been before, which was only safe *enough*, and that was with the security of law enforcement."

I go back to the topic at hand. "This is Chicago; why is it so hard to find someone to patrol me?"

"It's rather easy, really. You're the one who makes it hard."

I can't argue with him. In fact, the last time we argued, I fired him. "So this" —I motion to the candlelight, to the restaurant— "was all to butter me up in hopes of getting back on the case?"

"And also so you'd eat something that wasn't take-out." He takes a sip of his water, and I notice the stubble on his jawline has grown out a little. "I never left the case. I just stopped parking outside your apartment and stopped being so visible in safeguarding you."

So it was true. He didn't stop. He had gotten to me just in time when I needed somebody. "How do you know what I've been eating, by the way?" I start the process of unraveling my scarf and bending out of my coat. Looks like I'm here to stay.

"I was hired to watch you before you demanded I stop. And your habits—they're easy to memorize."

To watch me. To memorize. That triggers me, and he knows it.

"Some people aren't getting paid for that." I bite my tongue to stop myself from saying more. It has been a mistake every single time to bring up my intuition that someone is stalking me. Bradley can tell right away that I regret what I said. He waves away the subject, but bringing it up makes me realize I'm not ready to let it go, mistake or not. "It's not irrelevant what Lockheed thinks. He's got every reason to think I'm crazy, and God, if he ever had a hunch, I'm sure he'd cuff me, you know."

"Not without a warrant."

"Welch's people kept Ben under circumstantial evidence."

"You don't have the same circumstances."

"Then why does Lockheed make me feel that way?"

Bradley flops both elbows onto the table, the candle causing shadows to warp on his face.

It's the only movement in this dark and tranquil restaurant. Like the car ride, just the two of us, tucked into a crook of dim light. "I didn't come here to talk about Lockheed, Jessica. I came here to tell you I'm back, and I hope you won't ask me to leave again."

The flame flickers and snaps. "Then don't look at me through my window, anymore."

"Good. Lockheed thought you might try to fight me on this." He pulls his glass of water to his lips and takes a swallow.

"And no more popping into my apartment without my knowledge of it."

"You'll be very aware when I'm there. I've also been instructed to drive you to work every day."

"How—" But he already knows I'm going to work again because he's been snooping on me this whole time.

"It's a simple fix, Jessica."

"What is?"

"Close your curtains."

Our waiter glides to the side of our table and sets down a metal basket of small bread loaves, then hands out two white plates. "Your dinner will be out shortly." He disappears, and Bradley snaps a loaf in half. One side for him, and he hands the other over to me. I snatch it from him, finding his eyes starting to bend from a grin.

"Eat, Ms. Knight." He pulls a knife out of his rolled-up napkin and digs in the small bowl of butter.

"You never answered my question," I say.

"You didn't ask me one."

I had barely eaten my soup this afternoon after Bradley texted me, and I haven't tried taking a bite of food since. After I make sure he isn't looking, I grab my knife and start buttering a slice of bread.

"I asked you at the station why you want to help me," I say.

He stops chewing, his knife hanging loosely in his hand, then he goes back to swiping his bread. "I told you I understand."

"That's not a very good answer."

"Look." Putting down the bread and knife onto his plate, he leans over the table, and for a moment, the mummers of surrounding couples fill the silence of our space. "I know the situation. Alright? It's impossible for you to believe someone else has been through something like this, but they have."

"They've got a serial killer after them?"

"That's not what I meant. I mean I understand you're not guilty, so let's leave it at that." Even though I've gone weeks without any hope, a new feeling of relief smooths over me.

"So you said full-time. What does that mean? Eight hours a day?"

"No." Bradley moves his plate to the side, knocking the knife off it. He fumbles as he grabs it, and places it back on his plate. "Full-time means twenty-four-hour protection."

My knife clatters onto my plate now, and I swallow what bit of bread I've got left in my mouth. The smooth relief I felt two seconds ago peels up at the edges, tempting to flee.

"And that entails what, exactly?"

He chuckles again, sliding his utensils back into perfect place in front of him. "I hope you think well of me because I'm taking over your sofa for a while. Starting tomorrow."

~

After dinner, Bradley drives me back to my building, parking parallel on the street.

Tightening my scarf, I position toward the door, ready to get out. "Thank you for dinner."

He looks right at me, hand on the gear shift. "I'll be back tomorrow morning before you go to work. Got some things to do at the office before we start."

Before we start. It sounds so intimate. "I'll clean for you and get a space ready."

Bradley doesn't respond with the clever comeback I expect. Instead, he looks past my face, fixated by something in the distance. I turn to the window and see a man loitering under the light by my building's lobby door. Wide shoulders. Thick build. Not the Collector.

Bradley reaches under his coat to his ribcage, and I see the strap for a gun, his badge catching the light from the streetlamp.

"What's going on? Who is that?" I say.

He leans over the armrest, and I press into my seat so he can see past me. "It's Lockheed."

Bradley jerks the car keys out of the ignition and throws open his door, forgetting about reaching for his gun. I follow suit and chase him across the street. As we make it to the sidewalk, Lockheed moves away from the door in his long black coat and hat, and I place myself behind Bradley.

"Sergeant," he says, "how are you?"

Lockheed clears his throat, and a puff of white air blows out. Eyeing me from in front of Bradley, he says, "I've come to talk to Ms. Knight." He sidesteps to see me. "Ms. Knight? Would you let us inside, please?"

"Of course, yes." I shuffle through my coat pockets first, then my purse, and finally find my keycard attached to my door key. With a shaky hold, I swipe my card and the double doors unlock. Bradley pulls one open, but Lockheed lets himself in before I do.

The three of us take a silent ride up the elevator to the fourth floor, and I take them into my apartment, scouting right away for a kitchen knife I might've left out or a pair of panties from a sloppy load of laundry. Neither pop out anywhere, though the awareness of the messy state of my living room makes me self-conscious.

Bradley and I drop our coats and take a seat on the sofa, and I spot not one, but two leather straps that hold handguns hanging on the side of his torso. *Those were there all throughout dinner?* I think.

Lockheed remains standing by the dining table.

"What's on your mind, Sergeant?" Bradley says. Meanwhile, I mutter apologies as I unclutter the coffee table, but they both ignore it.

"Well" —Lockheed nestles into his coat, not bothering to take it off— "we've just made a new discovery."

His dark stare points right at me, and I find myself nudging closer to Bradley. "It's another family member, isn't it? You can say it." I stand so I can look at him head on when he says it, prepared to take a hit and not get blown down.

"No, it's nothing like that. Ms. Knight, but you might like to take a seat to hear what I have to say."

Lockheed's solemn voice sets off an alarm in my head. Bradley glares at me, silently commanding me to do as I have been told. I comply and situate myself on the edge of the cushion.

"What is it?"

Lockheed's coat bustles with his slow movement. He puts his hands behind his back, then he freezes as if he is unsure how to proceed. Lifting his chin, he focuses on the wall, a spot above my head, rather than making eye contact. Something about it says *coward,* and while it's probably only my imagination, I take note that when he's about to tell me something important, he won't look at me.

There's a roughness in his voice, one that I've noticed only comes when he's upset. He drops his volume to a near whisper. "There's no easy way for me to ask you this."

His body doesn't move, but I catch his glance shift to Bradley, whose face is unreadable.

Lockheed lingers there for a long moment, then moves his attention back to me. "Ms. Knight, what were you doing the night of June seventeenth?"

A hurricane of puzzle pieces whirl around me—the dates on the news, the photographs of Robert, the sex with John, sneaking away from my neighbor, and the unsuspected days following the Button

Collector's first murder. That was back when no one had pinned yet what had happened. Who had done it? Why had he done it? The puzzle comes together in one cohesive, seven-day accumulation, a week I hadn't expected to remember but did because of Robert. A week I'd started with John and ended in my storage unit staring at my dead cousin's school picture.

"I—I don't know," I lie. "That was months ago. That was right before Robert died."

"It was hours before he died. He was killed early on the morning of the eighteenth."

Lockheed glares at Bradley for a half-second before stealing a yard between us. "You have alibis for most murders. I'm just following protocol. Things are just getting a little foggy in the investigation. You should also know we checked for cameras at the storage units. There are none."

"Why do you want to know what I was doing?"

Bradley and I stand unanimously, my tunnel vision locking in on the sergeant's black eyes.

Lockheed doesn't answer, and I look up to Bradley. His arms swell with a tense flex, his mouth in a firm grimace that stripes through his five o'clock shadow.

I target my gaze back on Lockheed. "What did you think I was going to do with that rifle?"

His practiced composure doesn't budge. "We believe that since you didn't tell Officer Susan Welch what you were doing…"

"Welch? You thought I was going to kill her? I didn't take the gun. You can call the cab driver who picked me up. I didn't have a rifle with me."

Lockheed nods to Bradley, who makes his way out my door without making a sound, cell phone in hand and up to his ear before the door closes. When he slips out, his back is hunched with shame; he knows I didn't bring my father's gun back with me, but dialing the cab company to verify my story is part of his job. I choose to not be upset with him about it.

Without him beside me now, I lose a little confidence in myself. I need him back in here to support my weaknesses.

"I'm not saying you stole the rifle and brought it back," says Lockheed. "I'm not saying anything; we don't know where the gun is. We don't think you have it, Ms. Knight, so I've got a team of investigators at your storage unit trying to lift prints, or anything, really. Without surveillance cameras, we've got little to work with."

"Then get out of my apartment," I say.

"It's why you went to the unit and came back with nothing. What some of us are thinking is that you went to get the gun for some" —he tilts forward on his feet, landing back on his heels— "obscure reason and saw that it was gone, which is why you called. With all due respect, Ms. Knight, no one in your position would sneak out of their safehouse to get some photo albums. And then come back with nothing."

"Why are you questioning me like I'm a suspect? Because I'm the closest relation to the victims, and that makes me associated with the killer? I told you why I went there, and then I freaked out and immediately called the authorities. I dropped what I was doing and came to *you* people."

"Perhaps your paranoia has altered your thinking."

"You didn't assume that until my rifle went missing, and now you're questioning me because I walked out of the building one night? I was stuck in there forever. I didn't even have a TV—"

"Let's get back on track about the night of the seventeenth. I need to know where you were that night." His thick sleeves rub together as he takes a journalist's pen and pad out of his inside pocket, and I think, *When did I become the story?*

"That was a long time ago. I don't know," I lie again. "I remember that week being at home when Deborah called me to tell me about Robert, and it took a few days before it hit national news."

He jots down some notes. "You were here on the seventeenth?"

Heat spreads under my sweater, and my upper lip begins to form a dot of sweat. I wipe it away but smear my lipstick all over my thumb in the process.

"I don't know," I say. "I was here, probably. I don't remember."

"Police checked the footage of your building the night of the seventeenth, shortly before Robert was killed, and while there aren't any cameras outside this place, the interior surveillance showed you leaving the lobby on the night of June seventeenth around eight p.m. and walking down the street."

"What—"

Bradley opens the door, pausing to shake his head at Lockheed before he steps back inside. No, the lady who got in the cab did not have a rifle case with her.

Lockheed continues, "Robert was murdered around two thirty on the morning of June eighteenth in Hermann, Missouri, which would put our suspect leaving town around eight p.m. the night of the seventeenth. If that suspect were leaving from Chicago, of course."

Our suspect? *Our suspect?*

Bradley comes between us. "What's this about?"

"The case has taken a turn, Detective. We've got footage of Ms. Knight leaving her building at ten-after-eight on the night of the first victim's murder."

Bradley snaps around to face me, but I can't look at him. I search the floor for answers, for another lie, for anything that would put me in my apartment on June seventeenth of last year.

"Why wasn't I filled in on these developments?" Bradley asks.

Lockheed takes a firm dodge past Bradley to keep his aim on me. "It's fresh off the burner." He goes on, "Ms. Knight, we've also got footage of you walking back into your building around six a.m. on the morning of June eighteenth."

That doesn't mean I'm guilty, I want to say. *The killer is setting me up. Making you consider the little things that don't matter.*

"That's only hours after the first victim was murdered. What we don't have is video footage of you beyond here. Given the economic state of this area, security cameras are hard to come by," he says. "So where did you go at eight o'clock that night?"

I stumble back to the sofa. My knees don't support me, and I collapse down on the cushions. "You won't find video of me in Missouri or anywhere else. I wasn't there."

"You sound confident, Ms. Knight, but you could've taken the back roads the entire way to Robert's house if you'd gotten into a car and driven there, which is the only way you could've pulled it off. It's a five-hour drive to Hermann, Missouri, from here and five hours back. That would've given the killer about an hour in Hermann to take care of things and would put him back in Chicago around six a.m." He steps forward. "May I see your driver's license?"

"I don't have one." Before he can ask why, I say, "Because my parents both died in a pile-up when I was a kid. I've never driven a car."

"Hm."

"You're—" I choke on my own dry voice, hacking on the brink of truth. "You're accusing me of murdering my cousin, but I have alibis for the rest of the crimes. You said so yourself. That doesn't make sense."

"What doesn't make sense is your secrecy. Why you went for the rifle, but someone else beat you to it. Why you virtually disappeared between eight and six on the night of the first victim's murder. You weren't home the night he was killed, and that doesn't put you in a very good place."

Lockheed walks to me, the hem of his coat grazing over my coffee table. His large body blocks Bradley from my view.

"The mere fact that you're the only one left alive—and without an alibi—raises a red flag. Another thing: the killer isn't watching you, Ms. Knight. You're now legally required to speak to a psychologist because this deals with multiple homicide cases. Detective Bradley will drive you to the doctor's office in the morning at nine forty-five." He turns around. "Bradley, your full-time position starts now."

I force myself to stand. Lockheed is too powerful for me to object, so I straighten up, but confidence is the last thing I encompass. My sweat makes my armpits slippery and itchy, and I want to claw at them, but that might make me look crazy too.

"I didn't kill Robert. I just don't remember what I was doing that night."

"You don't remember being out for ten hours all night?"

My panting quickens, and the patterns on the rug skew into kaleidoscope shapes, objects, jewels of red and orange colors, the shades of hell.

"When you remember where you were," Lockheed says, "you'll know where to find me. And if you can't remember, talk to the psychologist. She specializes in mental illnesses and traumatic experiences that cause memory loss." He tips his hat at me. "Enjoy your session tomorrow morning."

15

I have to get to John. His wife is still in the hospital, so he's home alone tonight, and I need to see him.

"Bradley, I need to talk to John. I need to go right now."

Pacing the rug from the coffee table to the window, Bradley runs his fingers through his blond hair. "What does Lockheed mean, Jessica? What haven't you been telling me?"

"I've got to get to John."

He grabs me by the wrist and jerks me toward him. "You're not leaving unless I say so."

"It was John, Bradley. I was with John that night." Tears spring from my eyes, and I pull away, hoping he'll drag me back in, but he drops his grip and walks away.

"Oh, my God, Jessica."

"I know, but if I just speak to him, we can come up with a plan. He can help cover for me and prove I wasn't in Missouri that night."

"How? What's he going to say that won't throw you both under the bus, huh?"

"I don't know."

"You were under the sheets of a married man, and there's nothing else to it. How did you get to John's that night? Why does surveillance show you walking out of the building? Does it show you getting into a car?"

"It was Melanie, my neighbor. She's nosy, and I didn't want her to see me getting in a cab right outside my building. She's used to seeing me walk places, so if she saw me getting a ride somewhere, I was afraid she would notice that I wasn't coming back for the night, and I knew she would ask me questions."

"And why'd you come back so early in the morning?"

"The cab dropped me off a couple blocks down at six o'clock so I could get ready for work within the next couple hours. That's when the cameras show me walking back inside."

He shakes his head, pacing once more.

"Please help me, Bradley. You said you understand that people go through these things all the time."

"No." He comes face to face with me again, and I want him to grab me, to hold me up against his chest, to either punish me for my wrong-doing or praise me for the fact that I'm not the killer Lockheed thinks I am. "I told you people get accused. I didn't tell you it's okay to lie to the sergeant and sneak around in secret with your boss. You might not be guilty of murder, but you're guilty of too many other things to get away with another lie."

"It's not another lie. That was months ago, and if it comes out that he's sleeping around, it'll ruin his career and his marriage. His wife is dying from cancer, Bradley. I can't do that to them." Crumbling onto the sofa, I cover my eyes to block more tears from falling. "Please help me." Then I look up at him.

He comes to a steady halt at the coffee table and sucks in his lips, puffing them back out again. "I'm not sure there's anything I can do."

My eyes, blurry as I stand and walk toward him, burn for a resolve. "Drive me to John's."

"My car needs to stay out there in case Lockheed finds himself in this neighborhood again." He points to the door even though his car is below my window. "And you can't go anywhere alone."

I turn my back to him and circle around the table. "The Button Collector hasn't made a move on me…ever, actually. It was Ben who shot at me."

"But the killer's got your gun. Probably. There are too many risks, Jessica. You're the only one left he could want, so you're too vulnerable alone."

"Which is why I wanted my rifle."

"Well, it's too late for that. Anyway, the only way you could get to John's is by a cab, but I'd go with you."

I pull on my coat and pick up my purse from the couch. "Then we need to go now. Before Lockheed digs too deeply into this."

I start murmuring to myself, *A plan. We'll make a plan. We'll make a plan, and John will cover for me. A plan.* If Bradley hears me, he pretends not to, even though he marches out the door right in front me.

"Wait," he says.

I won't wait here while Lockheed finds a reason to convict me, but I do pause for Bradley with my hand on the doorknob.

"Are you sure you know what you're doing? With John, I mean?"

"Of course I do."

Bradley sits in the back of the taxi with me, and I tell the driver John's address, whispering it almost so Bradley might not hear how well I've got it memorized. I've been reciting it under my breath for years.

After twenty-five minutes in the dark backseat of the cab, the driver pulls in front of the locked iron gate. "What's the code?" he says, chewing his gum.

"Six one seven," I tell him.

He punches it in, and the gate slides open, letting us in. I show him to the glossy-windowed condo building where I spent the evening of June seventeenth, and I take out my debit card to pay the driver, but

Bradley interjects, handing him a wad of cash. He tells me it's so we don't leave a paper trail.

Inside the lobby of John's building, the floors shine sleek and white with a strip of cream-colored carpet along the hallways.

Beside me, Bradley straightens the collar of his coat, and I try to sneak a peek at his gun holsters again, but they're tucked securely under his arms. He nods to the lady at the front desk then ducks behind me so I can lead the way to the elevator, to the eighth floor, to John's door that's painted a flat gold color.

"You'll need to stay outside," I say. "I have to speak with him alone."

Bradley sighs from his nose, blowing hot breath and discontentment down on me. But, like I had hoped he would, he backs away until he's around the corner. I'm too busy staying alive to feel guilty.

I knock, even though I have a key. I'm the only journalist who got one. Guess he trusts me the most out of all the girls to not come unannounced on account of his marriage.

The other side of the door is quiet in the absence of John's wife, a space that's empty now, but commonly filled by *Chicago Post* journalists. His footsteps resonate from behind the door. Closer. Closer.

He flings the door open, supporting his weight on the edge of the wide frame, and rests his head there when he sees it's only me.

"Knight. Dear."

I let myself into his pearl-white apartment, and he closes the door behind me. "Have you been crying, John?"

"It's Mary." He collapses onto a chair that was already pulled out from behind the granite bar. His voice wobbles. "The doctors spoke to me today. I'm so glad you came by, Knight. They told me she's only got three months to live."

John arches his back and falls over the countertop, descending into a heap of bellowing sobs. One after another.

I drop my purse and run to him, hauling him so he is upright again. "I'm so sorry, John. Come here."

"It's a waste, Knight. She's not ready to die, she's too smart, she's too young. A fifty-five-year-old dying from cancer?" He shakes his head. "She's brilliant, Knight. Just brilliant. Amazing writer. Kept a hundred journals. She's got that Yale degree but barely got thirty years out of it. Could'a had thirty more."

John stands and walks to the opposite wall where a wooden table stocks a line of liquor bottles, tall and short. He pours a glass one quarter full then leans against the wall.

"She was top of her class. You know that, Knight? I'm seven years older; it should be me with the cancer."

By the counter, I turn the light switch down to dim the room and meet him against the wall.

"John, I came over to talk with you."

He sets down his drink and rubs his face. "I'm sorry, dear. Christ. I haven't even asked about you. Can I get you a drink?"

"No. Please, no. Listen, this is a bad time, and I wish I could come back when Mary's okay, but" —hooking my finger around his belt loop, I tug him off the wall— "are you okay? Okay enough for me to talk with you?"

He starts to agree by placing his forehead against mine but then he pulls away. His eyes widen, making visible all the red lines striking across them. "Oh, Knight. Oh, sweetheart. It's the killer again, isn't it?"

My tears sting, bubbling to the surface, so I blink them away and look down. "Yes, but it's also me. Me and you."

He touches my shoulders as if to brace himself, and I have no choice but to hold on to him too.

"The night the Button Collector took his first victim, I was with you," I say. "The police know I wasn't in my apartment that entire night, and they saw me leave and come back early that next morning, and they think I snuck away and killed my cousin. They don't know I was with you, and I can't tell them."

A single tear slinks down my cheek. "Tell me what to do, John."

"They think you've killed people?"

179

I nod, and John turns away from me and takes a step closer to the coat rack by the door. The coat rack wobbles back and forth while he digs through the pocket of his suit jacket, taking out a white carton of cigarettes.

He tries the lighter three times before getting it to spark a flame. "You can't smoke in here, John. Mary's oxygen," I say.

"The tank's in the bedroom." Next to her side of the bed, I recall.

He sucks on his cigarette, and it quivers between his shaking fingers. "Knight, what'd you tell 'em?" he exhales.

"I said I couldn't remember where I was that night. Sergeant Lockheed already thinks I'm mentally ill, and I don't know what to do. I don't know what to do, John. Tell me what to do."

He lets the cigarette hang from his dry lips that warp from his age and rubs his chest with both hands. Looking down, he's silent for so long I expect him to start weeping again. Instead, he takes the cigarette between two fingers, pulls it from his lips, and says, "Be honest, hon. Tell 'em where you were." John shrugs and taps the tip of his shoe on the rug. "Not too scary."

The door behind John isn't locked, and I sense Bradley is there at the peephole listening in. I want to run to him and tell him we need help because John doesn't know what to do either. Maybe we're all going crazy.

"Tell him? John—"

"What?" he asks.

"I can't be honest, John. I haven't been honest since I've lived in Chicago, and neither have you."

"No, dear," he says. "Tell the cops you were with me. Mary was in the hospital last summer when you came over, so I'll call those guys at…at where? What station?"

"Fuller Park."

"I'll call those guys at Fuller Park and say I needed you here to help me with some paperwork for a story we were working on. They'll believe that, Knight, won't they?" Chuckling at his plan, he takes a long drag from the cigarette. It's painful to watch him try to survive me and the COPD and the other affairs and the cancer in Mary. "They've got no proof you went to kill anybody." He smiles sadly. It makes me want to cry. For him, for his wife, or maybe even for myself.

"But they've got no proof I didn't," I say.

The coat rack wobbles again when his shoulder brushes against it as he walks away from the corner and heads back over to his liquor bar.

"If I say Mary was in the hospital and you were helping me here all night with work, that'll give you an alibi that I can back you up on." He flings the cigarette into a crystal ashtray and comes within inches of my face. "It's not physical evidence, but it's my word against their weak suspicion."

"I need to be the one who talks to Lockheed."

"Lockheed. That's right. I thought it was *Smeed*." He shakes his head at himself. "That's that guy in charge? Met him once when I was talking to that detective."

"Yes," I say to cut off his mumbling. "He needs to hear it from me, that I remembered where I was that night. He might call you to confirm."

"That's alright, Knight. You know I'll take care of you." He sniffles from his tragic news, and I cry at mine.

"It's a weak alibi," I say. "They'll think you're just covering for my murder."

"No, dear. We've got cameras outside this building." He pinches the tip of my nose and blows me a burnt kiss. "And remember, I'm editor of one of the largest papers in the city. My word is strong."

Bradley doesn't ask questions in the taxi on the way back from John's but thanks me once we get in the car. "That was fast."

I watch the gates to John's complex close from the backseat in the side mirror of the taxi as we head back to the main road. "Well, it was a quick discussion."

Bradley hums a little laugh under his breath, his expression trained toward his dark window. "I guess you two don't do much talking on a normal occasion."

"We talk plenty."

"So there's more to your affair than what meets the eye."

Even though I know I won't be able to spot it, I still look in the mirror for John's lights shining from his living room window on the eighth floor, but I can't count the levels of the building quickly enough.

"There's more to us than what meets the private eye of a man from the street." But that's a total lie.

Bradley adjusts his seatbelt and leans toward the center of the back seat, just out of the view of the driver though the rearview mirror. His voice low, he says, "You told me there were more women. It's not just you in the office that he calls when he's lonely."

The driver keeps his eyes straight ahead. He's probably heard a hundred love stories from the backseat of his cab, details of their failures and successes.

"Can we—can we talk about this—"

"So," Bradley says, somewhere on the bumpy line of a whisper, "where were all the other girls tonight if it's not just you?"

"He calls me the most. I'm not married like some of them."

"Like he is."

"Like the other girls."

The darkness in the cab keeps his face invisible. "Look," I whisper, "it's nothing. We're nothing."

"Does he love you?"

I stop breathing. Bradley can't tell through the dark, but my throat clogs when I try to say, *No.* I've never associated love with John. Only affection and fondness. He comes to me most outside of the office when he wants a woman, and in office, he steals Della away. The other journalists call him when their husbands are out of town, and John gladly heads to them. That process has never changed.

What has stayed the same all those years is John's affection when he's with me, and on the mornings that he leaves my apartment or I his, I've entertained the idea that perhaps I am his favorite.

But no one could ever love a whore.

"He's in love with his wife," I say. Bradley doesn't respond.

Back inside my apartment, I pour Bradley a glass of water and tell him to make himself at home. He takes off his coat and unstraps his guns, slinging it from his torso and placing the belt on the coffee table. Good. He's already comfortable here. It's as though he's lived here for years, the way he casually drops his crap, ready to unwind after a long day at work.

Bradley takes a seat on my sofa and rolls up his sleeves before sliding the magazines out of his handguns. From the kitchen, I can see both magazines are full of gold-colored bullets packed snugly, one on top of another, just waiting to be shot. He clicks them back into place again.

I set his glass of water beside his gun. "I'm not going to that appointment tomorrow morning."

He wipes his hands on his legs and lifts the glass to take a swallow. "Appease Lockheed. If you don't go, that's the hunch he'll build on to arrest you."

Taking the seat next to Bradley, I slip out of my shoes and dab at the remnants of my lipstick. "He can't arrest me over that."

"He can cuff a suspect who doesn't cooperate, Jessica."

Bradley's weight on the cushion pulls me toward him, so I scoot as close as I can to the other arm of the sofa.

"It's already midnight," he says. "I'll be up for a while, so you should go ahead and get to bed."

"Why will you be awake?"

The gap I created between us seems to widen when he pauses. "I'm going to stay awake until two or three."

Oh.

He goes silent and starts wiping down the barrel of his pistol. I want to hear him say the words he thinks I can't handle.

The base of an argument begins to build, but I think better of it. Bradley would win a debate as to whether I'm capable of protecting myself.

He doesn't say anything more but keeps his focus on cleaning his gun. I take the opportunity to excuse myself and go to bed. The underside of my pillow lacks the mild chill that my kitchen knife would provide. Since I've been home, I replaced the knife with a baseball bat stashed next to the bed where I can reach it.

When I was young, my father used to take me to our neighborhood sandlot and my mom cheered me on from the empty stands. They had talked me into trying out for the team at the elementary school, and I would have played all the way to Portsmouth High, but in sixth grade, I quit and never hit a ball again.

After my parents died, Coach had said, "They'd want you to keep playing, you know. Your parents would be proud if you kept it up."

But I'd found a new group of girls who hung out in the bathroom smoking weed and introducing me to boys with long hair. Two of the girls overdosed before graduation, one hung herself junior year. I had stumbled into my first relationship as a freshman. He weaned me off drugs but turned me on to his parents' alcohol. I had thought that he was the one for me, but before we left for college, he wandered into the bedroom of another girl and I started my freshman year of college alone.

My old baseball bat is tucked between my bed and the nightstand, and I feel safe enough to drift off to sleep with the bat's handle beside my temple.

He can't see me in here.

The Collector can't see through my shaded windows, but I know he is out there somewhere. I focus between the wavy line of my pulled curtains and stare right back at him.

"Have you ever seen a counselor, Ms. Knight?"

After Mom and Dad died, my foster parents made me see a therapist, and only for a brief four weeks, I went every Wednesday after school.

"No, I haven't."

Dr. Smith's sofa and chair sit in the center of her office. The openness of her room keeps me from screaming *I don't need you* because I'm afraid it might echo too loudly.

A skinny table with three legs stands beside me, a rosy scent coming from the bowl of dried flower petals. It's winter. The smell is artificial. It comes and goes with the draft of heat that swifts past every once in a while. And there's that oil painting on the wall behind her, a blur of brown and blue and rust shades that don't make any sense. Just an ocean of colors.

"Do you think you need to be here this morning?" she asks.

She reminds me a little of Welch, if Welch's hair was browner and laid on her shoulders. My psychologist's high heels add a few inches to her short height, and her fingernails are painted blood red, nothing like

Welch's unpainted ones. They're both stern people, which I don't love about Dr. Smith but admire about Welch.

Dr. Smith's petite wrists anger me. Her small size is immeasurable to the extent of my case. If Lockheed can't crack me, what makes him think this woman can? PhD or not. "I don't think so. I didn't schedule the appointment," I say.

Her office is too high in the building to see the clumps of iced-over snow on the sidewalks. The neighboring buildings don't reflect the burning morning sunlight like my floor at *The Chicago Post* does at nine forty-five. Outside, the air is gray, and instead of snow floating down, it's heavy drizzles of cold rain. I cross my arms, not cold, but not warm either.

"That's right," she says. "An officer from the Fuller Park Police Department scheduled this meeting. Why do you think they did that, Ms. Knight?"

"They believe I might be mentally ill."

"Do you think you have a problem?"

"I do not."

"So is this the only reason you are here? Because someone else thinks that you might be sick?"

Dr. Smith doesn't smile or move around at all. She didn't even show her teeth when I walked into her office earlier, and when she sat down, she crossed her legs and hasn't repositioned once. Her stillness doesn't encourage me to trust her.

"Right, I probably wouldn't have come," I say.

"May I call you by your first name, Ms. Knight?" Without making a sound, she puts her pen in her lap and squints her eyes at me. "It's Jessica, isn't it?"

"Yes."

"Jessica, I want to know your point of view. What you think the problem is. How you feel about someone else deciding you need psychiatric attention."

She must know about the case and why I'm here and that I think a serial killer is watching me all the time. Lockheed had to have sent her my information so she would know to tread lightly. But she's probably dying to ask me those direct questions about being the Button Collector's target. Our session has only ten minutes left because today is short, an introductory day. They had to ease me into this slowly or else I might be scared.

"An attempt on my life could be made any second," I say. "I wake up every morning thinking I could die that day, and yeah, that takes a toll on me. I'm not mentally ill. They just think that because I feel a little paranoid. Of course I feel paranoid."

"Yes," Dr. Smith says. "I was informed about the case, and the sergeant mentioned that you feel like the Button Collector watches you. Do you believe the Button Collector watches you, Jessica?"

When I got into Bradley's car this morning, I'd felt the killer's eyes cross over me in the gust of wind that rushed through my legs and blew my hair back. Bradley had noticed and asked what was wrong, but I told him nothing and buckled my seatbelt.

"Sometimes I do," I tell Dr. Smith.

She jots down a note on her leather pad. "Do you feel like you have control over your life anymore?"

"Yes," I lie. "I still have control."

"Then let's move on to something else. Jessica, do you sleep well at night?"

Last July, I started waking up sore from restless nights. After Deborah's daughter was killed, I couldn't sleep at all. That's when the Button Collector got his name.

I reach under my sleeve and rub over the stiff line of skin that has healed from the knife cut. Stroking the scar, I say, "Yeah, I sleep fine."

"Because the lack of sleep can cause things as severe as hallucinations. Have you experienced anything like that?"

"I've never seen anything out of the ordinary."

Dr. Smith moves for the first time, uncrossing her legs and resting her elbows on the arms of her chair. "The sergeant also told me about your aunt Deborah. I'm glad she's going to be okay."

"Yeah, well," I mumble, "she's probably going into a ward, so."

The rain outside picks up. It pelts against her office windows. I'm grateful for the distraction.

"The sergeant said he noticed you began to seem ill after your aunt Deborah's incident," she says.

Her question is flat, but maybe it's just a statement that needs my answer. "He didn't know me before then," I say, "so his observation isn't accurate."

"He filled me in on the case." Dr. Smith sets her pad aside and locks her hands together. "Jessica, you're aware, and often reminded, that the Button Collector is most likely after you, and no one knows why. That can cause extreme paranoia, and luckily, yours seems mild. It could, nonetheless, cause you to think the killer is watching you."

"I suppose so," I say.

"Since the serial killer has attacked other members of your family, you automatically formed the conclusion that he must be after you too. While that does seem likely, we still just don't know what the Collector will do next."

I study the slim waterfalls of rain trickling down the window. She knows I'm the last of my family and that's who the killer wants; she's just trying to make me feel better.

"I believe, Jessica, you can put to rest the idea that you're being watched. If you accept that, you also can start to take comfort in knowing you've got protection from the sergeant and his people. After all," she says, "he cared enough to contact me about you."

～

At the end of my session, Bradley drives me to the Fuller Park station and parks facing away from the building. He keeps the car engine cranked with his hand on the gearshift. The veins in his wrist stream under his skin, and I follow them to his fingers and back up to the cuffs on his forearms.

"Listen," he says, "Lockheed's been doing this job for a long time. He knows how to break people to catch them in the middle of a lie."

His face is closer to mine than I anticipated, and the spicy scent of his mouthwash from this morning lingers on his breath. I lean over the armrest to meet him halfway. "Will he know I'm lying?"

"He's already pinned you as a liar. Just" —Bradley glances down, just below my nose, and I smear my lips together just as I remember I didn't put on my lipstick this morning— "don't mess up."

Bradley comes with me into Lockheed's office and closes the door behind me. He stays behind me, so I back up a few steps until I am almost leaning against him. His hand brushes into my back, and he taps me on my lumbar to either comfort me or push me to follow through.

"I came to tell you what I was doing on June seventeenth. I remember now."

Lockheed's reading glasses slide down the bridge of his nose, his mustache blanketing his mouth. The glasses are too thin for his face, and the temples attached to the hinges bend at obtuse angles.

He removes them and tosses them onto his desk. "Talk to me, Ms. Knight."

Bradley clears his throat. I put my hands behind my back, thinking he might take one of them to indicate I'm getting through this just fine. To mean that Lockheed can't see through me. Can't see me at all.

"I was at my boss's apartment in Oak Brook all night. He's the editor at the newspaper where I work, and his wife was in the hospital that night because she has cancer, so he called me in because he needed assistance with some paperwork."

Lockheed's mustache twitches.

"It had built up since he couldn't be in the office. Because of his wife. We worked long into the night to sort through the work."

"You two were alone together all night in his apartment? Why didn't you come home?"

"By the time I had finished, it was late—about three a.m., and John was already asleep in bed. So I took the sofa and headed home after a short nap."

"Wait a second." He pushes his glasses out of the way to make room for his chest and thick arms as he leans across his desk. "John—that's the name of the guy we called in about some suspicious text messages." Lockheed's rolling chair whines as he looks beyond me to Bradley. "You conducted the interview."

"Yes, sir, I did. John's text messages were work related, so he checked out clean. Nothing on him."

"You can call him," I say. "He can tell you everything, and the hospital between my neighborhood and Oak Brook can confirm his wife was there."

"How did you get to his home? You were shown walking away from your building," Lockheed says. "You hitch a ride?"

"I didn't want my very nosy neighbor to see me leaving that late in a cab. She would ask questions if she knew I was out that late, so I just walked out of sight and got a cab."

He rolls back in his chair again and stretches out his legs, crossing his arms over his chest.

"Truly, she's a pest," I say.

He looks past me. "Bradley?"

Appearing at my side, Bradley clears his throat again. "There's nothing that indicates her story isn't true, Sergeant."

"I've got that man on my radar," Lockheed says. He sighs, and it sounds more like a whistle. "How was your doctor's appointment this morning, Ms. Knight?"

"Fine. It was fine."

He scans me from my shins to my head, taking heavy breaths through his nose. I catch him searching for my hands, tilting in an obvious way to see behind my back.

"Did you get anything accomplished?" he asks.

My arms fall to my sides at once. "That's a question for Dr. Smith, but I'm sure she can't share her client's info."

"Then you tell me. Did you come to any conclusions?"

Bradley says, "Sergeant, please. It was just a thirty-minute—"

"That's enough from you, Bradley. I want to hear from Ms. Knight." Lockheed stands, and his chair rolls away, hitting against the cabinet behind his desk.

I jump a smidge, and Bradley flinches.

"This case hasn't budged since Martha Pax was killed, and you, Ms. Knight, are our only hope of getting a few steps closer to the serial killer who, according to you, is lurking around our neighborhood, but you've done nothing but complicate things with your careless behaviors. It's entirely my business to know what that psychologist asked you because I can't have you keeping that killer around my city for much longer, if he's even here at all, because in your little world, he's always looking at you." He puts a fist on the desk. "You're either guilty of something or just plain psychotic, so until I know which, you're on my radar."

"She's not a suspect in these homicide cases, Sergeant Lockheed. Let's think logistically, here," Bradley says.

"Detective Bradley, please. Ms. Knight, did you come to any conclusions with the doctor?"

"Yes," I say. My tongue dries with the sudden loss of moisture. "She said I'm just paranoid, and no one is watching me, and I have good protection. But, Sergeant Lockheed, I'm having trouble deciphering whether you think I'm still a victim. I—"

"I don't know what you are. You might not be the killer, but you don't strive to earn my trust, and that concerns me and this case. You also don't seem concerned about your well-being." He pauses. "Would you mind pulling up your sleeve, Ms. Knight?"

"I'm—I'm sorry?"

"Pull up your shirt sleeve."

Bradley steps partially in front of me. "Sir."

"Ms. Knight, have you been physically harming yourself?"

"I—no."

"Show me your arms."

Bradley puts the length of his arm over my front side and nudges me back. "I don't believe this is your call to make, sir."

Lockheed bends over the desk and grabs my wrist, his strength firm and his hand coarse.

The lamp on his desk shutters from his sudden movement. He pulls me to him and slides his grip up my arm, rolling up my sleeve and revealing the scar from the knife. His short, thick fingers wrap all the way around my skinny forearm, his callouses scratching my skin.

"I can explain that," I say louder than I mean to.

As quickly as he took me into his grip, he releases me, and Bradley doesn't move, but in my peripheral vision, I can see his disappointment in me.

"I don't think you can," Lockheed says. He straightens his shirt, his brows slanting inward. "Now, please excuse yourselves from my office. I have a phone call to make."

I wake in the morning light to the clatter of pans in the kitchen and reach under my pillow, finding only my soft, wrinkled sheet. Beside my bed, I get the baseball bat and throw myself on my feet. Then I hear Bradley, and he's whistling to a faint rhythm of music, reminding me he's still here. My scar singes with the memory of Lockheed's hand scraping over it. Bradley had believed my story about the accidental cut without saying much. His response to my explanation had simply been, "The sergeant is hard to convince."

I concluded last night that Welch must have told Lockheed she'd seen a scar on my arm—a fresh one, and suspicious one to keep tabs on.

Opening my bedroom door, the music converts into a song that defogs a memory from my childhood. My dad used to play that song in the car, and he'd poke my cheek on every syllable when the singer said, *So darling, darling, stand by me.*

I charge into the living room to shut it off, to keep me from storing that song anywhere but in that memory of my dad, but Bradley doesn't even flinch when the music goes off. An apron hangs around his neck and is tied at his hips. I've never seen it before. When I told him good-night last night, he was still wearing his work clothes, so I wonder why I didn't hear him change into these pajamas he's still wearing. For the three nights after my meeting with Dr. Smith, I stayed awake until I heard Bradley's belt fall to the floor and his stiff shirt crinkle off of him.

Last night, though, I'd pulled the sheets over my head because yesterday was the first day this week I felt the Button Collector watching me again.

Bradley turns around with a spatula in his hand. His white apron hardly covers the front of his tee shirt, though that seems to be the only part of his chest that's spotted with grease from the splattering eggs in my skillet.

He grins and goes back to scraping the eggs. "You can put down the bat, Jessica."

I forget I'm even holding it. I set it against the same wall that John had pushed me against the night Bradley saw us through the window, and I examine the breakfast spread. Bradley has assembled four slices of toast and a pound of bacon, which he has already plated and laid out on the kitchen counter.

"I packed my apron a few days ago when I ran home. Thought I'd do the cooking since I'm staying in your lovely home for free."

"You're getting paid to be here," I say, trying to make it clear that he's not here for the fun of it, and we both know that.

My dining room table is set with two placemats that I usually keep rolled up in a kitchen drawer. They are already prepared with forks and two empty glasses.

Bradley flips an egg in the pan, and he laughs a little to himself. "Consider this a thank you. Or a rent payment."

I pick up a plate beside the toaster and move along the spread of food. "You weren't invited here."

Bradley meets me with the skillet and scoops a serving of fried eggs onto my plate. His tee shirt sleeves stretch higher around his biceps than his uniform reveals.

"Then I suppose a thank you to Lockheed is in order," he says, "since he's the one who put me here."

Standing in front of me, Bradley's apron is flush against my plate, creating only a dish's width between us. I close my mouth to breathe through my nose so he can't smell my morning breath, then dart to the living room with my plate, telling myself our awkward interactions are easing up a bit.

"My coffee cup—I left it by the window in here, I think." Bradley sets down the skillet, and I stumble to the window.

"So," he says, "your neighbor knocked this morning. Melanie. She asked me who I was and asked to see my badge for proof."

The curtain has already been pulled back; the February chill seeps in from outside, reminding me that I'm supposed to be searching for my mug, which I'm now certain is not by the window.

"I see what you mean about her," Bradley says. "For sure the nosy neighbor type."

The steam from the eggs on my plate makes a haze on the glass, so I stand on my tip toes above the fog to see the empty street below. In the snow on the sidewalk, three lonely words are scratched into the thin layer of white.

YOU ARE NEXT. BC.

"You wouldn't happen to think she's assuming that you and I are sleep—"

My plate shatters into porcelain fragments on my bare toes. A scream burns my throat from a force that presses through me and detonates in my apartment, an earthquake and explosion all at once.

The walls blur together, and before my knees hit the ground, I'm suddenly pressed against Bradley's apron and counting backwards from ten, clasping my hands over my ears, warped as far as I can go into his body.

"Nine, eight, seven—"

One of his arms lets go of me, his other one still cradling me into his neck. His skin is wet where my face lies, but I'm not crying. I can't be crying, not in front of Bradley again. *Am I crying?*

Five, four, three, two…

A muffled ringing comes from above me, and then: "Sergeant, get down here. We've got a message from the killer."

"Ten, nine, eight—"

"'You are next.'"

17

IT IS GOING ON A year since the serial killer known as the Button Collector has been on the loose, murdering members of who is believed to be a targeted family. In these nine months of investigation, five murders have taken place, and one attempted murder occurred that left a woman in critical condition last January.

The latest murder of Chicago resident Martha Pax in December did not reveal any evidence or surveillance footage at the crime scene that could lead authorities to identify the killer. The Button Collector is believed to be a bald male of short stature. CPD officials claim they are surprised the killer has been quiet recently, which, according to Detective Michael Bradley of Fuller Park CPD, "might be dangerous. This man is organized, so he could be plotting another murder during, what we might consider, down time."

The *Post* asked Bradley for a quote a few days ago, and Lockheed made him agree to an over-the-phone interview with a temporary journalist who's filling in during my absence now that John has demoted me to part-time. Bradley had to lie, though, for my safety. Even Lockheed told him to keep all the tormenting and sporadic acts of the Button Collector away from the media.

He wants to avoid unnecessary risk of me becoming famous for being alive. He and Bradley both believe that this waiting game is part of the Collector's plan to make me suffer before he kills me.

Just a couple weeks ago, Bradley was walking me to his car to drive me to *The Chicago Post*, and he was the one to see it first—all the chiseled letters in the sidewalk and the Expo marker lines all over the street signs. The Collector knows my path to Bradley's car and knew exactly where to scribe *you are next you are next you are next.*

I had skipped work that day and gone straight to Lockheed with the picture of those words on Bradley's phone.

"You still think I'm the killer now? You still think I did this? That I wrote this? He sees me every second of the day and knows exactly where to write things like this."

Lockheed had stayed calm and let me scream at him while everyone in Fuller Park listened.

"You're right to be afraid, Ms. Knight. He does know where to attack. Detective Bradley and I have been discussing the behavior of this serial killer. He's getting bolder and acting out now. It's like he's got nothing to lose."

I'd left the room and heard Lockheed say to Bradley, "That friend of hers—John—has the voice of a man who can lie right through his teeth. It was a cover, Bradley. You stay on Ms. Knight, and you stay on her close. I've got a feeling about her. She was up to something last June."

"Didn't you check the surveillance at his apartment? He said they have cameras."

"It erases after six months. Bradley, don't let me start thinking you're defending her for no reason."

Since then, they've placed more patrol units around my neighborhood, and they've lied to the media about the killer's silence. At least three officers are scouting my area at all times, day and night, now. They check the grainy video surveillance outside my neighborhood, but I am certain that the Collector knows the exact streets with no cameras. How else could he evade so many watchful eyes?

What the newspaper says is a lie—the killer has not been quiet. The Collector, actually, has been very loud. He's been under my nose, under Bradley's, under Lockheed's. Every morning, Bradley looks out my window for a message from the killer, even though the snow has been gone for weeks now, but no threat has been found and spelled out with spring flower petals. Bradley checks for me, anyway, and then he makes our breakfast, has my mug clean and ready for coffee, and three out of five mornings, he drives me to work. John keeps to himself in his office like a recluse. Our only contact is professional, and the last time we actually had a conversation was when he called me in on a rainy morning to give me the latest update on his wife. Still dying. Me too.

Behind the media's back, Bradley and Lockheed converse in my apartment about how the Collector is acting rash, out of character, ready to pounce. He's always watching me, the killer. I can feel him on my way to work, always lurking when I leave the apartment, and at times when I don't expect it, like when I oversleep and he's there, or when I get out of the bathtub and he's there. Bradley knows it too. The note in the snow was the beginning. It was a terrifying first confirmation that I am indeed next.

Fuller Park called my extended family, some of whom I've never even heard of, and informed them they are no longer in danger of being harmed by the Button Collector for undisclosed reasons. The search for the killer is called off except in Chicago due to the specific threats directed at me. I'm convinced that every cop in the city knows my name now.

My appointments with Dr. Smith haven't amounted to what Lockheed must've thought.

Questions and answers, and her conclusions all come out the same. "Are you feeling comfortable today? Scared?"

"Fine, since I learned I was only paranoid."

"And the live-in detective? How do you feel about a man you don't really know being with you all the time?"

"I feel safe with him."

She pauses here every time, taking her notes. "Have you developed romantic emotions or feelings for this man? It would be okay. Natural, actually."

"He's just doing his job."

"Have you ever been in a situation where he's physically had to protect you?"

My brain always goes black; her questions trigger the memory of Ben's bloody body lying on top of me. Bradley had stood at my feet and taken the shot that ended Ben's life.

"No, never." Another lie.

"It's been since the end of February that he's lived with you, and, Jessica, it's the last week of March. Besides his occasional hour-long absence to go to his home for a new set of clothes, he's been with you for over a month. Your situation is unconventional. You're living with a man whose job is to do all he can to keep you safe. A man who has a duty to protect you. It's only natural for you to feel something for him."

After my sessions with Dr. Smith come to a close each week, Bradley drives me back to my apartment, I kick out some lazy articles that a fourteen-year-old could write, and I wait for my next sign that the Collector is one step closer to killing me. The anticipation eats through my walls and through my flesh. I'm not the only one waiting. The entire Fuller Park station is waiting. CPVC is still involved and on call for when something does happen. Bradley was told by Lockheed that the FBI has been informed of the situation, made aware that the serial killer known by the nation is inching closer to Jessica Knight, Chicago journalist, with every sunrise. Thank God the media has stayed out of it. If they hadn't, the whole country would've been anticipating my survival too.

We've settled into a routine, Bradley and me. He turns on the television when the sun starts to set, and I draw a bath, leaving the door unlocked in case I need him. Just in case. It's been like this ever since the morning I received my first threat in the snow.

Tonight, when I get out of the tub, I wrap in my bathrobe, and the oval mirror is steamed gray like a winter morning. Using my middle finger, I write on it *you are next.*

Just for fun.

I can control things too.

Bradley sits on the side of the sofa that's nearest to the window, already in his sweatpants and the same tee shirt he wears most nights. He pours a glass of wine and holds it out to me, picking up a second glass for himself. The wine is a dark red color and reminds me of waves of blood. When I swallow it, it's almost as if I am tasting my own.

I take the glass over to the window and peek down at the sidewalk through the curtain. "You're not allowed to drink on the job, you know. Especially *with* me."

Behind me, I hear him set his glass on the table. "Come sit, Ms. Knight."

At this hour, the room should be lit by the television flashing, but now we've only got the yellow shades of light from the kitchen.

"The TV isn't on," I say.

"I thought we would enjoy a glass of wine instead of the TV tonight," he says. "And I'll drink whatever I want."

He picks up his glass again and sprawls on the corner cushion, feet propped on the coffee table, so I take the middle seat and cross one leg under me, closing my robe over my lap.

Bradley turns toward me, our drinks almost chiming together, and I resist my usual impulse to back away when he comes close.

"You took a quick bath," he says.

The wine spirals around in my glass, giving me something to focus on other than into Bradley's eyes. "I didn't hear the TV on and thought you needed company." Bradley flashes me a grin and takes a sip.

"You were married," I say.

"I can't tell if that's a question or statement." Amusement flirts with his words, drawing my eyes to his.

"Welch told me at the safehouse."

The wine in his glass goes still. "You sound like you have questions."

"I don't. Not if you don't want to answer them."

He places his drink on the table and rotates himself to face me, to share the middle cushion with me. Taking a breath, he readies himself for the conversation. "She left."

"How long were you together?"

"Two years. I worked too much, she got bored with me. You know that old story."

"Right." Actually, I don't. I can't imagine a married version of Bradley, or the type of woman that he would be interested in settling down with.

"You aren't married," he says. "You're in your mid-twenties, have a good job, got plenty of men after you. I know of three in the past year."

I wondered if he counted himself as the third one or if he was adding the Collector along with John and Ben.

To steady my shaking wine, I put my free hand on the neck of the glass and hold it still. "Settling with someone doesn't seem like an option."

"But are you content where you are right now?" The scruff of beard shadowing his jaw moves with tension, but I bring my eyes back up to his so he won't think I'm looking at his lips.

"Are you?" I ask.

His Adam's apple bobs as he swallows, and he looks down at my robed knee that is just barely grazing the fabric of his sweatpants. Bradley's hand rests on his leg, and the tips of his fingers brush against my bathrobe. I nearly let go of my wine glass but instead fumble with one hand to tighten the belt around my waist and adjust my hem.

Bradley's volume drops into a whisper. "I can't answer that."

"Then neither can I."

I grab Bradley's glass of wine from the table and hand it to him. "Dr. Smith keeps bringing up Ben," I say to change the subject.

"And?"

"She wants to know what I think of the coincidence of having two people trying to kill me. I can't help but wonder how Ben knew I was in the alley that night since he wasn't the one stalking me."

Bradley sighs and takes a sip of wine. "The department has discussed it, but there's nothing that connects him to the killer."

"So what should I tell Dr. Smith when she asks?" I say.

"Well, what do you actually think about the situation?"

His fingers stretch out and curl over my knee. I finish my wine and set down my glass, which widens the split of my bathrobe across my lap, air creeping up my thigh.

"I think you and Lockheed missed something," I answer.

"What could we possibly have missed, Jessica?" His thumb grazes my knee and stays there. I start to feel a tingle under his light touch when the shrill ring of my cell phone interrupts the moment. I jump up from the sofa and head to the dining table. Bradley offers to refill my glass while I rummage through my bag to find my phone.

When I find it and walk to Bradley, he hands me back my filled wine glass. "Who is it?" he asks.

The phone vibrates in my palm with each ring. "Nobody."

"You can answer it. He's on your side, you know. And he's probably worried."

I put the phone to my ear. "Hi, John."

"Knight," he says, loud enough for Bradley to hear.

I set down my glass and walk over to the window, turning my back to Bradley to separate myself as much as I can without being too obvious that I know why John is calling. Usually, there is only one reason he calls in the evening, and it isn't about working late.

"I needed to hear your voice."

In my peripheral, I catch Bradley crossing his legs. He sips his wine, peering at me from above the rim of the glass. I duck into the kitchen and face a corner cabinet.

"Thank you. I—I'm a little busy now, though."

"You okay, Knight?" His draw on his cigarette crackles through the phone.

"I'm okay, just with the detective."

"He's still there, eh?" A chalky laugh leads him into a coughing fit. "Remind me to buy him a drink, sweetheart. He's taken good care of you."

"I need to go. You're okay too, I hope?"

"Home alone." I hear him fumbling through some dishes. "Would've come over, would've invited you over, but—"

"It's too dangerous, anymore. You know this."

The dishes quiet down, and I can see him—feel him—hunching over his countertop, a cigarette perched between his fingers, and suspenders pulled over his shoulders. His after-work apparel with a burn hole in the sleeve, with a repaired tear on his belt loop.

His voice strains with the weakness of an old man's. "I'll let you go, Knight."

Bradley's concentrated silence stretches all the way to me, listening to what I have to say when I hang up the phone.

"John, I—"

Before I know what I'm doing, I have my head covered at the sound of a shot stabbing the apartment with the piercing boom of shattering glass. The cabinets shake, and wood splinters spray to the floor. Bradley leaps off the sofa and onto the floor, already on his chaotic way to me. My window, the spot where I was standing a mere minute ago, is now only a gaping black hole in the wall, curtains blown into ribbons.

Pieces of drywall shower down on top of me. The gunshot resounds through the air, a dying echo outside of the dark void.

I crumble to the tile and crawl away from the wall, dropping my phone and keeping my hands over my head. The phone screen goes black, and a line cracks across the corner of it.

Another shot blasts through the building, striking above the row of cabinetry that meets my ceiling. Chips of my apartment rain over me to match the explosion roaring through the kitchen.

The blast of the gunshot evaporates back out the window, but my apartment is distorted under the thumping of my heartbeat and haze of dust that fogs my vision.

Bradley calls my name and appears before me on his hands and knees. "Are you hurt?"

I shake my head.

He takes his phone out of his pocket and gives it to me, getting to his feet. "Call Lockheed, now."

My grip quivers on the phone, clicking buttons until it rings his number. On my elbows and knees, I bend around the corner. Bradley is lifting the sofa cushion where he was sitting, and he slips out his pistol. He stands against the wall by the window and aims his gun down to the street then straight at the building across from me.

"This is Lockheed," the voice says over the line.

"Sergeant Lockheed, it's Jessica. There was a—a shooting. Someone from outside shot into my apartment, and we're okay. Bradley is fine. I—I don't know. . . I don't know what happened."

"We're on our way." He hangs up, but I remain frozen.

Bradley rushes back to me and swoops me lower to the floor, stealing back his cell phone.

"What's going on?" I croak.

He brings the phone to his ear. "I'm calling Lockheed again. The killer is across the street."

~

The entire block is shut off with yellow tape despite how little traffic travels by here, especially at this late hour of night. Blue and red and white lights spin from the grills and windshields of police cars, bouncing from building to building and waking up the neighborhood under their ominous lights. My neighbors above and below me have their blinds closed, and they wait in the lobby with me and Bradley, forming their own circles to whisper about why a cop is standing with me and only me.

They point their whispers to me without trying to hide it, but I don't look at anyone and try to hide behind Bradley to shield myself from their gossip. He didn't have time to change out of his sweatpants, but he did manage to grab his gun and to throw his bullet-proof vest over his tee shirt. I got to put on a sweatshirt and jeans before I came down as Bradley stood outside my half-open door.

The lobby door swings open, and everyone wrapped in blankets or jackets stops chattering long enough to watch Lockheed approach me and Bradley.

"Thank you for being patient, Jessica. I'm sorry you two went through such a scare," he says. "We've got our teams still searching the streets and building across the street. Bradley, take her home with you until further notice."

The elevator on the opposite wall delivers a ding as it lowers to the lobby, and Melanie steps out with a suitcase rolling behind her. She tugs her daughter behind her, who carries a pink tote bag.

Melanie merges her shoulder into the gap between Bradley and Lockheed.

"Jessica, I'm leaving this building," she says, "and I'm taking Marge with me, and it's all your fault. I know it is. You're related to that family, and now look at what you've done." Her brown hair falls in strings beside her reddened cheeks. "My daughter could've been killed, and that would've been your fault. How does that make you feel?"

Lockheed turns to face her, to block her from me. "Ma'am, this isn't Ms. Knight's fault. We're still investigating what happened here tonight, and we strongly advise you to stay in this building and not enter the street."

"It doesn't matter. What's done is done. Goodbye, Jessica."

Her daughter cranes up to look at me just before she and her mother charge out the front doors. Even though Rosa was fourteen when she was killed, something about Marge reminds me of her—the innocence, and the fact that she could've died just because she was near me.

"Bradley," Lockheed says, "get her to your place. I'll drop by when I'm done here. Jessica"—he looks down on me, and the bulk on his chest swells and sinks with each exhale—"keep your head down."

He permits me to go back upstairs and gather a suitcase worth of my things while a crew of officers photograph my apartment and measure the bullet holes in my walls.

When I'm through, Bradley shuffles me to his car with his arm draped over my shoulders, the weight of his hold keeping my head ducked as Lockheed instructed.

Across the road, he opens the car door for me, and I throw myself inside, looking over the hood at the building where the shots must have come from. It's got five floors with slim windows, built of dark brick. I went inside there once, right before I chose to rent my apartment instead of the moldy room they had offered me.

Tonight, the police stormed inside that building first, instead of mine. They're still there questioning the residents, but the apartment directly opposite of mine is vacant. If the police would listen to me, I'd tell them that the Collector popped in for a minute, took his aim at my silhouette behind my curtain, and left before Bradley and I were even off my floor.

Bradley swerves onto the road and flashes his badge so the officer will let us through the roadblock, closed off with yellow tape at the end of the block. As soon as it is safe enough to do so, he picks up speed to escape the blue lights and curious crowds.

A woman's gentle voice sings on the radio, but the volume is only a subtle hum of background noise floating into the dark air between us. He clicks the off button.

"He won't know where you are," Bradley says.

"Are they going to check the roof of that building?"

"Yes." His hand hovers over the gearshift, and I prepare for his touch on my pant leg, but he drops his hand on the knob instead. "They'll take care of it, rest assured. You're going to be safe at my house. You okay?"

"The killer isn't over there. They're wasting their time questioning those people."

"They're making sure no one was harmed. They have no choice but to question the residents."

"I know he's not over there."

"You don't—"

"I *do* know," I say. "He doesn't want to hurt any of them. It's me he wants to hurt."

B radley's house is tucked into a suburb with cul-de-sacs and large trees, with neighbors whose lawns are mowed under the black iron streetlamps. Brown vines slither up the two brick columns on his small porch, a cozy appeal only a wife would suggest. She must've done it all—plant the shrubs along the foundation, place the rug in the living room, set the candles on each corner. The intimate space is too warm for my cold and unpleasant presence.

Throughout his house, empty areas on tables and walls are plain and bare from the removal of what I can only assume were photographs of Bradley with his wife. I run my hand over his bare mantle above the stone fireplace.

"Like what you see?" he says.

I spin away from the mantle, and Bradley stands in the wide-framed entrance to the living room, setting my bag down in the doorway.

"This isn't exactly a city apartment," he says, "but, you know."

"Neither is mine," I say. "This is, like. . . a home."

"If you say so." He puts his hands in his pockets and drifts toward me. "You can make yourself at home. Take my bed." He nods toward the hallway to my right.

"No, the sofa is fine. I don't want to keep you from sleeping in a bed any longer."

"Actually, we'll both be sleeping in a bed."

I take a step back, my neck burning with a red heat that I know will spread to my face.

Tucking a brown wave behind my ear, I look anywhere but his face. "I'm sorry?"

"I've got a guest bedroom," he says, going back to my duffel bag. "It's just that my bed is bigger, and I thought you might want the space."

"Oh."

He picks up my luggage and slowly steps toward me. Looking anywhere but his face, I lock my gaze just past him at a wooden clock hanging on the wall. It's getting close to midnight, close to the killer's hour. Except he's already made his move for the night. Acting reckless.

The only people who know I'm here are Bradley and the Fuller Park police, and the only person who is watching me tonight at midnight is Bradley. For the first time since he's lived with me, it's only the two of us. The Collector is not present. His eyes are not on me.

Bradley cocks his head. "You seem to have misinterpreted what I said."

My breath shutters on the way out, but I account it to the previous events at my apartment tonight. "I didn't."

"Then let's go get in bed, Ms. Knight."

Bradley hums an amused little laugh, then he motions for me to follow him through the hall. I do, but I wish I would have carried my duffel bag because now I have nothing to fumble with.

"I thought you insisted on using my first name, not 'Ms. Knight.'"

"Yeah," he says. "Especially after I met John."

My neck burns again. "I still prefer my last name."

"Well, I prefer Michael. But I guess a lot would have to happen for you to call me that."

In his bedroom, he chucks my bag on top of his pale green comforter—another leftover decoration of their marriage, I assume.

"Right, Jessica?" he asks.

I stumble into the room and twist my arm around the corner bed post, hugging it from the side. How many times has Bradley laid on this mattress and watched his wife get undressed?

Given the way Welch had talked about his divorce, I had imagined at the time that he'd probably had a few women over as distractions. But being in here now—in this room riddled with the touch of a wife whose biggest complaint was that her husband worked too much—makes my skin prickle with the notion that I might actually be the first woman to sleep here since they signed the divorce papers.

Bradley backs away, rubbing his palms together.

"The bathroom is right there, and the towels are by the shower, so make yourself comfortable. It's, uh—" He motions to the bed. "It's safe here, so try to sleep. It's late."

He says *safe* in a tone that irons out any room for me to think otherwise. "I know," I say.

We stand in the silent awareness that even though the killer doesn't know I'm here and though he's made his move for the night, it's clear that he no longer cares where I am or who I'm with or what I'm doing—he's willing to attack any time of day now.

"I'm in the next room over," Bradley says, "so come get me if you need me."

I nod, and he closes the door behind him. All the small windows have the blinds pulled and curtains drawn. One less thing to worry about, though I'm not a fan of being on a ground floor level.

The bed is hard at first when I sit to take my shoes off, but when I pull back the comforter and sink deeper into it, I realize how tired I actually am and how soft this mattress is. I shimmy out of my pants and crawl under the sheets, with no energy to rummage through my bag and pick out pajamas.

Sleeping in Bradley's bed in nothing but my underwear—it makes me feel like an imposter. The woman in this bed should be Bradley's ex-wife, should be a woman he's sleeping with, at the very least. I'm not good enough for this. I'm too grimy with years of filthy affairs to be in a good man's bed.

I roll onto my side, and the sharp scent of his cologne digs through me, alarming my senses that deserve the smell of cigarettes instead.

In the morning, I slip into a pair of lounge pants and go to the kitchen, where I hear Bradley chatting with Lockheed. I comb through my hair before I approach them at the round table. Bradley's sparkling clean windows above the sink show off the bright green azalea shrubs in his neighbor's well-kept yard.

"Morning," Bradley says, sliding an empty white mug to me. I choose to sit in the chair right next to him so I can avoid looking straight at his face, but he stands and walks toward the coffee maker.

Lockheed's posture straightens in the chair across from me. "Good morning."

I try to smile at him, but my mind is elsewhere, my eyes studying the rim of my mug to check for lipstick stains, and there are none, of course. The sunlight streaming through the windows makes every-thing seem brighter, but I can't help noticing all the feminine touches left behind in the divorce. I see a green ivy plant growing along the windowpane behind the kitchen sink and think Bradley must be de-cent at keeping things alive. After all, he's kept me safe all this time. I admit to myself that Bradley has a delicate touch that I don't have, and because of that, there's more life in this house than my apartment has ever seen.

Bradley pours a black stream into my mug, and I take a sip as he sits next to me. "So how long have you been here?" I ask Lockheed.

"Long before the sun came up."

I remember he'd said last night he would stop by after he finished at my apartment, but I must have been knocked out cold and missed most of his visit.

Both men stare down, trying to think of how to proceed, drumming their fingers on the table. I must have walked in on a conversation they didn't want me to hear.

"I, um—I'm sorry if I interrupted something," I say quietly.

Lockheed shuffles in his seat, rearranging his legs underneath the table. "We're having a theoretical discussion about catching the serial killer." It almost sounds comedic—*a theoretical discussion*—so I partially expect Bradley to laugh, but his expression is flat, so serious around Lockheed.

I turn to face him, hoping for an explanation.

"I'm not on board with this," he says, raising a brow at Lockheed. "It's dangerous, but Sergeant thinks otherwise."

Lockheed glares back at him, and neither of them acknowledge me. "My point is exactly that it's getting too dangerous. For you, Jessica, and for others."

"I thought that you thought I was involved with these murders," I interrupt, despite how lost I am in their conversation.

Lockheed slouches over the table, and his coffee breath makes a direct draft to me. "What I thought isn't relevant right now. And neither are you and whatever you were doing with your boss last June." He sighs. "Last night, we found your father's rifle on the roof of the building across the street. Everything was left there. Shells, gun—whatever evidence a killer would usually be careful enough to take with him. Up to this point, the Button Collector has been very meticulous. Last night, he was not concerned with what he must have known we would find. In fact, while he left a big crime scene up on that roof, the one thing he didn't leave were his fingerprints again. He's not so reckless to forget gloves or leave a single boot print. I had my guys ask the residents if they'd seen anyone suspicious, but they only gave descriptions of each other. Most of the people have lived there for at least a couple years. Not one matches the subject description."

I nudge my mug away a bit so the steam won't clog my air; I feel like I'm suffocating under Lockheed's statements.

"Jessica," he says, "I need to ask you again: can you think of anyone at all who might dislike you?"

In my head, I run through faces, names, family, most of which are dead.

"Ben was the only one who concerned me. He was the only person who would maybe get—got—violent with me."

Lockheed flashes a look at Bradley, and he leans back in his chair, arms crossed. "The killer wants one thing and one thing only, and he's not stopping until he gets it."

"I don't understand it," I say.

"We've theorized a few things, but you're right. It's not really understandable unless you're the killer. And you're not, obviously."

I roll my eyes.

"We've profiled him as a psychopath. But he's slowly turning into the opposite—a sociopath. Sloppy, emotional. Nothing like he used to be. It's like he did a complete one-eighty. We've even theorized that it could have been a different subject taunting you these past few months, but ironically, the lack of evidence somewhat proves to us that it is the same person." He slides his coffee mug aside, making room for his hands on the table. "Ms. Knight, you trigger him. You do something to his brain that makes him rash. It's like he wants to kill you but keep you alive and terrorize you at the same time. We've speculated that you perhaps remind him of someone, and that's why he wants you. That maybe you unconsciously did something that altered his life in some way. We've even theorized that he's maybe even in love with you, which causes his obsession."

"Then why would he want me dead?"

"That's the mind of a killer, Ms. Knight. Love can make people do crazy things." Looking into my coffee, my heart leaps into my throat.

I ignore my nausea and nod for him to go on, but Bradley cuts in. "He's too rash anymore. Jessica, he's been clean since he started, only taking out people he's intended on. But last night was an example of his impulsiveness, of how he's not afraid he might take other people's lives while he's attempting to take yours. He's getting careless."

"What we're hypothesizing," Lockheed says, "is the idea of using you, his target, to catch him. The killer is desperate."

Suddenly, it makes sense. They want to use me as bait. "So you don't think I'm secretly involved anymore?"

He blinks. "Everything is up for debate right now. Some things more than others, and what I'm telling you now is more important to focus on."

I sip my coffee, holding the warm liquid in my mouth and then swallowing to try and slow my panic from seeping into my voice.

"How do you mean you want to use me?"

Bradley taps his fingers on the table again, bouncing his eyes between me and Lockheed.

Finally, he says, "Sergeant wants to outsmart the killer." I turn to Lockheed, waiting for him to continue.

"Do you feel comfortable with a set-up, Ms. Knight?" he says.

"You mean like the one I did in the alley the night Ben shot at me?" Neither of them answer.

"Last time I tried setting up the killer, I was called insane and suicidal. And now you want me to do that all over again because *you* deem it as appropriate now?"

"Ms. Knight—"

"Jessica," Bradley says, "I brought that up to him already. Listen, I told him I don't like the idea."

"I almost got killed last time."

Lockheed leans in again, forcing his opinion to the center of the table. "But last night you almost got killed. Again." His voice tightens and lowers. "If we don't use you as a ploy, then you're very likely going to be murdered. Probably very soon, at that. This is the only plan I can pitch to reduce your chances of being taken out by the Button Collector, Ms. Knight. So you and Detective Michael Bradley are getting on board with this or you're probably going to end up bleeding to death under a knife. Your choice."

Bradley sits back, and I close my mouth, considering the gravity of Lockheed's lecture. Threat, rather.

"We'll plan here at Bradley's starting on Monday if the pitch is well received at our meeting this afternoon. I'll bring a few officers with me next time. Everything settled?"

Bradley says, "Yes, sir."

"Good." He stands. "Thank you for the coffee, Bradley. Ms. Knight, I'll be back after the weekend is over."

Keep your head low, I wait for him to say. But he leaves the kitchen without saying anything, and a moment later, the front door clicks shut. The ivy plant above the sink blows in his hurried aftermath.

Bradley takes a large swallow of coffee, tilting it up high to drink the last bit, then sets the empty mug on the table.

"He pisses me off too."

Dr. Smith expects me to talk more, but there's nothing left to say.

It is her professional opinion that I'm only imagining the Collector is my stalker, a response to the entire situation.

"Have you cut yourself in the past, Jessica?" Dr. Smith asks at my latest appointment. Lockheed must have finally reported my scar to her, given her some material to work through with me.

"That was an accident. A misunderstanding."

"I'm sure that's what it feels like," she says. "I waited for you to bring it up in our sessions these past few weeks, but you kept it to yourself. Why is that?"

I watch the view out her window, the same spot I always daze during our meetings, but this time I almost anticipate a bullet flying through it and into my brain.

"Because I was paranoid, I kept a knife under my pillow, and it cut me one night."

"Did you feel any relief from that?"

Ugh. I shake my head and close my eyes to suppress my frustration.

"Even if it were an accident, Jessica, do you feel the need to harm yourself?"

"No."

"The sergeant contacted me to inform me that you have been deemed the killer's target. Without giving me much information for the sake of the active investigation, he did tell me that you've been fearful over this fact."

"Yeah."

"Do you feel peace with the fact that the individual is no longer after your family? Or only more afraid?"

Bradley tells me to appease Dr. Smith, make her feel like she's doing her job because I can't tell her the whole truth anymore. The media doesn't know the truth, and Lockheed has demanded that our—my—personal information and plans for me are to be shared only at Bradley's table. It would be helpful if I had some insight into just how much she knows about this case. This whole counseling thing—it's just a charade. I should end these sessions right now.

"Do you perhaps feel forgotten, Jessica, by the killer? The desire to cut yourself for attention is something many people struggle with, especially people in your situation."

Situation.

"Is attention something you've missed?" she asks.

So she doesn't know about the killer's attempt on my life last week. All she knows is what the media has been telling her—that the Button Collector has been quiet these past several weeks.

"I feel normal again," I lie. I blow an annoyed puff of air out of my mouth.

"I'd say that despite these circumstances, you're progressing in your

217

healing process. But let me ask you this: have you had less of a desire to harm yourself since the incident in the alleyway?"

"That wasn't the killer, though."

"That's my point," she says. "There were two people in the beginning. Now, one is gone and the other seems less interested in you. Perhaps there's a part of you that misses the attention. After that incident in the alleyway, did you briefly feel less of a desire to harm yourself?"

I play daft, disguised under a mask of sarcasm. "Yes. Less of a desire. I know the Collector's always watching. And if he's watching me, then I know I won't have to be the one to do the harming."

The clock behind her shows I have only five minutes left in my session, so I grab my jacket and stand to leave, wondering just how much or how little of my *situation* will get back to her when this is all over.

"See you next time, if I'm alive."

The weekend drags through a temperature drop and a rainstorm, keeping Bradley and me stuck inside. He spent Sunday afternoon and evening in his garage, working under the hood of an old car. Despite his multiple invitations to join him out there, I declined. I was happy to have some distance so I wouldn't have to keep pretending to be comfortable in his house, though I would have actually enjoyed spending hours watching Bradley work and talk about something other than my case.

He knocks on the door of my room tonight as I'm unmaking my— his—bed. "I'm sorry I was busy all day," he says. "It's Sunday, after all. Should've kept you company."

"Don't apologize, Bradley. I'm fine in here."

He leans on the wall and crosses his arms over his chest, placing one ankle over the other. "You've been quiet for a while. You okay?"

"I'm tired, mostly," I say, and he steps in, standing at the foot of the bed.

"I spoke with Lockheed a little bit today."

"You talked about me to him?"

"Yes."

I sit on the edge of the bed and rub my face, covering my eyes that burn to cry. "This doesn't make any sense."

I hear Bradley's socks patter toward me, and he sits at my side. "I know."

"I've just. . . I've never done anything that would warrant this."

"It won't last very much longer," he says. "We're working hard on this."

I don't look at him because if I do, he might draw the tears right out of me, so I stand and go to the bathroom door, hoping he will just leave me alone. Resting my head on the door jamb, I rub the back of my neck, trying to soothe a crick that formed there last night.

"I need to sleep," I say.

His gaze stays on me, a beam straight through the compressing silence. I fumble with the sleeve of my night shirt and wait for him to take the hint.

"Goodnight," he tells me and offers a sad smile, leaving and closing the door behind him.

I dive into bed and flick off the lamp.

Monday night, the doorbell rings. Bradley lets Lockheed and three male officers inside, all of whom nod to Bradley, all out of uniform and dressed in jeans and a jacket. They scan me as Bradley guides them into the kitchen. Standing next to Bradley, they're all three an obvious size smaller than he is.

When I hear the chairs start to scoot on the floor in the kitchen and everyone is settled, I try to sneak in without a sound.

The round table is circled shoulder to shoulder with men, so I make my way behind Bradley, but before their chattering begins, Lockheed glances up at me.

"Ms. Knight," he says, "we'll call you in when we're ready."

I flush a little; each of them trains their eyes on me. Bradley turns around and gives me a little wink.

"Just a minute," he whispers.

Oh, I think, plain and simple, annoyed as I walk to my bedroom—annoyed he had me leave rather than having me stay and listen to him defend me.

Instead of going to my room, I glide straight into the guest bedroom where Bradley's been sleeping. The bed is made perfectly. Mine I just throw together in the mornings. A rectangle mirror on the wall reflects me. No buttons on my clothes. My brunette bun has fallen low, and my jeans sag with age, and my black and gold college sweatshirt keeps me warm in the room where I imagine Bradley must've spent most of his nights during his divorce.

The silence here is harsher than in my room. These walls loom down, demanding a certain esteem for being the room that houses guests. Does Bradley feel like a guest in his own home? When he falls on this small bed every night once I've gone to sleep, I wonder if he feels relieved of his duty, of the ultimate stretch of protection.

I run my hand over his comforter just like I did with his mantel the first night I was here, and I feel sorry that he had been sleeping on my sofa more than in his own home.

Regret replaces my pity; I should have offered him the privacy of my room back when he was staying with me. He wouldn't have taken it, wouldn't have put me in the danger of sleeping by the front door and window. But I should have at least asked.

Dr. Smith's words float back to me: *You're living with a man whose job is to do all he can to keep you safe. A man who has a duty to protect you. It's only natural for you to feel something for him.*

On his nightstand, a trivial wooden box rests in a thin film of dust. Perched in the dust is a framed picture of Bradley shaking Lockheed's hand at some sort of ceremony and a skinny candle, both established in what looks to be their unmoving resting places.

I study the photo for a moment then steal up the box.

The lid twists off with a slight tug, and inside, a golden band twinkles with a layer of a final polish. I remember back to the first time I met Bradley in Lockheed's office, and he wasn't wearing a wedding ring. I'd thought it was strange at the time that a man his age isn't married, but he *was* married once, and it seems that maybe in a life before this investigation, being a husband would be right for him. Bradley embodies the protection every wife would want. Why would his wife choose to leave? So what if he prioritized his work?

In case of leaving a fingerprint, I close the lid and set the box back where it was, in its humble shade of the picture frame.

A burst of quick laughter bellows from the kitchen—heavy, male sneers—and one of the officers mutters something that includes Bradley's first name.

Michael.

Mulling over the sound of it in my head, I startle when he calls for me. "Jessica?"

I shoot into the hallway, and he meets me half-way to walk me into the kitchen. Like he had in Lockheed's office a couple weeks ago, he touches my lower back to guide me into the uncomfortable situation.

Bradley lets me sit in his chair and then stands behind me. He rests his hand on the back of my chair, and his fingers press against me. I expect him to move away, but when he doesn't, I lean my back against his touch.

Lockheed introduces me to the three men, whose names I'll choose to forget when this is over.

"Ms. Knight," Lockheed says, "these men are well acquainted with you and your situation."

"Hi," I mutter, shy like a child.

"Tonight is about discussing our outline and the dangers of this project, which we've already talked about back at the station over the weekend."

Bradley squeezes my shoulder, and in his fast release, I stiffen where he touched me. I recall his words only after he's said them: "And how to protect you against those dangers."

"Okay," I say.

"We're also considering all of our options," says Lockheed.

A flutter of hope lifts inside me, but before I can ask if there truly are more options, Bradley says, "We're trying to pin when and where to do this and pull it off successfully."

He winces through his teeth the moment he says *pull it off*. They all choose to ignore the implications of what he said.

"What exactly are we trying to pull off? I mean, I haven't been given any ideas or. . . or plans," I stammer.

"If the Button Collector really does keep tabs on you," Lockheed says, "then we're going to have you go to a park."

"A park?"

"He might not always be watching you, but we do know he knows enough about you to pin your location quite frequently."

Lockheed rearranges in his seat.

"When he shot at you, he left the rifle, so if he doesn't have another firearm, he'll have no choice but to get up close and personal with you this time."

With a needle.

The skinny officer with eyes sunken into his skull agrees with Lockheed. "Yes," the officer says, "but we'll be close to you on rooftops and have our sights on you and the killer the entire time."

"We'll do this in Winston Park. It closes at ten p.m., so you'll go in a few hours later, around one," Lockheed says.

"What else?" I ask. "What do I do exactly?"

They each shuffle in their seats, nonverbally deciding who should continue the conversation. Bradley wanders to the other side of the table to face me and Lockheed.

"The killer might be familiar with me and Sergeant by now," he says, "so we'll be out of sight and in your ear for the whole thing. We're sending Foreman to the park early to hide there, waiting for you to arrive."

He motions to the skinny officer.

"So he's going to be above you."

"Above me?" I say. "Wait, so you—you want me in the park to, like, lure the killer?"

Foreman points his thin finger upward, bypassing my question. "I'll be in a tree, armed in case anything might happen."

"Just one person in a tree? What tree? There're a million trees in the park."

Lockheed holds up a hand to shush me. "Those are details we'll discuss the day of."

"Also," Bradley says, "like we said, the killer is familiar with this—with you—by now, so at first, we were concerned that he might know this thing is a set up. So we're having you carry a bottle of wine with you to the park. Stumbling a little."

"You want me to act drunk?"

"Only so he'll make the assumption that you don't know what you're doing, where you're going. You get the idea. He might think you're just crazy enough to try to get yourself killed."

Lockheed's torso hiccups, and he catches me staring. "Again," he says. He waves away his amusement and meets the severity of our mood again.

"We've made the FBI aware that we're close to catching this guy," he says, "but we left out details about our plan. CPD have worked closely with them in the past, so we will handle the arrest and then hand over the suspect."

I look up to Bradley. "How many of us will be there?" I ask.

Lockheed answers me, though. "You, the five of us" —he points to Bradley and his three officers— "and a few more. We're going to have CPD surrounding the area and have other neighborhood stations on standby for our regular calls. But we'll be the ones in your ear."

"That seems a bit shy," I blab a little too loudly. "Just a handful of you guys behind this operation? On a roof?"

"We can't be overt, Ms. Knight," says one of the officers. He's young, has a mustache like Sergeant's.

"He's right," Lockheed says. "If the media makes any sort of discovery at all, you'll be in more danger than before. Dozens of Chicago PD officers are going to be present in the area to make the arrest and notify the FBI. You will be well protected. Okay? We've talked about this."

He asks me as though I've not only gone insane but lost my memory, as well.

"It'll all come together, Ms. Knight. I know it sounds confusing now, but it'll all be under control."

"When?" I say.

"A few weeks."

The three officers nod in agreement.

"There's a lot to plan. Bradley," Lockheed says, "I'm sure it's fine if we keep meeting here on Monday nights?"

"Of course." The warm, yellow hue of light from above the sink casts a homey radiance on Bradley. He must've felt so uncomfortable in my cold apartment with no sprawling ivy or stone fireplaces.

Lockheed turns his attention to me. "We'll meet once a week to keep you updated and content until we're ready."

"Okay."

"Do you have any questions?"

Bradley tilts his head and crosses his arms, and I stare at him for longer than I intend. An eagerness buds low in my belly for Lockheed and his team to leave. For the past week, I've been alone with Bradley, and the idea of that brings me a sense of comfort. I understand, now, why his wife wanted him home more.

Lockheed's mustache moves up and down with the scrunch of his nose, but I look down.

My only question is one he cannot answer: At what point will I tire of living and feed myself to the predator?

Week by week, they keep coming, making a circle around the table, and it's always the same. Bradley gives them coffee, and Foreman, the skinny officer, always avoids eye contact. They speak privately first, then make a slot for me to join them.

On the fourth Monday, I fall asleep on the sofa when the sunset casts neon orange streaks on the walls, and I wake up to a dim room and under a blanket I didn't have when I closed my eyes.

Stretching out, my whimper calls Bradley's attention to the side of the sofa.

"Good timing," he says. "I would've taken you to your bed, but someone new is coming over tonight."

I freeze under the weight of his words. A pinch forms in my chest when I think about how he would've transferred me to my room.

"Who's coming?"

A *ding dong* rings overhead, and he says, "They're here."

I roll up the blanket and stand, but before Bradley swings the door open, I whiz into the kitchen and steal my seat. From here, the voices of all those previous Monday night meetings flood into the room—

Lockheed and the other officers, Foreman and Neal and whoever else.

But I'll forget about them when it's over. I'll choose to forget everyone. Everyone.

A stealthy but familiar voice mutters from beyond the kitchen walls, awakening my memories of the safehouse, of my cold, upstairs bedroom, of Ben's dead weight falling over me, but mostly of Welch's lifeless legs protruding out from the living room.

Susan Welch's black shoes click all the way up to the opposite side of the table.

Her smile widens, revealing her coffee-tinted molars, and she puts both hands on the back of a chair, bearing her weight down on it. She ticks her tongue in my direction and assesses me from waist to hairline.

"Good to see ya, Jessica. Looking better than the last time I saw you." She pulls out the chair and slouches back in it.

"I—I could say the same."

"Looks like you were onto something when you tried getting yourself killed in the alley that night. Remember our first date?"

"They hated that I did that."

"Yeah, and look at 'em now. They're stealing your tactic." She smiles at me as if we are part of an inside joke.

Bradley and the four others pile into the kitchen all at once. A clattering of squealing chairs is followed by Bradley's welcoming of Welch to our table.

She cackles, and I notice for the first time there is a brown mole on her cheek. "Looks more like a night of poker than an investigation."

Lockheed and his officers laugh along, but Bradley gives me a close-lipped smile and waits with me for the moment to end.

"Jessica," he says, "Sergeant felt that since Officer Welch was familiar with the case, she should be invited to aid in our strategy. She's another set of well-informed, well-trained eyes and ears, and it's good to have Chicago Police Violent Crimes involved."

The entire table is listening, but I only talk to Bradley. "I thought she couldn't since she was injured."

"That was pardoned upon Sergeant's request."

Lockheed gets comfortable in his seat, and the seams of his pants rubbing together makes an irritating noise from under the table. "She'll provide good insight. Would you two like a moment to catch up?"

"No," I say.

"Fine," Lockheed says. "Before we begin, Ms. Knight, do you have any questions? Susan?"

She opens her mouth, and a deep, firm laugh spills out. "You tell me when and where, Sarge, and I'll be ready."

By the shallow details of their conversation tonight, I can tell it's our last Monday night meeting. I yearn to know what evening they'll choose to use me as a ploy, but I don't dare ask.

Thirty minutes in, Welch slaps her hand on the table. "I'm going outside for a smoke." She had never smoked at the safehouse or even walked outside when we stayed there together. How had I missed that she was a smoker? Granted, I had hardly left my bedroom.

I search the faces around me for a hint of surprise, but each of them ignores her statement.

"Jessica," she says, standing up, "join me. We'll have a nice chat."

I follow her out Bradley's front door, and she pulls out a pack of cigarettes from her back pocket.

"I didn't know you smoke," I say.

"Used to smoke. I quit ten years ago, then you almost got me killed by some psychopath ex-boyfriend, and I thought, 'God, I'd do anything for a cigarette.' And I'm gonna die someday, anyway, right? You should know that better than anyone." Welch laughs at her own joke. I fail to see the humor in it.

The mid-spring night still carries a bitter chill on its breeze, so I back closer to the door to seek the house's heat. She lights the cigarette, and the smell infused with the night air reminds me of John's easy knock on my door that would lead us to a night on my sofa or mattress.

"I didn't expect you'd be back on the case," I say, inhaling the smoke. A lungful of John. A lungful of all the weeks it's been since we've spoken. I haven't reached out to him other than to say I'd be absent from work due to the case; I want him to spend those last days with Mary.

"Screw the rules, Jessica. If people didn't break them, I'd be out of a job." She takes a drag and tilts back her head, blowing up a straight line of white. "So Bradley was living with you." Welch turns to me. "Now you're living with him. How's that? Not too much fun, I hope." She smirks, and I back closer to the door.

"What do you mean?"

"Well, Jessica, the man's wife left him not long ago, and you wouldn't want to go breaking his heart, would you?"

"I'm not doing that. Neither is he."

"Oh," she says, "so it's just sex, then?"

My gut goes hollow, and a faint numbness flushes down my arms. "What?"

She flicks her ashes onto the brick floor of the porch and muses in a bold laugh. "I'm messing with you, Jess. Now, go inside. I'd like to be alone with my bad habit."

The plan is simple, really. My last night at Bradley's will be Thursday, and on Friday morning, I'll wake up and move back into my apartment. Stay there for the weekend so the killer will find me, seek me out, and reclaim his hold on me again. He will re-familiarize himself with me, noting the new changes in our routine. Bradley's patrol car will be outside the entire time, just like it used to be, but with a substitute driver. And on Monday night—the least busy night of all in the city—I'll walk to Winston Park just near my block, "sneaking" past the squad car right around one in the morning.

If I'm right—as it seems now to Lockheed—and the Button Collector is watching me, he will follow me to the park.

They don't know how he will come at me. They only know that he will.

And I'll walk while Bradley and Lockheed and Foreman and Welch are all in my ear.

While they're all waiting for something to happen, they will be in position on surrounding rooftops with sniper rifles ready. Foreman will be perched in a tree above the spot where I am supposed to stand alone and wait. One other officer and another sergeant from CPVC will snipe from the other side of the street.

Where the four sidewalks come together from north, south, east, and west, I'll have five scopes watching me, five guns aimed, ready to rain down bullets on the center of the park.

I'd asked Lockheed, "What if he isn't watching me this time? How can we be certain he's going to be there?"

Lockheed compared the Collector to Ben and how he knew the exact moment I snuck out of my apartment that night so many weeks ago. If Ben could figure out where I was, then the killer would be able to do it too. I tried to harp on all my questions about Ben, but all Lockheed could say each time was, "We're going to look into that once we nail the real killer."

Thursday night, I pack my bags, but realize that not all my possessions I brought with me are where I'd intended on keeping them. I've made myself at home here, enough so that the cup where I store my toothbrush has developed a ring of bathroom grime on Bradley's counter, and my clothes are strewn about his bedroom, taking up space in all his drawers. I'd moved in here with the thought that I'd keep everything stowed in my bag, but as the weeks passed by, that line I didn't want to cross had blurred a little. Some of my panties are in the hamper, mixed right in with Bradley's clothes. We had decided the second week that it didn't make much sense to do separate loads of laundry, so I've been helping him wash and fold since then. With a reluctant hand, I fish out my things and bundle them into my suitcase that I've kept stored under Bradley's bed.

It's muscle memory, the way I know exactly what knobs to pull and what drawers hold what. I loathe myself for making a home here over the past six weeks. I loathe, even more, the fact that I have to go home. My routine with Bradley has become, well, *cozy*. I've watched the ivy over his sink grow several inches down the windowsill and liked the thought of watering it myself each morning if Bradley was ever allowed to leave me alone and go back to work.

The lamp on the nightstand sets a weak glow in the room, causing pale shadows to dance around, bouncing off the furniture, projecting onto the walls. My body's shadow lies motionless on the rug at my feet, and I wonder what it must feel like to disappear in the night.

When I look up, Bradley is standing at the corner of the bed. "Oh, I didn't hear you come in."

"I was going to see if you needed help packing, but I see you're almost through."

He wanders to the other side of me and sits on the edge of the mattress, crossing his feet, his calf resting against mine. I angle away to zip my suitcase, though I still have to pack the shampoo and conditioner that Bradley bought me when I moved in.

"There should be no traces in your apartment of the shooting. We took care of all that for you."

"I'm not afraid of going back," I say, but he knows that's the exact opposite of the truth.

"You shouldn't be." He tilts over so that he's able to glance up at me, and I have no choice but to look down upon him. "I'll be in my car up until the night of."

His five o'clock shadow is back, dusting his jawline with a dirty blond tint. It crawls down his neck then dissolves when it reaches his Adam's apple. Up close, a small scar on his bottom lip is barely visible, but I tear my eyes away only to land on his forest green stare that I don't believe ever left my face.

"Just outside your window," he adds.

A feeble vulnerability exposes itself in Bradley's tired grin. There one second, gone the next as I try to find his scar again.

He takes in a breath like he wants to speak, and I hold mine and wait to hear him say something, but we both ignore the emptiness of the moment that needs to be filled.

"Is there something you want to say?" I ask quietly.

"Is there something you need to hear from me, Jessica?"

I mean to say it louder, but my words come out in a crackling whisper: "Are you expecting a thank you?"

His eyes don't waver. "Not unless you think I deserve one."

I don't answer.

"It's your last night here. Just thought you'd want to do something different. Maybe watch a movie of your choice," he says.

I break away from the moment and set my suitcase on the floor. He stays against the bed, watching me.

"I want to take a shower," I say. The empty air fills.

In the bathroom, the door doesn't quite click shut, leaving open an inch gap. I turn my back to it, twist the shower knob, and give in to a small shiver of cool air from the bedroom that seeps through the crack and onto my skin.

I slide my shirt over my head and drop it to the tile floor. My bra snaps off, spreading over my feet in full length, so I nudge it away and pull down my jeans. I step out of them and stand in nothing but my panties, facing the shower. A plume of steam rises from behind the glass shower door, and it splashes onto the mirror that reflects my profile.

I look at my body. I don't have many close girlfriends, so I can only compare myself to the girls I see on television, but even I know that those women aren't real.

In the mirror, my thighs swell beneath my bottom and come together at my crotch. Both legs start to slim toward my knees and curve into my small calves. Nothing pudges behind my white panties, but I suck in my stomach anyway, and the illusion makes my C-cup breasts look a little bit bigger.

Thoughts of Bradley's wife creep into my mind, and I shy away from the mirror when I wonder how many times she'd gotten naked right here where I stand. How many times had Bradley come up behind her and scooped her into the shower?

I take down my ponytail and let my hair drape mid-way down my back. Then I move out of the view of the crack in the door and slip my panties down, tossing them away with my toes.

The water burns my neck, but I wait for the sting to go away and listen to the torrent hitting the shower floor. I keep my hair dry. In case. Because I don't like how I look when it is wet. Brushing it off my shoulders, I lather soap under my armpits and every other crease on my body before rinsing it all away.

I whisper to the killer one last time, but he can't see me in this humid corner of a house he's never followed me to. My words are overtaken by the water: *Why do you want me?*

I close my eyes and hear the pull of the shower door opening, feel the escape of the steam and the chill of the air blowing in, feel two heavy hands rest on my upper arms.

Last month, I would have screamed. I would have fought. I would have run away. I would have known it was the killer trying to sew me silent, and that person inside of me who still craves to live—she would have flinched between that firm hold. But tonight, she's ready to surrender.

I turn around and don't have time to take him in before he thrusts me through the stream of water and against the cold wall, pushing himself against me. The skin of our abdomens and our chests stick together, dry and wet. He is strong against me, steady.

Bradley puts his face on mine, and I inhale the breath he lets out. The scruff of his day-old beard rubs against my cheek, and I enjoy the burning sensation it creates as I frantically maneuver until I've reached his lips. He bears down on me with each kiss but strings his fingers up my neck to cup my head and keep me tilted upward. I brace myself around his torso and find the curve of his waist, and I glide my hands up his muscled back. My ankle twists around his leg, and he draws nearer.

A light stream of water runs down his nose and cuts in two at our lips. "Bradley."

I'd spoken through a kiss that was thick with his lips and warm from his tongue. He stays pressed against me, and I wrap my arms around him. The water on his dark blond hair drips down from his brow and on to my collarbone. We watch it descend between my breasts and disappear where my bellybutton meets the space just above his groin.

Bradley moves his grip back down my neck and over my chest, then rests his hands in the bend of my waist.

He says onto my lips, "Call me Michael."

When I wake up in the light of early morning, we aren't holding each other, and I'm not on his chest or resting my head on his arm. He's on his side, still sleeping, but he is facing my direction, and I try not to wake him as I roll onto my back. His presence is thick in this master bedroom, where just hours ago, there was a bareness that I'd lived in for weeks under this ceiling. He was Bradley then, and last night, everything changed.

Throwing the covers off me, I'm surprised at the sight of my naked body. Before Michael, it had never been touched all over, treated as though it's soft and fragile. Men have moved fast on top of me, here for a few minutes and out the door within the hour. Even John comes and goes when he pleases, but I let him, and I do the same thing. But Michael had touched me and listened for my breath, kissed me, and let me kiss him back. He hadn't offered to go back to his bed; instead, he leaned over me for what felt like all night, twisting my hair in loose curls around his fingers and coming down to meet my lips every few seconds. We didn't speak. Not once after I'd called him by his first name. In the dark when he was moving on top of me, I couldn't see him and he couldn't see me, but neither of us cared. We'd spent hours with his hand in my hair, with him stroking my face, and with my palm stroking his arm. Glints of light kept flickering in his eyes, reminding me whenever I lost his gaze that he was right where he wanted to be. I'd fallen asleep on top of him; I woke up on the other side of the bed.

Still facing me, Bradley—*Michael*—sleeps, but even unconscious, he wears the guarded look that I saw the first day I met him in Lockheed's office.

I pick up my pile of clothes on the bathroom floor and set it on the counter then step into my jeans and sweatshirt. I'll throw the rest of my things in my suitcase once Michael is awake.

When I'd said his name last night, I repeated it just to taste it. I liked how authentic it felt—a new flavor, a new side of the man I've lived with for months. For the past several months, I'd felt so close to death that I never felt alive. This morning, things feel alive. Better.

In the kitchen, I brew us a pot of coffee, hoping I'll be busy with a bowl of cereal when he walks in so I won't have to make small talk.

But he comes in just as I am rinsing the bowl and going back to the table to finish my coffee.

"Good morning," he says. A smile plays on his lips, and I can see that scar on his bottom lip perfectly now, and I can feel the ghost of it between my teeth and on my neck and trailing down my belly. His shirt is off, revealing how much of him I'd missed in the shower and in the dark last night. I could only feel the clefts where his muscles swelled and dipped. Seeing them gets my heart racing.

His sweatpants hang low on his hips, but I pull my eyes back up to his as he walks past me to pour himself a cup of coffee.

"Morning," I say.

With his back to me, I make out the shadows on his back that lead down to his sweatpants.

"You're all packed?" he asks, turning to face me.

"Not quite."

He sits in the chair beside me.

"I still have to pack my things from the—" *Shower.*

Michael takes a sip out of his mug and smirks into it, and I smile a little too. The morning after. . . is he Bradley again or is he still Michael?

"Would you like a hand?" he asks.

I bring my mug to my chest. "I think I can manage."

Once all the coffee is gone, I wheel my stuffed suitcase to the front door. The keys jingle as he opens the door for me. I reach for my suitcase, glancing around the living room one last time before I head out, then he locks up behind me.

"You act like it's the last time you'll ever be here. You never know."

I look up at him, wondering what might happen next, but he only smiles, double checks the lock, and walks us to his car. As we drive away, I don't look back. I would like to believe I'll be back.

The ride is silent, a different noiseless half-hour than last night. This time, it calls for something. An explanation.

The radio takes the place of anything helpful either of us could say, and for the first time in months, I can unwind with a little relief that Michael Bradley won't be following me to my apartment. I like us better together in his house. In his home. My apartment isn't the right place to grow a budding relationship, or whatever last night was.

He'll be just outside my window.

But he does come in to help me unload, explaining that the officer who stayed here in my absence has been called to leave. Inside, I drop my suitcase right there in the living room because seeing my clothes balled up on my bed might jar a memory that's too familiar. Still too tempting. Bradley hovers by the dining table, and I linger by the sofa, and I try to speak but he interrupts me by accident. He goes first.

"I was just going to say that I won't be seeing you for a few days."

"Right. He can't know you're here." The word *he* peels up a new emotion—the killer is about to be killed.

"I'll see you in three days. Lockheed will take it from there."

"Four days, if you include the rest of today."

We've never smiled right at each other with any sort of intention, but today, we both stand there just feet apart and leave each other with a slight grin.

He bobs his head and lets himself out. And I don't lock the door in case he chooses to come back inside.

Michael Bradley sits out there for three days, not including the day he dropped me off at my apartment, taking two shifts a day and having Officer Foreman take his place for the morning shift. When Foreman is out there, I keep the curtains shut. The windows on his patrol car are tinted darker than on Bradley's, and he never gets out of the car once, probably because Lockheed is sensitive about the Collector putting a face to a new officer on patrol.

The three days that I'm alone in my apartment are quiet, but there's a blaring silence that the Button Collector brings. He comes and goes. It's a subtle disturbance during the day when I stop what I'm doing in the kitchen and run to lock my door and close the curtains. Sometimes, to hide from the killer, I descend into a bath of hot water and wait until I'm certain he's gone—always around seven in the evening. Both nights before I go to sleep, I peek out the window and let Michael see me. From up here, he doesn't look like Michael, though. He's the same Bradley who used to sit down there all night and let himself into my apartment without my permission whenever he felt like it.

I've kept myself occupied by a bottle of my darkest wine. That, along with coffee, curtains, and baths.

My phone rings while I'm cooking in the kitchen. It is a number I don't recognize, but it says, *Wisconsin, USA.*

I answer the call.

"Jessica Knight?" a female voice says.

"Yes?"

"This is the Jones Creek Psychiatric Unit. We're calling per request of our resident Deborah Wilson, who would like to speak with you."

The sound of her name fleshes out a series of memories from the Spooner police station. Deborah comes to the phone as I say, "Sure. That's fine."

"Jessica? Jessica, is that you?"

"Yeah, Deb, it's me."

"Jess, these people are crazy. They don't believe anything I say about the killer."

"I think you're just feeling overwhelmed, Aunt Deborah. They're just trying to take care of you."

"No, they're after me. They think I'm crazy, and *I'm* the one who was attacked by a maniac. These people don't believe anything. They don't believe me. Everything I tell them, they ignore because they don't listen to the people in here, Jessica. I don't belong here. I've got to get out of here. They're the crazy ones. I'm telling the truth about h—"

I hang up on her. I hate to do it, but I can't listen to her anymore. I close my eyes and try to forget that she ever called.

Monday afternoon, Bradley texts me to say he's going to meet me at the police department, so I hail a cab to the police station as he drives away in his patrol car. I have my driver take me in the direction of my office to send the killer a message: *Just going to work. I'll be home in a little while.*

At Fuller Park, Lockheed, Foreman, Welch, and Bradley are there to hook an earpiece onto me. They practice a few times to make sure it works seamlessly, then they fit me for a bullet-proof vest.

My knees buckle under the weight of it as Welch straps it around my ribcage. "You good, Jess?"

"Is there a lighter vest?" I try to hold my breath when I say it so she won't smell the full bottle of wine I have already downed to calm my nerves, but her height undermines my efforts.

She laughs, and a scent of liquor sifts past my nose. At first, I mistake it as my own, but it comes from up high.

"No." Welch slaps my chest. "This feel fine?" Suppose the day calls for a drink for both parties.

"Yeah. And you smell like booze," I say.

"Well, you smell like wine."

"I was trying to calm my nerves."

"So was I. You're not the only one who got attacked by Ben and was left with PTSD. Had to ease my memory somehow."

I touch the speaker in my ear and reach for the microphone on my sternum, but the dense vest blocks most of it. I sway a little on my feet but catch myself before Welch notices. Anyway, they want me stumbling.

"Will you be able to always hear me?"

Welch turns away from me to check her own gear on her body. "No need to be scared, Jessica. Especially now that you've eased your memory too." She smiles at me. "There are seven of us and only one of him, not to mention all our back-up on call."

"How are you going to make it look like I'm not wearing this?" I pull at the thick edges of the vest.

"A coat. It'll be fifty degrees outside; what'd you think?"

She leads me to a room with dark walls and a high ceiling, a room I've never entered. Lockheed, Foreman, and the other men look down at a wide sheet of paper on the table, but Michael—Bradley—watches me walk in behind Welch. I must not think of him as Michael today.

"Ms. Knight," Lockheed says, "come over here."

All I see is Michael disguised as Bradley, dressed in all black with straps along his chest and shoulders for handguns. His eyes linger on mine as Welch leads me between Foreman and Lockheed. Sergeant spreads his hand over the page. "This is for you. It's a map of the park."

"I don't need a map. I've been there before," I say. Bradley looks from me to Lockheed.

He goes on without acknowledging I have said anything. "You'll come in here. We're going to have Foreman here, perched in this tree. There's a plaque at the base, so you'll recognize it. The closer you get to this tree after you've exposed yourself in the center of the park, the safer you'll be."

As Lockheed's pointing all over the page, I peek up at Bradley standing opposite of me. He's following Lockheed's finger along the map. The radios on everyone's hips start to fill the room with fuzzy, short sentences that I can't make out, but they turn them down until they're almost muted.

"Sorry," Foreman says to me. "The rest of CPD and CPVC is getting ready." I catch a note of fear in his voice. Maybe I'm just too tipsy.

"Now," Sergeant says, pausing, "Ms. Knight, remember—the killer is psychopath. He's obsessed and started to encompass sociopathic tendencies. Since you were gone for a few weeks and he didn't know where you were, he probably went even crazier. And because he's so anxious to get to you and control your fear, we are counting on the fact that he knows you've been back in your apartment for three days."

When I don't speak, Bradley says, "That's just how psychopaths work, Jessica. They calculate and manipulate. This guy is smart, and you're his target, so we can assume he's been waiting for you to come back for all those weeks you were with me."

A current of heat washes over my face, and he looks down. "Okay," I say.

Lockheed's low voice sucks me back into the plan. "So we're going to have eyes on you from all directions. No one should be in the park at one in the morning. It closes at ten, and that park is deserted, anyway. And we'll have men on the ground ready to make an arrest. As soon as we've got him, he's going in cuffs and into the FBI's custody."

"How does that work?" I ask. "I mean, you're going to shoot him but not kill him, and then arrest him? How do you do that?"

"The FBI is expecting some news from Chicago PD tonight. We are expecting Foreman to alert us the moment he lays eyes on the killer, and our officers will swarm the place. We'd shoot him only if we had to, and only to detain him, not kill him. The plan will change if you're attacked. Then we will do whatever it takes to take him down. But once he's down, we will take him to CPD downtown to stay in custody overnight before we fly him to Quantico. The FBI would also request to see you shortly after the arrest, so that's something you might want to be prepared for this week."

"Don't think about that," Bradley interjects. His eyes draw me in, dense with what they've seen, and they hold me in that secret place that only he and I know of. I hope mine reflect the same place. "You just focus on the here and now." He nods to me, slowly, and I know he knows I understand.

"But Ms. Knight," Lockheed says.

I tilt back because his mustache is only inches from my face. "You do exactly as I say when I say it."

"What if you kill him? Then what?"

Welch's heavy hand lands on my shoulder. "Killing anybody is always our last resort, but Jess, protecting you and taking him down is our priority. You have to trust us."

"Shouldn't we have practiced?" I ask, and Bradley pulls the paper toward him.

"No," he says. "There's no practice for something like this."

Welch circles around to Bradley and says, "Plus, we don't need practice. All we need is for you to stumble into a park late at night and present yourself to the killer." She crosses her arms and gives me a wink that only I can see. "Nothing you haven't done before."

Bradley dismisses her with a slow eye roll. "Jessica, we won't let you get hurt."

"Lighten up, babe," says Welch. "You're working with professionals."

One of their radios lets off an unclear voice that says something like *Set up on Morgan and Wallace, west of Winston Park. Let us know your whereabouts, Johnston.*

"How do we know for sure that he's going to try to attack me?" I say.

Welch rests her weight on one leg. "She's asking a lot of questions, Sergeant."

"Ms. Knight," Lockheed says, "it's our job to know and to predict how a serial killer is going to pursue his next victim. I told you to trust me. Now, I'll see you at one a.m."

Hours later, a cab takes me back home with my earpiece in and my vest strapped to my body, hidden under my thin jacket. Lockheed has a new officer patrol outside my building. They told me to leave my curtains open so the killer will have a good sense of where I am, what I'm doing. That I'm alone. Every time Lockheed brings to light that a psychopath is watching me, a hundred *I told you so*'s burn on my tongue. I want to ask him, *How can I trust you when you never trusted me?*

Once the sun has set and I'm out of my vest, I leave on a single lamp so the Collector can see me inside my living room, getting used to me again. I think about taking a bath, but I'll just have to go out into the cool May weather afterward, and I think better of it. Then I think about drinking, though I can hear Bradley in my head warning against it. I can also hear Michael saying, *Pour two glasses.* I think about calling John because I'm lonely, because I don't have much to lose, but then I hear Michael again: *Don't choose him.*

My bottle of red is half-empty in the cabinet above the microwave, so I stay in the view of the window and pour myself a glass that I drink too fast. At the end of that drink, I pour the second glass and finish it too. And when the bottle goes dry, I'm three glasses in and warm under my skin. I open a new bottle and pour a fourth glass to the rim. What could it hurt? A little over two bottles in one day. In college, I passed a test with more alcohol in my system than that.

Then I start hearing Bradley again, this time his voice in my ear, not just my thoughts. "Hello?" I say.

"Jessica."

A handful of different voices beat against my eardrum. "Ms. Knight?"

"Let us know if you can hear us, Jess."

I cup my ear. "I can hear you. I can hear you."

"Perfect," Welch says. "Start walking."

"Ms. Knight, don't move," Lockheed says, overriding her.

My window reflects only the inside of my apartment, and in the reflection, I'm hunched over my coffee table, picking at my ear.

"Don't leave until I say so."

"What do you want me to do?" Though I can't see outside, I still try to look for the Collector out there, pacing, waiting, wondering when he will have me.

"Stop talking, first of all. Now, go somewhere private and get your vest on and put on a jacket or something. Then make it a point to take your time gathering your things—keys, phone, whatever. Just make sure you spend some time in the living room. And get the bottle of wine."

I do as he says, waiting for Bradley to chime in as I reach for the half-full bottle and miss, hooking it on the second try. He doesn't speak until I'm out the door and in the hallway.

"Say, Jessica, how are you feeling?" he asks with a touch of sarcasm. It's enduring, like an inside joke I'm finally a part of, something else shared only between the two of us.

Stepping into the elevator and pressing the button for the ground floor, I wriggle under the weight of the vest. "It feels like I should have a weapon. In—in case."

Welch hums in my ear. "Well, you didn't need one last time, did you?"

I remember that she hadn't known I was carrying a kitchen knife under my sleeve that night in the alley. "No," I muster.

Bradley makes a tapping noise as I step into the empty lobby. "Foreman, you there?"

"Here, sir."

"Ms. Knight," Lockheed says, "walk straight to the park. When you get there, enter from the east side, but walk slowly. Twirl. Do whatever you do when you're drunk."

I hear Bradley laugh under his breath.

The coolness of one a.m. Chicago air wraps around my ankles and neck, but my veins buzz with heat and my adrenaline is pumping. I can't tell if it's the alcohol or Lockheed's assumption that my getting drunk is a common occurrence that is feeding a growing twinge of irritation. A hundred questions pry at me to ask, but the risk of annoying everyone in my ear is too high.

As I walk, an age-old question picks at my scabbed wounds. *What if this doesn't work?*

Then Dr. Smith was right—he's not actually watching me. I am only paranoid. I am Aunt Deborah.

One block away, I say, "Where are you?"

"Above you," Bradley says. "Just four, five floors high."

"You can't see us," Welch says. Her speech slows, and I can hear her zeroing in on me. "Doing great, Jess."

The sidewalks are spotted with yellow circles of light from the streetlamps, so I walk close to the buildings and out of the faded rings of light. As I move closer to the park, my ear rings with their quiet voices.

"I've got her, Sergeant," Bradley says.

"In my sights."

"Got her."

"Foreman, she's on her way to you."

"Roger."

I take a swig of wine out of the bottle.

The park across the street is dark beyond the last of the streetlamps, and I hesitate before I cross the road. Something black breezes between the trees in the park, but it fades away just as fast. It's only the wine. Only the wine.

I whisper, "Does anyone see him?"

Welch says, "Shut up, Jess. If you're talking, you better be slurring."

Lockheed butts in. "Ms. Knight, go straight to the center of the park. You should see four benches, each facing the other."

"Jessica," Bradley says, "Foreman will be in the big oak on the east side where there should also be a plaque by the base of the tree. Don't look for him or the Collector might get suspicious."

His voice sounds more affectionate than professional, which surprises me, and makes me think of when I was lying underneath the weight of his body. I miss the feeling of his strong embrace, and I wish he were here now instead of on top of a building somewhere.

"More slouching, Jess, and more wobbling," says Welch.

Starting to cross the street, I stumble into a trashcan but keep tripping forward until I have to take a moment to collect myself, thinking, *The wine.* The bottle in my hand swings low beside me, empty—how did it get this empty?—but I tilt it into my mouth, anyway, and the heavy vest strapped to me makes my knees buckle.

"Good job, Jess," Welch says.

From my corner of the city block, I look into the park trees and can't recognize anything beyond them, but the next time I blink, I'm across the street and surrounded by them. Then Foreman mentions something about my location.

"Ms. Knight? Ms. Knight?" It's Lockheed.

"Yes," I whisper.

"Foreman, she's here. Ms. Knight, can you hear Foreman?"

"Yes, sir."

Bradley says, "Foreman's in and out, Sergeant. His signal's no good."

My fingers lose grip on the wine bottle, and it crashes to my feet, breaking into two pieces. All the voices in my ear silence, and I stop breathing. The beginning of a question sputters out of me, but I go silent with them and wait for their instruction, for the killer to respond to my disturbance. I start to bend down and pick up the pieces of glass, then Bradley says, "Jessica, leave them. Keep going."

As if answering my next question, Lockheed begins a one-way conversation.

"You're briefly out of my sight, Ms. Knight."

Sight, Ms. Knight, I sing in my head, closing my eyes and trying to walk straight. *Out of my sight, Ms. Knight.*

"Keep moving forward so you'll be out from under these trees. My men on the east side have eyes on you."

"Confirmed, Sergeant," one of them says.

Lockheed says, "Foreman, can you hear me?"

Foreman crackles on the other end as I come to the center of the park, where all four sidewalks meet. A lamppost stands erect in the middle, casting a halo of light around me that keeps my shadow short at my feet. I investigate the canopy of trees above me and see only a starless sheet of black.

Welch's voice comes through the line, scratchy and stressed. "Foreman, do you copy?"

"Stop looking up, Jessica," Bradley says.

A mixture of tight breaths from everyone cuts through the line.

"Just stand there and keep your eyes peeled. We've got you in our sights."

All four sidewalks spread their own direction, and each vanish into the depth and darkness of the woods. I back into helpless loops, around and around, until I've lost track of the path I came from.

In the trees, a rustle of leaves calls my attention upward, and I ignore Bradley's instruction.

"Jessica, it's just Foreman. He's letting you know he's there."

"I don't know," I say.

"Sergeant," one of the officers says, "I've got movement on the west side. A man is entering the park."

Welch confirms that she's keeping her sights on me, and I hear snippets of Foreman in my ear. *She's. Below. Me. Got. Her.*

I crane up at the tree but can't see beyond the light.

"I've got eyes on the man," Lockheed says. "Ms. Knight, remain where you are."

Bradley begins, "Sergeant, Jessica should move—"

"Stop, Bradley. You and Welch make sure all four sidewalks are clear leading to her." They go quiet again, and I tear my eyes away from the tree in which Foreman should be.

"Sidewalks are clear, Sarge," Welch says.

"Clear," Bradley repeats.

Another officer says, "The man is moving fast, Lockheed. He's running." All voices rise in pitch, creating a chorus of chaos in my head.

I spin around. "Which way?" I say. "Where?"

"Stay where you are, Knight."

"Don't move."

"He's under the trees and on the west path."

Bradley becomes the only recognizable voice I can hear. "I'm staying on Jessica."

"Sergeant," an officer says, "he's running toward Knight."

"Someone tell me what's happening," Bradley shouts. "I'm staying on Jessica."

I back against the tree that Foreman is in and stretch up, hoping he'll pull me up with him, but he's probably strapped in too high.

"I need to leave," I say. "I can't fight him."

"Knight, don't move an inch."

Welch says, "Jess, stay with us, hon. Don't panic."

"Where is he, Welch?" I say.

Lockheed says, "Get under the lamppost. Now, Knight."

"Can we determine if he's a suspect?" Bradley asks.

"Could just be a runner," says one of the officers.

"Jessica," Lockheed says, "we need him in the open to detain him with a shot if that's him. He's on his way to the center of the park."

"Foreman, do you copy?"

My ankles tremble under my clumsy body as a scampering of dull footsteps charge my way. The earpiece vibrates with commands.

"Everyone focus in."

"If they go out of sight, we need Foreman."

I inch backward to the center of the park.

Bradley says, "Does he have a weapon? Does the suspect have a weapon?"

"Don't panic, Jess."

"He's blocked by the trees. Who's got movement?"

"Does he have a *weapon?*"

A thump bangs behind the curtain of black behind me, and I spin around.

"I hear something. There's a person," I whisper. "Someone is in the woods."

"Knight, stay put," Lockheed says.

There's a shuffling of noise on Bradley's end, and he says, "Someone is on Jessica, guys. He's in the woods. She's being cornered, guys. Jessica, leave the park now, through the north entrance."

"Knight, you take commands from *me*," Lockheed says. "The subject is not in the woods. I repeat, the subject is *not* in the woods."

"Sergeant, there are *two people* out here," Bradley shouts at him. "There is a second person in the woods."

The other officer says in a low tone, "I've got the subject again. He's going to the center of the park. I don't detect a weapon."

From the location where the first thump seemed to come from, I see a flash of movement behind me, and a figure splits through the dark. Short. A thin sliver of light bounces from a long blade in his hand, and I back away, toward the north exit, but the north is gone, lost among south and east and west. Disoriented, I look back to the person with the knife.

The running footsteps are getting louder, closer as they plow from behind me, and I press onto the lamppost dead center of the park. *The wine. It's just the wine.*

"Knight, where is the other person?" an officer says.

But I can't squeeze anything out of my body other than my own pinching breaths as I wait for the running man to appear behind me or the short man to slither out of the darkness. I keep my eyes locked on the short one, the only one I can see. He steals an inch forward, his knife flickering with white light, and Bradley screams in my ear, "She sees two people, Sergeant. Get her out of there, *now.*"

"She's not going anywhere, Bradley. Knight, we're taking the shot on the suspect if he gets much closer."

The words are dry on my tongue: "It's not him. That's not him. The killer is right in front of me with a knife. He's in the woods."

"Jessica," Bradley yells, "get out of there. Turn around and run."

"Detective—" Lockheed says.

"This wasn't planned, Lockheed. We're not taking the shot on the runner. She says it's not him."

"He's charging straight for her."

Welch says, "Shut up, Bradley. She doesn't know anything."

"Foreman," I scream, "Foreman, can you hear me? Do you see him? He's right—"

"Foreman's mic is dead," Lockheed says to me. Then to Bradley, "We can't confirm she's seeing someone else."

"Sir—"

"You're through, Bradley."

"He has a knife," I say. "He's in the woods." I push away from the light post and away from the sprinting feet that continue to close the distance behind me. "Lockheed, I'm sure. The killer is in front of me."

"Jessica, is the person with the knife running?"

The only words I can repeat is *The killer is in the woods. He's in the woods. Help me.*

He's in the woods.

And all I can register through the crackling voices is Bradley's on repeat saying, *Run, Jessica.*

Stay put, Ms. Knight, or you'll ruin everything. I stay against the lamppost, ready to die, ready to live, I can't even tell anymore.

Run away, Jessica. Bradley's desperate voice tempts me to follow only his instruction, but I know he will pay the price for going against Lockheed's orders.

In my earpiece, I hear a rifle cock, pulling a bullet into the chamber, and it signals everyone to prepare for a rupture of gunfire.

All at once, the veil of darkness on the path spits him out—the running man.

He's not the killer.

And then.

Oh, my God.

He stumbles to a stop and wavers from his momentum, his mouth open and stammering on wheezing coughs. Dressed like he came from the office. Not a cigarette in sight. Strings of gray hair tumbling down, matted by sweat on his forehead. We stare at each other until he breaks away to see into the woods, to see the man with the knife.

It can't be him.

"John."

Instinct pushes me toward him. He throws himself at me.

"Clear," the voices in my ear say.

"Clear."

"Clear."

Then two outbursts of gunfire shred through the park.

John falls, but I dive the other way and hit the ground hard. Scampering to my feet, I dash down the path closest to me, and John cries out a long, hoarse weep. The knifed man escapes through the woods, crunching leaves as he goes, but I've already got a head start. Wind wizzes past me, overwhelming the angry shouts in my ear. Among them, Bradley's voice is absent, but I yank the earpiece out and let it dangle over my coat. If John were still shouting, I should be able to hear him, but the wind roars past me, my breath whimpers out of me, and my feet pound the sidewalk to get as far away from here as I can.

It can't be him.

And it wasn't. Because he didn't have the knife. He didn't have anything except a pathetic, desperate look on his face.

He calls out my last name, and it's combined with Bradley's voice cutting through the darkness demanding me to run.

Knight. Run. Knight. Run.

I can't tell which one is in my head or which is real, but the dark world hurls past me in a streak of black and brown. The streetlamps at the edge of the park appear through the trees, and I race straight toward them but crash into Bradley's hard chest. He scrambles to keep me steady, to keep me from escaping down the street, and he grabs me by my forearms to hold me up.

"Jessica, talk to me. Talk to me. It's okay."

My cheeks burn from the contrasting warmth of hot tears against my cool flesh. "You shot John. You shot John," I scream at him. "He's not the killer. I saw the knife and the man in the woods. He was walking right to me."

"I didn't shoot him," he says. "It wasn't me."

"Well, it wasn't John. It's never been John." And I collapse in his arms and let him hurry me into the center of a budding crowd of armed police officers and blue lights.

They close off a four-block perimeter around the park and light it up with an army of scouting officers and flashing blue and red lights. I don't see John again, but his ambulance flies in and out to take him to the hospital. Bradley tells me he's alive. Lockheed says he doesn't know where he hit him. Welch tells Lockheed to shut up and then she asks me what I saw. I explained that John didn't have the knife. He wasn't going to kill me. "John, your boss?" she says.

"Yes," Lockheed says. "The man who she spent the night with when the first victim was killed."

I think I hear him whisper, "Supposedly," but can't be sure with the sirens, with the people, with the wine.

"Jess," Welch says, "you can pop by the jail and see him once they patch him up."

"So he's not dead?"

"Didn't you hear him screaming after you? The only thing he would say was your name. It was bloody violent."

Foreman comes up to us on the sidewalk. "Boss, I'm so sorry. Something happened with my signal, and it just shut off. It'll never happen again, sir."

"Not your fault, Officer."

"I couldn't take a shot at anyone without your orders, sir. And I didn't see the man with a knife."

"Stop whining, Foreman," Welch says. "It's done, now."

Lockheed whistles at Bradley to get his attention over all the noise. "Bradley," he says, "go take care of your report. I'll be in soon. Everyone else, when we finish up here for the night, go home. The suspect is going to be locked up for the night once he's patched up, so we'll have CPD investigate and search his residence first thing tomorrow. Alright?"

"He's not going to the FBI. . ." I mutter, somewhere between a question and a statement.

Lockheed blows air out of his nose and looks down the sidewalk. "He didn't have a weapon. We can't be sure it was him, especially with you saying it's not. I've already had someone alert the FBI."

Bradley leads me to his car, and Lockheed follows, eyeing me before Bradley shuts my door. He stands with his back to me at the hood of the vehicle, facing Lockheed. The sergeant hooks his thumbs around his belt and mutters through his mustache at Bradley, whose neck is lined with worried veins. Lockheed's stiff face reddens, his cheeks setting in a permanent-looking frown.

Go, his lips read. I imagine the rest: *Take her to the station, and I'll be there shortly.*

Bradley turns on the siren and speeds through the film of media cameras and journalists who probably got word on their police scanners that a shooting went down at Winston Park.

At the station, Bradley takes me down to the basement where I spent the night on the cot a couple months ago.

"I have to report what happened tonight," he says.

"I'm not going to be able to sleep. Let me come with you."

"Good," he says, and I can hear the relief in his voice, "come with me."

We go to an empty floor, and he turns on a row of fluorescent lights over some cluttered desks and takes a seat. The desktop computer clicks on, and I pull up a chair, stripping off my coat and ripping through the Velcro on the bullet proof vest. I set it beside my chair as Bradley unbuckles the handgun from his hip but leaves his vest and his badge where they are.

"Bradley," I say.

He stays focused on the screen and starts typing, unyielding. "I told you to call me Michael."

But that night seems like years ago. "John being involved in—in this.... Ben is the only connection between us."

Bradley ignores what I say, choosing to focus on his report. "Ben is dead, and you saw someone with a knife. You're sure about that?"

This time, I ignore him. "Can you pull up the records on Ben? I just want to see his file."

He heaves a long sigh and waves me in closer, probably realizing I am not going to give this up.

"Is it okay for tonight's report to wait?" I ask.

"Yeah. Lockheed will just have to deal with it."

"Shouldn't this be a job for some officer, anyway?"

"You'd think."

The computer screen displays five different windows before Bradley clicks on one and the printer under his desk churns to life. He reaches down and retrieves a stack of pages the printer shot out.

"This is the report. Evidence is in the basement."

He hands me the pages, and I flip through to the *Details of Event* portion and skim over the summary of Ben's breaking and entering, his attempt on Welch's life, and his attempt on mine.

The perpetrator made excess phone calls to the victim on her cell phone.

"How did you know this?" I point out the sentence to Bradley.

He takes the paper for himself and reads the entire paragraph before answering. "We knew from your phone records."

"You didn't check *his* phone records? No one thought to even flip through his messages?"

"Foreman. He's the rookie, the one who bagged the evidence on this one, and to be honest with you, Ben was an early suspect, so he dropped off our radar pretty quickly. That is, until he popped up at your place and got shot." He nearly chokes over the word *shot*. Looking back down at the paper, he sucks in his lips.

"Foreman's a rookie?" I ask.

"He's been here a year. This was just his first big case."

"Can you get the phone records?" I say.

"We can order them with a warrant, but we didn't because you said he had already verbally threatened to kill you, so we didn't need that evidence after he was dead."

"You can order them, though?" I take back the page from him and add it to the rest of the report in my hands. "Never mind. That'll take too long. And I've waited long enough." I stand. "Take me to evidence. I need to see Ben's phone."

"Jessica—"

"No. This is too coincidental, and between John and Ben—I just know, Bradley." Then I correct myself. "Michael, I just know."

His eyes soften around the edges when he stares up at me, but dismissing my leads, he starts to type on his keyboard. "We saw your correspondence with Ben already. But do you think Foreman missed something?"

"It's not the texts or calls to me that I'm wondering about. It's the texts and calls he made to John."

"Foreman investigated his phone and said it was clear."

I walk to another desk and fumble through the drawers. "There's bound to be an iPhone charger around here somewhere," I say, because I know that phone has been dead for months now.

"Jessica, what are you looking for?"

"Something that has to do with John. He's not the killer, Bradley. I know John, and I know he didn't do it, and he wouldn't do that to me. John is not the killer, but it could still be Ben."

Something clicks in Bradley's head. I can see it happening underneath his confusion, the realization that a newbie on his first big case might have missed a beat. Bradley delays his typing, and his fingers curl into fists on the keyboard. He pulls out a drawer and takes out his white phone charger and a laminated keycard with a silver clip attached.

"We need to go before Lockheed comes back." He rolls up his sleeves and stands. "I'm on a clock."

He takes us to a locked room with lines of shelving that's stocked with large boxes from floor to ceiling. A library of evidence only accessible with the keycard.

Following him through the alphabetized rows, the skin on my hand catches on my shirt fabric. The concrete in the park must have scratched me up when I fell. It reminds me of when I slipped against the tree bark the night that I ran in on Ben at the safehouse.

"Here," Bradley says.

We squat to the concrete floor, and he pulls out a white box. He opens the lid, and I rummage through the plastic bags he sets out. The fluorescents burn a humming light over us, flashing and dimming every few seconds. It gleams down an ominous tone on the palm-sized photograph of me. My headshot that prints in the back of the newspaper every week is torn at the edges, and my weak smile looks distorted through the plastic. This is the picture that Ben had set out by the box of bullets Bradley told me about.

At the bottom of the box, Ben's coat and gloves lie in a clear plastic evidence bag, but Bradley leaves them in there and picks out a thin, rectangle box.

"His gun," he says.

Though I almost ask him to open it so I can see the steel he held against my head, I ignore him and unzip the bag that holds only Ben's cell phone.

"Get the charger," I say. "Where's an outlet?"

He takes me around a corner to a thin sliver of gray wall, and I stick the charger into the outlet and put the other end into the phone. In a few minutes, the screen come to life, and I tap on Ben's recent call list.

Jessica.

Jessica.

"These calls were all made on the same day," I say.

Bradley stands against my back, looking over my shoulder. "When?"

I point with my thumb to the date beside my name. "The night he broke into the safehouse."

"Scroll to the night from the alley, a few weeks prior."

The list slides upward, revealing only my name, random numbers, and John's name. "There," he says. "Stop. This is the day."

Ben had called me a few times that day and then that night, which the list shows, and the rest is John's name in the afternoon, outcoming and incoming calls. All the way from morning to evening.

"Oh, my God."

Bradley takes the phone from my hand and yanks the charger from it, inspecting the call list for himself. "Does John call you this much?"

I shake my head, my eyes stinging with the hotness of tears, and the strangulation of betrayal. Bradley backs out of the call list and checks Ben's messages to John. Together, we read them from the night Ben was killed.

Ben: *I'm doing this myself. She's mine now.*

John: *You're a coward. Touch her, and you won't have time to put a bullet in your own head.*

Ben: *You've had years to kill her. At least I have the guts.*

"Foreman called this 'clear'?" I ask.

Bradley pushes himself off the wall. "We need to see John's phone. Immediately. I've got to order records for him and Ben."

"How could this happen?"

"Foreman didn't investigate this damn phone. He threw it in evidence with all the rest of Ben's things and called it a day."

"John wouldn't say all this. He wouldn't do that. I didn't tell either of them that I was in the safehouse, Bradley."

"Lockheed's got the phone by now."

"Isn't John in the hospital?"

He puts the phone in his pocket and goes back to the box of evidence to pack it up. "We have to look over the report again. We missed something the first time. Lockheed was right from the beginning."

"About what?"

"About John being involved." He places the lid on the box and slides it back into its slot.

"That's impossible. The murders were too far away. I was with him the night Robert was killed, remember?"

"Then Lockheed had suspicions for good reason. He just dropped Ben as a suspect too quickly, and Foreman didn't gather evidence from the cell phone because your records had already been ordered and looked over. We've got proof now that John wanted to kill you."

"No, Bradley. No. Lockheed probably assumed John and I were part of Robert's murder together when he found out I was with him all night. Whatever he thought about John, he also thought about me."

"It doesn't matter, now."

"You actually believe John's the killer, Bradley?"

"Don't let your bias get in the way of facts. You're sleeping with your married boss. Okay? Your judgment is clouded, Jessica."

I trail behind him through the room and out the door, and he scans the keycard. The bolt clunks into place.

"I can't believe you would say that to me after—"

We stop in the hallway. "After what?" he says. "After we slept together?" His alteration from nervous to annoyed turns him into a person I barely recognize. "It didn't mean anything to you then, and it doesn't mean anything to you now that John's back in the picture."

"How am I supposed to act like I don't care about him?"

"By not sleeping with the next man who enters your life."

"Hey" —I step toward him— "it takes two people, Bradley."

"Yeah, Jessica. One man who loves you, and one woman who can't admit she's in love with her boss."

He spins around and leaves me standing alone. His statement pierces me right where it *should* hurt, but I feel nothing. Not even excitement that he just admitted he loves me. I've become numb to pain and joy. Or maybe that's a result of being too shaken over watching John get shot and seeing the killer come toward me with his knife. I take a step forward to run after Bradley, but now I can't recognize *myself*, so I don't go any further. I can't. I can only know I'll never convince Bradley I don't love John. And I'll never be able to convince him I'm falling in love with Michael instead.

At three in the morning, Lockheed enters the room and turns on the extra rows of lights in the office. I look up from a few desks over and tuck Ben's phone between my legs to keep it out of sight. As Bradley types away on his report, I have been reading through Ben's messages and reviewing part of the report on Ben's crime spree and his death. I've been watching Bradley review the second half of Ben's report, and analyzing how I could've misinterpreted what he'd said earlier.

He flips the report upside down on the desk as Lockheed approaches. "Sergeant."

Lockheed breezes straight between our desks, and without looking at me, he says, "Ms. Knight, please give Detective Bradley and me a moment. We've got something to work out."

Bradley sits back and crosses his arms, and my shoes make a pattering noise on the thin carpet until I'm out the door. Pulling it closed it behind me, I realize I left the report on the desk. Guess it doesn't matter now.

The skinny window on the door allows me to see only Lockheed towering over Bradley.

They start off quietly, but then Bradley stands, and their voices raise.

I hold my breath to hear better.

"You went directly against my orders tonight."

Bradley mutters something, too low to hear from out here.

"You don't make the call during life and death situations like this, Bradley."

"I'm sorry, Sergeant. I believed her when she told us he wasn't the killer."

"If she had stayed right where we wanted her, we actually could have determined whether there was another man with a knife in the woods. Thanks to your orders, Ms. Knight fled the scene, along with the potential killer who also, *somehow*, disappeared through the south exit of the park."

"I'm sorry, Sergeant. I was concerned for her safety since she saw two people there."

"You've gotten too personal with this case, and I'm wondering now if it was a mistake to put you on duty protecting her."

"Things haven't gotten personal, sir."

That stings, but I know Bradley is protecting me by lying to Lockheed. I replay his words from earlier—*one man who loves you*—which are left resonating in my thoughts.

"Then when it comes down to obeying orders from me or using your own judgment at the workplace, you listen to me. From now on, Jessica Knight doesn't exist to you."

I gasp and clasp my hand over my mouth, and a moment passes without either of them speaking, or perhaps I just cannot hear them over my heartbeat.

"You're through here, Detective."

"I can't go home now. I'm in the middle of—"

"No, Bradley. I mean you're fired. Effective immediately. Finish the paperwork and leave your badge and your gun on my desk before you go. You can come in tomorrow morning to clean out your desk. Have a good night."

"Sergeant."

I put my back against the wall, and Lockheed storms through the door beside me. As it closes, Bradley's voice breaks through the stone-cold silence.

"*Sergeant.*"

Lockheed says to me without looking, "You'll be able to visit John in a few hours in the jail. I'm sure you two have some things to discuss."

At seven the next morning, I realize I had dozed off. From my spot on the cot downstairs, the first thing I do is check my phone, but Bradley hasn't called or texted me. It hurts to know that he left me here without so much as a "goodbye." I don't let the thought settle in my mind, though; I know last night wasn't our last discussion, but the sudden dread of being without him in this big building sinks me, and I want nothing more than to melt into my mattress. First, I have to find John.

I somehow locate the front desk in the lobby and ask the desk clerk how to visit someone in jail. Her flat look intimidates me. She must recognize me based on the way she glares at me. She has an officer show me to the small, gray room with five cube-shaped cells inside that are nothing like what I had expected. Despite his gunshot wound, John sprouts up the moment he sees me, and the officer nods at another uniformed man sitting at a desk in the corner.

I jog over to his cell door, on a mission. John's left hand is wrapped around a silver bar. His right arm hangs in a navy-blue sling, and white medical tape sticks out from around his shirt collar from his bandage.

"Oh, Jessica. Dear. I'm so sorry. You've gotta believe I'm sorry, dear."

"John, John," I whisper, and a foundation of confidence builds on top of whatever nonsense Bradley said about him. "I know it wasn't you. They don't know what they're talking about."

"I'm okay, Knight. I am."

"No, you were shot, John. That's not okay."

"It got me just under my shoulder blade, dear. Don't worry about me. I can handle a few surgeries, love."

I look into his cell and the cold metal bars between us, comparing John's actions to the alleged text messages between him and Ben.

"What, sweetheart? What is it?"

"They found evidence. We—we found evidence."

He releases his grip on the bar and rubs the elbow in his sling, backing away. "Knight, what did they find?" Then he dashes back to the cell door. "I—I need a cigarette." Looking past me and to the officer, he says, "Can I have a cigarette?" His voice cracks and wavers, and his back hunches over as if he is standing in a fetal position.

The officer doesn't respond, and John doesn't ask again, which I know must be killing him. He comes to stand next to me again, and I take my chance. "John, you were calling Ben. A lot. We found the call log on his phone, and you two were messaging. Messaging. . . bad things," I whisper through the distance of the bars.

He turns away again and covers his face, hugging himself with his bandaged arm. "Knight, dear, I haven't got an excuse." He rests his forehead against the bar and closes his eyes, but this time, I'm the one backing away a microscopic centimeter.

"You and Ben were calling each other."

"No, dear, we weren't," he mutters.

"Tell me it's not true. This can't be real."

"Knight, I'm so sorry. I'm so sorry." His shoulders shake while he coughs out a sob. "I don't have any excuse for what has happened."

"It's impossible." Lower, I say, "We were together on the night of Robert's murder."

He sighs, then shivers as he takes a deep breath. "I know we were, Knight. I know we were."

"Then what are you saying, John?" My heart jumps, and he looks right at me, but there's a truth in his eyes, an unwavering knowing that turns the whites of his eyes a dark, bloodshot red where tears begin to puddle.

John leans in, glancing from me to the officer sitting at the desk in the corner. He thinks for a moment before licking his thin, wrinkled lips. His breath is an opaque warmth that hints at the last cigarette he smoked several hours ago.

"You need to go to my apartment, Knight. Take that boy who's always protecting you and have him take you to my apartment."

"Why?"

"There's something I can't say. I—I just can't, Knight."

"What is it?"

"My wife isn't there, so you should be fine, but please, don't ask me any questions. I just—I just can't say anything right now. Give me your word that you'll go to my apartment, Knight."

"I don't think I can. The police might have already been there to investigate."

"No, Knight, they couldn't have been there. Not yet."

That's right. Lockheed said they would investigate his apartment this morning, but it's barely daylight now, and the sky is ten shades darker due to rain.

"Just go, dear. Please."

The way he looks at me—the intensity of his stare. I've been sleeping with it for years, and after seeing him here, I know. I am certain that John is not the killer.

"I'll go."

I let myself inside his apartment and am grateful that his door doesn't creak the way mine does when I open it slowly. The rain blows in pelting sheets against his windows, making spotty gray reflections dance around on his white living room floor.

I press the door closed behind me and listen for the record player to be on or his coffee machine to be buzzing. There is no fresh cigarette smoke lingering in the air for the first time since I can remember. Nothing. No police have been here yet, either. With Lockheed's promise to investigate the residence today, I anticipate them barging through the door any moment.

I walk through the kitchen and scan the counter tops, but the only objects that lie upon it are the espresso maker and a wine rack. The white, sparkling granite is wiped clean, and the dining room table and china cabinet appear the same as usual—bare, untouched, unused.

Down the corridor, the bathroom door is closed, so I edge my way toward it and press my ear against the cool, fogged glass. The silence reminds me of being in Deborah's cabin. The sound of an aftermath. The glass turns everything on the other side of the door into a shapeless blob, my body's reflection in it just a frightened figure, terrified about what I might find behind the door.

I push it open.

The tightness in my throat eases when I don't see a body or vibrant streaks of blood. The shower looks spotless, without even a hair clogging the drain, so I go head into his bedroom.

Maybe whatever it is that he wants me to find is there.

As I step through the doorway, a wave of rain blasts the window, causing me to jump.

Thunder cracks from outside, vibrating the floor. I didn't know we were expecting a storm. The lampshade on John's nightstand rattles, which draws my attention to a book on his comforter. Beside it, a faded antique box is wrapped in yellowing lace. The journal is spread open, showcasing its creamy pages filled with lines of black cursive.

Amazing writer, John had told me in a conversation we had not too long ago. *Kept a hundred journals.*

I reach to pick it up but see a hand-written letter sitting beside it and pick that up instead.

I read the only two sentences on the page.

I love you, John, even if you don't love me back. And I'll love you until I die tonight.

Apr. 30
She's back home.

May 1
She's alone today.

May 2
They're planning something. That newbie officer says they'll be in the park at 1 tonight. It's the park where John and I had our first date, but Foreman didn't know that when he told me. He only said that he'd cover me while I lure J out of sight and into the woods.

It hits all at once. *Foreman,* Bradley had said at the station. *He's the rookie, the one who bagged the evidence on this one.*

I flip to the front of the journal, dated a year and a half back.

Went to the office Christmas party tonight and met Ben. Apparently, he's in love with J, just like John is. We chatted, and it turns out she dumped him. What kind of slut sleeps with a

*married man but won't date her co-worker? Ben kept staring
at her. We both were.*

I turn a few pages over.

*Ben's a freak. He can't have one woman, so now he says he's
going to kill himself. I was starting to question our secret
friendship, but since John doesn't know about our obsession
with the same slutty journalist, I came up with a brilliant
idea.*

*I asked Ben to help me before he ends his life. He's pissed
at J, same as I am, and if he's going to kill himself, he might
as well help me commit my own ultimate murder.*

Ben, on the verge of suicide the whole time. . . I flip to another page further into the journal.

*It's been a seamless five murders. John doesn't even notice
that they happen every time I insist on going to my "out-of-
state treatments" by myself. My chemo ended long before I
made my first kill, but John's so wrapped up in life outside
this apartment that he doesn't question when I have my "pe-
riodical treatments" far away from Chicago. He only notices
me when he has to drive me to the hospital himself because
I'm actually sick.*

Another page.

*Ben's distracted. I keep expecting John to come home from
work and tell me that his reporter has killed himself already,
so I have to use him quickly.*

Another. This one dates back to early January.

*Tonight, she will die. I'll be in Ben's ear the entire time on
John's old Bluetooth earpiece. While John's working late like*

he said, Ben is going into the alley, and I'll be behind him in the shrubs with my gun. It's perfect. It'll look like he's the one shooting her with his handgun, but it'll really be me with John's old pistol. And then, when it's over and she's dead, he said he's going to hang himself, even though I said shooting himself with his gun would be quicker.

Anyway, if my plan doesn't work? He'll be the one to go to prison. Not me. The perfect crime. One shooter, two guns, but only Ben will look guilty.

I turn to the entry from a couple days later.

I gave Ben fifteen-thousand dollars in cash from my savings account that John doesn't know about. This way, he will stay alive since our plan in the alley didn't work. The moron shot at her with his gun, missed, and then ditched his coat with the residue on it. He'd taken the shot before I even raised my gun in the woods. Couldn't help himself. I don't even know why 15k would keep him from killing himself, but to each his own. Maybe he worships money as much as he worships J.

Since he took that shot at her, J is gone, and I can't find her. More importantly than that, I didn't get to kill her because of that hasty idiot.

A week later she added another entry.

I should've just killed J in the alley and run. Yesterday evening, Ben dropped the cash back off to me and decided to take J out alone. The idiot got killed, and the slut survived. At least he knew where to find her.

I flip through, page after page, wondering how Ben knew where I'd been hiding at the safehouse.

John hasn't slept with me in months.

I gave the cash to a young officer at the police station. He's going to help me now that Ben's gone. Foreman said he was in charge of stocking Ben's evidence at Fuller Park. He told me not to worry about the cops catching me through Ben's idiotic death since he handled storing the evidence from that fatal night. He also said Ben's phone was dead when he stored it in evidence, plus, Ben put my contact under the name "John." But the cops know Ben wasn't the Button Collector. They're still searching for me.

Foreman investigated his phone and said it was clear, Bradley told me.

I've got three months to live.

The cops are making a plan.

I'm going to kill her before I die, and I'm tired of waiting.

She and her family have to suffer for what she's doing to my marriage.

The media is calling me "sloppy." I don't care. I'm going to kill her if it kills me. I'm going to die anyway.

I drop the journal, and it falls closed onto the little box, tipping the whole thing over. The lid pops open, spilling a collection of buttons onto the comforter.

Yellow. Blue. Green. Black. Among the collection of buttons that come vomiting onto the mattress is one crystal button that catches my eye. Julianne's button.

And here is one of Rosa's pink buttons from her cardigan.

And here is the copper button identical to the one from Uncle Josh's jeans. "Oh, my God."

I run out of the room and tear through John's apartment, slamming the door on the way out without bothering to lock it. A person is waiting for the elevator at the end of the hall, so I turn around and shoot to the stairs at the other end of the hall. I yank the door open and sprint the entire eight flights down. Once I reach the bottom, I pull out my phone and dial Bradley.

He answers with a slow "Hello."

"Bradley?"

"Yeah?"

"I'm at John's apartment, and it's not him." The lobby doors split open, and rain blows in on me. I wave my arm at a yellow cab across the street. "I knew John wouldn't do this. Bradley, it's his wife. Can you meet me at the station?"

"What? Jessica, what do you mean?"

"It's John's wife, Bradley. Her name is Mary, and she has cancer. Oh, my God, it all makes sense. She wrote everything down, all of it. Ben was helping her, and Foreman knew about this too. He was working with her the whole time. She was paying Foreman to help her kill me. That's why his mic went out last night. It was all fake. She wrote it all down in a journal. Foreman was faking it in the tree last night, Bradley. He was on Mary's side, and she was using Ben to act like he was going to shoot me in the alley that night, but it was really her that wanted to kill me."

The cab pulls up, and I hop in, scanning in every direction to make sure that I'm not being followed. Lightning flashes a white crack in the gray sky, and the thunder rumbles as we drive off. I tell the driver, "Fuller Park Police Department," and tap him frantically on the shoulder.

"Can you meet me at the station?" I ask Bradley. "I have to see John."

"His wife? Did you get the journal?"

"No, no, no. I don't know. She knows about the affair. She knows I'm sleeping with John, but he's sleeping with a hundred other journalists. Why me? Why is she after me?"

The background noise thickens with jingling keys and heavy breaths. "She doesn't know about the others, then," he says. "Okay, Jessica, go to the station and meet me at the back entrance and don't call Lockheed. And don't go inside without me. Are you in a cab?"

"Yes."

"Stay in it until I get there."

When we arrive behind Fuller Park PD, a deep green Jeep Wrangler hydroplanes into the parking lot, stopping at the curb behind the cab. Bradley jumps out, and he jogs to me under the torrent of rain to open my cab door. He puts his arm around me as I get out.

"Why aren't you in your car?" I shout through the rain.

"That is my car. I'm not on patrol today."

He's also not in uniform, and there's no bulge on his belt where his gun and badge used to be. In the rapid confusion of the last few hours, I had almost forgotten that Lockheed fired him. Surely that wasn't serious.

We go inside, and I trail behind Bradley as he walks straight into the room with the cells, with no questions asked. The officer on duty sits up at the desk, and John, lying on his thin cot, stands and comes to the cell door.

"Keaton," Bradley says to the officer, "is Lockheed in?"

"Not right now, sir. Would you like me to call him?"

"No. Is Foreman around?"

"I'm not sure he's in yet, sir."

"Where is Sergeant?"

"At a crime scene. A homicide."

I tear my eyes away from John and walk up to the desk. "Who was killed?" I ask.

"I heard on the radio it was some woman in the city. Della some-body. There was a stabbing at her residence. Why are you asking?"

I grab Bradley's arm. "Della is John's receptionist. We work to-gether."

The officer says, "Yeah, there were about three other murders throughout the night. Their bodies are being discovered and reported like crazy this morning."

"Were they all women?" I ask, but I already know how he will answer. He nods.

Bradley looks down at me, asking with his eyes a question I can't bring myself to answer here.

Yes, Della and John were sleeping together.

"Keaton, go upstairs and have a detective track down Foreman," Bradley says. "Tell them Lockheed and I need him in the office, but don't make it sound urgent."

"I'm not sure I can leave the cells without permission from the sergeant."

"Lockheed's not here, so you're taking orders from the next rank above you. Go." The officer leaves, and Bradley and I rush over to John.

"Jessica, dear, come here. What's happening?" He falls against the cell door.

I reach through the bars and put my hand on his wrinkled cheek. "I knew it wasn't you, John. I'm so sorry."

"You went to my apartment?"

"I found the journal and the buttons. What's happening?"

"I don't know, Knight. I honestly don't know. I've gotta get outta here," he says. "I need to get to my wife."

Bradley walks to the filing cabinet behind Officer Keaton's desk and pulls out a key to unlock the desk drawer.

"I need to see that journal," he says. He shuts the drawer and comes back to the cell with a card in his hand. Swiping it against a block by the cell, he causes a bolt to click.

"You're not allowed to do that," I say.

"I also wasn't allowed to give an officer orders."

He slides the door open, and John wraps his body around mine. His bones are hard and sharp.

"Jessica," Bradley says, ignoring our embrace, "call Lockheed."

John lets go of me, and we head back into the storm. The three of us pile into Bradley's Jeep. I take the backseat and find Lockheed's name on my phone.

"Yes?" he says when he answers. I plug my other ear with my finger as Bradley drives through the rain.

"Lockheed, it's me. The woman who was killed—Della—she worked with me. She was John's receptionist."

He doesn't respond.

"The killer isn't John. It's his wife. She's after all the women who he's been cheating on her with. Myself included."

Out of the corner of my eye, I see Bradley in his rearview mirror glance my way, but I stay bent over with my finger in my ear.

"Are the other victims from the past few hours employed at *The Post?*" I ask.

Lockheed brings his mouth close to the phone. "I'm elbow deep in four very bloody scenes, Ms. Knight, so I need you to stay away from your home until I can get back and talk to you. Stay at the station. Do not move from that station, Ms. Knight. Call Susan Welch and inform her of the situation."

"But it's not John, Lockheed. It's his—"

"John's staying where he is until this mess is sorted out. I'll talk to you when I'm back at the station later. Call Welch *right* now."

He hangs up the phone.

I throw up my hands at Bradley in the mirror. John leans against the door, muttering words that are drowned out by the pounding rain.

"I saw the note," John says. He uses his one mobile hand when he talks, bringing it to his face and down to his lap again. "I was digging around for a robe in the closet when I got home from work and found her diary and that—that box of buttons in the very back. Then I went to call her, and I saw that note she left by the bed. She never answered her phone. God, can you believe it?" He claps his palm over his eyes. "Can you believe I found those buttons before that letter? She stopped hiding it. She had it all right under my robe 'cause she knew where I'd go when I got home." He lets out a painful wail from his dried-out lungs. "I was with Carly in my office before that. If I had just come home at five or six like normal—"

"What did you do after you saw the note?" Bradley says.

"I went straight to the park. That's where the diary said she would be. Knight, dear, I almost got you killed. It's all my fault. I almost—"

"No, John." I rub his shoulder and hold back what rotates around in my mind: *It's my fault. For Robert. For Rosa. For Uncle Josh. For Great Aunt Julianne. For Martha Pax. For Aunt Deborah.*

"She said she was going to die tonight," he says. "Is she going to die tonight? What does that mean?"

Bradley grips his steering wheel tightly, rubbing his hands up and down the wheel. The veins in his neck pop out again. "I don't know what that means," he says.

"I do," I blurt. "She said she was going to kill me last night even if it killed her. She just wants me dead, no matter what."

Bradley parks under the awning at the front entrance of John's building, and John leads the way to his door eight stories up. We flood inside the apartment. Three pairs of wet shoes sprint through the white hall, leaving a trail of dirt and destruction. John stands in the doorway of his bedroom, touching at the wound under his sling and shirt, and Bradley grabs the journal I left open on the bed. Water drips down my cheeks, and I can't determine whether it's my wet hair or my tears.

"All these dates add up," Bradley says. "Did you know Mary had a secret savings account?"

John only shakes his head. "I didn't know anything, son."

"Foreman's got fifteen-grand lying around somewhere as a bribe to kill you," Bradley says to me.

John interrupts and goes to his nightstand by his side of the bed. He digs through the drawer and pulls something out. "This." He holds up a small, laminated book. "I kept track of all her treatments on my personal calendar. Take it, son."

Bradley leans over the bed and lets John hand it to him. He turns the pages. "January eighth. Treatment at MD Anderson Cancer Center in Houston, Texas."

275

"Aunt Deborah was attacked on the ninth," I say. "Mary was lying to you about where she was going out of state. She wasn't getting treatments."

He turns back more pages. "June sixteenth. Treatment again in Houston."

"Robert."

"There's more," he says, shuffling through the pages. "These are the weeks the others were murdered."

Closing the calendar, he stares down at it, and I pour out the box of buttons on the bed. Three needles spread out, each rusted with brown gunk. I pick up one of them and hold it close to my eyes.

My hand shakes when I realize it's not rust. It is the caked-on residue of my family's blood.

"She was lying to me about the treatments the whole time," John says, shaking his head. But the whole time, it all should've made sense. The wife who kills the mistress. I didn't recognize that all it took was a needle and thread and a hand who knew how to work them. I can connect all of the dots now. She was brilliant, John had said, with her Yale education. Mary was given only months to live at the same time the killer started acting as if he had nothing left to lose. In the hospital, Deborah wasn't referring to the killer as *He*. She was saying *She* because of her bandage and because it was true. And when Deb had called me a few days ago, she was telling me that they wouldn't believe her about the killer. That they were saying she was crazy. Nobody would believe a person who's going insane. That the Button Collector is actually a woman, a bald female.

Mary could watch me because she knew my schedule. Because her husband was my boss.

And she knew Ben was obsessed with me. They were partners in this crime. And Foreman couldn't turn down fifteen-thousand dollars in cash. And Ben would've stayed alive for it. Anything to make me taste my repercussions. Her strategy was actually brilliant—attacking the victims at night because she's weak from her cancer. She kills while they're asleep, unconscious, and then leaves her skilled trademark upon their lips. No evidence. Spotless. Wiped clean.

The voice that pipes in from behind us is unfamiliar, dry, and aching for moisture: "Here they all are."

I drop the needle and turn around.

She's short. Bald from months of chemotherapy. Her arms are stained a deep red, splotchy all the way down, where the blood has been washed with streaks of rainwater. The face that I know only from a frame on the corner of John's desk is now before me, pale white and speckled red with the blood of my coworkers. Her paper-thin skin is lined with spidery purple veins, more indication of what the cancer has done to her.

The knife in her petite hand has been washed clean from the storm outside, but blood encrusts the blade where it meets the handle. I expect Bradley to reach for his pistol, then remember that he turned it in to Lockheed last night.

"Here they all are trying to pick me apart," she says.

John slowly holds out his arm to her but at the same time backs away. He covers his mouth.

"Mary. Oh, Mary. What have you done?" His words are tear-stained, heavy with a disbelief I'll never understand.

Her teeth come together when she talks because she's shivering, and her shoulders wobble with each syllable. "What I've been doing since I found out about you and Jessica, darling."

"I'm so sorry, Mary," he whimpers, crumbling into his thin frame.

"Who are you going to sleep with now, John? They're all dead."

"Oh, Mary. Mary. Why, dear? Why couldn't you have just divorced me?"

"No, not that easily. I couldn't let you get away with it that easily." A pink puddle forms under the hem of her long, black skirt. "And I couldn't just *allow* Jessica to continue to sleep with my husband."

She pins her eyes on me, and I withdraw back toward the bed. When the backs of my knees hit into it, I buckle and barely catch myself before I fall.

"I'm not the only one," I say.

"I know that. Now. And I've taken care of the others." Della, Rylee, Grace. Carly should've been next. "Haven't you noticed the blood stains by now, Jessica? They're all over me. They're all over you. They're everywhere."

"But—" I start, then look behind me and Bradley, who gives me a microscopic nod. "But how did you know about them? Why did you go after my family?"

"Because he loves you. Don't you see that? What kind of man would cheat on his wife who has cancer if he didn't love the woman he was cheating with?"

"I told you I'm not the only—"

Mary stomps her foot on the ground. "But you were the first I knew about. It's been you the longest. It's been you the most." She closes her eyes and looks up, giving in to a brief chill that shakes her entire body. "Yesterday." She points the knife at John. "Yesterday, before I went to the park—before you were there to stop me from hurting your precious Jessica—I stopped by the office to see if you were really working late. Jessica wasn't there. I knew that because Foreman was keeping tabs on her for me. And you only worked late to get your hands on her." She points her knife at me, now.

John reaches out to her again. "Mary."

"Don't touch me. I saw you with another girl. You were in your own desk chair, John, and you never even left the bed with me."

"Mary, please give me the knife."

"And if you were having sex with some woman in a chair, you were having sex with all the other girls too." She watches John weep, her lips curling into the start of a sneer. "They're dead now."

"Mary, give me the knife, dear."

Mary takes aim at Bradley and says, "What—your cop friend doesn't have his gun?"

Bradley lifts his hands a bit and takes a slow step away from the bed, toward her. "No, I don't have my gun, Mary."

She keeps the knife straight out, blade-up. Her bald head is small on her frail neck and pure white under the spray of red blood. "I know. Your pal Foreman doesn't keep a lot to himself." Mary's smile shifts into a frown that warps her face. "I see you've found my journal."

John tries going to her, but Bradley pulls him back. "Darling," John says.

"We also found your texts to Ben under John's name," I say. "It's like you were trying to sabotage your own husband."

"No, Jessica, if I were trying to sabotage him like he was to me, then I would have told the whole country that the editor of *The Chicago Post* was spreading HPV to all his journalists." She looks to John. "I was using you against your lover the whole time."

A grin tries to force its way upon Mary's face, but Bradley pulls us back on track.

"We know about Foreman and Ben," Bradley says. "It doesn't have to be this way, okay? It never had to be this way. If you set down the knife, we can take care of you."

"No, it did have to be this way. I had to watch her—*her*—suffer for months before I could begin to think about a divorce, but it wasn't even worth it after the cancer started eating away at my time. I made the best with what I had to work with, and I'm finished waiting to kill her. I've seen her suffer, and I loved every second of it—the tormenting, the stalking, the killing. From hundreds of miles away, I was still making her suffer, making her think she was next any minute of the day."

I push myself away from the bed and inch toward Bradley. "You waited too long to kill me," I say.

Bradley holds out his arm. "Jessica."

"Ben couldn't do it."

"Ben could've done it if he wasn't such an idiot."

"If he was such an idiot, then how'd he know where to find me at the safehouse?"

"He might've been an idiot, but he was still a journalist. Remember that domestic violence rape story you assigned to him when you were out of the office, Jessica? He brought it up to CPVC when he learned they got involved in this case. He inquired about their tactics to keep domestic victims safe. Then he dug deeper and learned what side of Chicago they have their safehouses on. A few days of scouting that neighborhood's streets. . . it didn't take long for him to locate you. Imagine his relief when he saw you standing out in the snow before that woman yanked you back in and he realized he got the street right."

The day I'd gone out for some fresh air in my snow boots, when Welch had made me come back inside—

"It's all your fault, really. You deserve to be dead."

"You don't want me dead. You want me alive so you can keep controlling my life."

Bradley looks at me, pleading.

"Jessica." But I ignore him.

"You can't keep going," I say.

"You think I don't know that?" Mary lowers the knife. "Didn't you read the rest of the book? I've been done since they gave me three months to live. I've been ready to have your blood on my hands since I knew I was dying, and I didn't care about getting caught as long as you were dead. Answer one question, Jessica: did you suffer?"

Her eyes turn up with an artificial joy, and the shivering makes her skirt wave at the ends. "Did you wake up with nightmares?"

I look at Bradley, then at John, but neither can break their gaze from Mary.

"Huh?" she says, voice shaking, cracking right down the middle of each word. "Did you keep your curtains closed for me every night? Did you go to sleep scared? Did you wonder how the Button Collector could find you and watch you and tell you over and over that you're next?"

"How did you watch me?"

"I was in the building across the street for ages, Jessica. It only took two hundred bucks a week to hang out in that crappy neighborhood, in a building that's falling down around me, in a room that has water damage and paint peeling off the walls. You people are so blind."

"You stole my father's gun."

"Oh, how miraculous. You saw the empty case."

"How did you know?"

"I wanted to know everything about you, Jessica. The moment I saw you get in that cab the week I killed Robert, I knew I'd have to call the cab company, see where it took you. It doesn't take a genius to pose as you, kindly ask if I had left my purse in the car when they drove me to. . .oh, where was it? Yes, My Storage in Crestwood. My Storage, who reminded me of *my* unit number when I called to tell them I'd forgotten. You know, all the trauma *I* suffered when I had to stuff all my dead parents' things in there made me forget, and between the new job at the newspaper and the move into a new apartment those years ago, the information was easy to lose. It was so simple. Give a good sob story, and they'll tell you anything you want to know. A name and an estimated date of rental was all they requested from me."

"How did you know?" I ask. "How did you know I had a rifle in there?"

"Oh, I didn't. That's the good part. All I did was happen upon it as I was going through your things in the unit." She laughs, showing all her yellow teeth—another sign of chemotherapy.

"It looked like you knew exactly where to find it."

"I'm sure that's what it looked like, Jessica," she says. "I'm sure it looked like I didn't touch a single thing in that unit except for that gun, and I'm sure that scared you even more. And when I was finished, I cleaned up my mess just enough, so you'd know the rifle was the only thing that was long gone."

My mind, made up of strenuous webs, finally pulls together a story that makes a hundred little pieces into a cohesive whole. The room distorts around me, bending and folding in at the corners. I struggle to keep my footing.

John uses his good arm to hold his hand out to his wife. "Mary, sweetheart, please."

"No, John. You put me through hell, and it was Jessica's turn to always wonder. Always be scared. Always have knots in her stomach like I did when you'd come home late smelling like someone else's flesh."

"Why didn't you just torture *me*, honey?" John says. "Why?"

"John." Mary's red eyes drop a tear as she lowers her arm that's stained brown with dried blood. "That's the thing. I still love you. That's what my note said." She bites her bottom lip. "You just stopped loving me."

John whispers, "I love you, dear."

She looks away, tucking her chin to her shoulder, still biting back a moan.

"I love you," he says.

"You can't say that."

Bradley glances back at me, and I let him see me exhale. *I'm fine.*

Then he says, "Mary, let us help you. No one has to get hurt here today."

"Oh, I've been getting hurt for years. I'm not afraid of pain."

I almost speak, then suck it back in, but Mary notices my hesitation and says, "What, Jessica?"

Bradley snaps his head back to look at me, and John stays arched over in a desperate plea for hope.

"You can't kill me, Mary. I shouldn't have slept with your husband, but I lost my parents when I was really young, and I got into drugs in high school, so I've been messed up my whole life. I'm just a drunk. It's no excuse to hurt you or anyone else, but. . . I'm just a slut. You said it yourself. I've been this way my whole life. I never meant to hurt you."

Mary readjusts her grip on the knife. When she talks, I can barely see through her tight lips. "So why can't I kill a whore who drinks?"

I motion to Bradley and John. "There are two men here to stop you. You can't win."

"I've already won so much."

She's right.

Something clatters from the hallway, and Mary turns around, but before Bradley or John or I could make a move, a man steps in the doorway. I don't recognize him in this scenery, not without Lockheed beside him, and not without his uniform. Then his form begins to take shape in my tormented memory.

"Foreman, don't do this," Bradley says. "This is crazy. It's not you."

He holds a pistol behind his thigh as if ashamed. Without his uniform, he somehow appears bigger, scarier. I'd met him out of uniform at Bradley's house, but here, he's not a cop. Here he's just a civilian with a gun.

"I'm just here for the money, Bradley. Don't make this bigger than it is."

Mary moves away from him and stands by the chest of drawers against the wall. "What do you mean?" she asks. "I've already given it to you."

"No, the rest. I need to be able to afford to get out of here," he tells her. "Lockheed keeps calling me, Mary. Give me the rest of your savings, and I'll be gone." His eyebrows twitch, his shoulders jerking as though he can't decide whether to shoot us all and run or negotiate right here and now.

Bradley takes a slight step in front of me. "I can't believe you would do this. You took an oath, Foreman."

"I need the money, Bradley. You don't understand. I got a pregnant girlfriend at home. I got loans."

"You won't make it a day, Foreman. Think about what you're doing. Think about the logistics it would take to escape."

With a weak grip, he holds up the gun, pointing it at Mary, then at Bradley. "With all her savings, I'll be in another country with my girl-friend before Lockheed would even know I'm gone."

"Keaton already has Lockheed looking for you. That's why he's been calling you. It's over, man. Give up now and they'll go easier on you."

He moves his fingers around the handle of the gun and sucks in his lips. The rain pounds on the window again with a gust of wind, and, keeping the gun aimed at Bradley, Foreman's eyes start to shine with tears as he looks at me. I try to swallow but come up dry.

"I'm sorry, Jessica."

Mary stomps her foot to the ground again and points her knife up at Foreman. "Shut up. You're pathetic. I've given you the money. Now, leave."

He ignores her fragile command and looks to me again. "I don't even know you, Jessica. I'm sorry. This isn't about you, okay?" His cheeks redden, glossed over from his tears. "It's the money. I just—I need the money."

John backs against the wall, and the limp wrist that hangs out of his sling is pressed to his chest. He wears his fear unreserved.

"Foreman," I say, "it's okay. Just don't shoot us. Mary's the one who doesn't care about you. We want to help you."

Bradley holds out his arms in a surrendering pose. "Arrest Mary," he says, "and you'll be a hero for ending the Button Collector. Okay? We'll forget about the rest. It's done. Forgotten."

With a quick swipe of his sleeve over his eyes, Foreman's tears are gone, and his cheeks are pale and splotchy red, but he shifts his aim to me, and I throw up my hands. Bradley steps in front of me in one swift movement.

The muscles in his back harden, his voice matching the strain. "Foreman, stop," he shouts. Foreman closes his eyes, turning his head away from the gun, preparing to blow us away.

But Mary sweeps to the center of the room, in front of the gun, between her husband, Bradley, me. She screams and raises her knife into the air, making a full circle and stops in front of John.

Turning back to me, she yells—screams at the top of her lungs—the words I've known for months: *I've already won,* and she drags the knife across her own throat. Her fingers stretch out, frozen at the base of her neck, and the blade falls, catching flickers of light on the way down and bouncing with five heavy *clinks*.

Blood spits in a line across the wall where John stands, and before Mary drops, he's there, with blood on his face, catching her, falling with her, scrambling to bandage her neck with his hand.

Foreman lowers the gun and stumbles backward, contorting into the shriveled coward he really is.

Stripping off his sling, John screams at us to help as he wraps the cloth around Mary's neck, but Bradley leaps over her body and crashes on top of Foreman in the doorway. I hear the gun clatter on the floor and run to them. Bradley pins Foreman's arms under his knees, and the gun slides out from behind Foreman, hitting the wall in the hallway and coming to a stop out of his reach.

No one answers John's cries for someone to call an ambulance for Mary, but they would never arrive in time.

I jump over Bradley, but my foot catches on his waist and I slam to the ground near Foreman's head. Pain throbs in my hip bone and elbows as I push myself up a few feet to reach the gun. Foreman brawls under Bradley, and when I grab the gun and bring myself to my feet, Bradley has his arm under Foreman's chin to stop his fighting.

"Jessica," Bradley breathes out.

Michael, I want to say.

Mary's choking sputters to a wet gargle from her bedroom, a mixture of blood and her drowning last words: *I won.* A bitter symphony of Mary claiming her victory, mixed with John's desperate begging for someone to call an ambulance. John buries his face against her chest, exclaiming, "Mary, I love you. I'm sorry. How could this… How could this have happened?"

I use the wall as a brace to lean on, and I point the gun at Foreman's face. He tilts back his head to look at me, and the whites of his eyes reflect surrender. Bradley nods at me, a wordless *Thank you*.

All this time, after all these months, I'm finally the one with the gun, and all the bad guys are down. After all Bradley's protection, I can finally offer him mine.

Behind him, Mary's body lies motionless in John's lap. Her blood oozes through his fingers as he drapes over her chest, her gurgling replaced by his weeping.

Then everything goes silent except for the rain.

Five months later.

FIVE MONTHS AFTER THE death of the Button Collector, former Fuller Park Chicago Police Department officer Spencer Foreman has pleaded guilty to attempted murder and assisting in the plot to murder Chicago resident Jessica Knight.

Foreman claims to have been offered fifteen-thousand dollars by Mary Stoll (Button Collector) last winter to assist in her final crime that would conclude a series of murders of those belonging to the same family name. Foreman has been sentenced to fifteen years in prison for accessory to murder and an additional twenty-five years in prison for attempted murder.

According to Detective Michael Bradley, who was present at the time of Stoll's suicide and Foreman's attempt at murder in early May, Stoll had been killing members of a related family to scare Knight with the intent to eventually come for her life.

Stoll was pronounced dead at the scene.

According to authorities, Stoll had caught her husband, John Stoll, having an affair with Knight, which triggered Stoll to execute a series of five murders and two attempted murders in the span of ten months. During that time, Stoll hired an employee from *The Chicago Post,* where Knight was a journalist and John Stoll was Editor in Chief, to help plot the murder of Knight. The employee who was hired by Stoll, Ben Madden, was fatally shot by an official in Knight's home after his breaking in and attempted rape on Knight. Both Knight and John Stoll have since been dismissed from the *Post.*

I set down the *Daily* and check my phone, but it shows me only a blank screen.

Back in May, the newspaper explained every detail of what happened that night, and this October, they've got Foreman's prison sentence to bite on.

But as the investigation of Mary and the trials began over summer, they moved on from my life and on to the next big thing. My name is ruined. John's name is ruined. The *Post* earned thousands of new subscriptions.

When John was my boss, I never called him by his last name, but seeing it beside Mary's name humiliates me.

Mary Stoll. Mary stole. Knight. Night.

Maybe we aren't all that different, she and I. We're both killers, both stained, both thieves.

A small travel magazine has hired me to write, but I'm limited to hosting only over-the-phone interviews for now because my new boss thinks people might be afraid to let me in their home or office. John has been thrown back into the pressroom at a small, neighborhood newspaper. I've even had to change my professional name, and now my byline reads H. Knightly under the title of all my published pieces. H is for Hanley, my father's middle name.

My phone buzzes on the table, so I snatch it up, but it's only a notification for an email from my new boss. She's a woman, something I subconsciously assumed would be best for me, for John, for a conversation if Bradley ever decided to call me. The last time Bradley and I spoke was at Foreman's sentencing two weeks ago, and before that, we'd only seen each other for minutes at a time during interviews with police and then for an hour at a time in the courtroom.

He'd asked how I was doing once we had stepped outside of the courthouse.

The wind was blowing, so I had to tuck my ponytail into the hood of my jacket outside on the street.

"I'm doing okay."

He'd put his hands in his coat pockets and stood with his back to the wind. "Where are you staying these days? Same place?"

"I've been staying with John." I'd looked down at my shoes when I said that. "He had to get a smaller place outside the city, and I couldn't afford my apartment anymore."

"Right." He'd looked down, then, too. "Still a writer?"

"Barely."

He'd told me that he'd gotten accepted to work for the homicide department at NYPD. Lockheed tried getting him back, but Bradley declined and said he'd already applied to too many promising jobs to go back to Fuller Park. He'd even said he'd been accepted into a program to become a crime scene analyst. But he likes getting his hands dirty. He likes being in the thick of an investigation. So he took the job to investigate murders in Manhattan, a city far away from this one. He was done with Chicago PD, and he made his future sound exciting and hopeful.

Michael Bradley seemed relieved that it was just a one-night fling with me. He was ready to move on with his life, away from me and his former boss and his marriage and that ivy above his kitchen sink. This was the beginning of a new life for him. I was happy for him. Really.

"That sounds good. Like a good job," I'd said.

"It is. It will be."

"I—"

"Listen," he'd cut in, "I'm sorry. For what happened."

I didn't know what he was apologizing for, or which event needed a "sorry" from him. "No," I'd stopped him. "Let's just—"

"I know."

"I know too."

"It's just. . . Jessica."

"Yeah?"

"I. . . I'd said once that I loved you."

"I remember," I'd said, embarrassed but overly hopeful.

"That was true back then. You're loveable, Jessica. Believe that."

"So are you, Michael." Then I'd added, "Bradley," with a swelling ache in my chest that I was sure would stay forever.

I had remembered in that moment that I never gave myself the chance to say *I love you* back to him.

We'd stood there in the wind, letting it blow around the small talk, until he said he had to go. "I'm meeting someone for lunch."

Some inexperienced part of me had wanted it to be his ex-wife; someone needed a happy ending. Some relationship needed fixing, and I'd hoped it was Bradley's.

I walked away first so I wouldn't give myself the opportunity to watch him go. He didn't say he'd call me, but I still keep my phone close to me just in case he wants to check in on me one day.

I leave the *Daily* crumpled on the table and walk to the bathroom to take a shower like I have every day since Mary told me that I was stained. At the mirror, I use toilet paper to wipe off my red lipstick, but it makes an ugly smear across my face, a blemish that water won't take away.

I'll remain forever stained with the blood of my family. The survivors should destroy me. They should break down John's door and come find me and tackle me down to this damp carpet. They should force knives into my neck and watch me bleed. They should finger through my clothes and collect my buttons.

I would lie there and let my life seep out of me, and I wouldn't scream when they threaded the needles, when they stuck a button to my lips. I hope they'd watch me suffer, and I hope I'd be unrecognizable under all my blood. No number of showers, hot or cold, can cleanse me of the stains because I'm the one who tattooed myself with them. The moment I let John take off my clothes when I was twenty-three started seaming together what would be the rest of my life. It determined the lives of my family.

Every night when I crawl into bed with John and he whispers into my ear, "Goodnight, love," all I can translate it into is the laughter of Robert, Rosa, Uncle Josh, Great Aunt Julianne, Martha Pax, and Aunt Deborah.

This is what you get, they would tell me. *A life of hell for killing your family.*

And Deb would say, *For killing my daughter. For forgetting about me in this asylum.*

John leans over to kiss me, turns off the light, and the room is swallowed up by the dark, but I hope my family can still see me drowning in their blood. I hope they drink my tears, and when I'm certain they aren't watching me—that they're still just bodies in graves scattered all over the country—I open the curtains, wanting to see the words *you are next* on the sidewalk below and wishing it had been true the first time.

The End

About the Author

M. M. COCHRAN is an award-winning journalist and fiction writer. She is the author of young adult mystery romance novel *Between the Ocean and the Stars*, which was named a finalist in the 2023 National Indie Excellence Awards.

She lives in the foothills of South Carolina and can most commonly be found watching sunsets, making homemade lattes, or seeking out the next adventure.

Keep up with M. M. Cochran on Instagram @m.m.cochran_writer.

Photo by Alli K. Photography

IngramElliott Publishing

IngramElliott is an award-winning independent publisher with a mission to bring great stories to light in print and on-screen. We publish stories with a unique voice that will translate well into film and television. Visit us at www.ingramelliott.com for more information.

Our *IngramElliott* imprint features full-length fiction and non-fiction titles designed with the book lover in mind.

Our *IE Snaps!* imprint features novella-length fiction in popular genres that are designed for a quick read on the go.